PRAISE FOR
THE GISAWI CHRONICLES

———

"With an **authentic and unique** voice, Voelz masterfully delivers a suspense-filled and highly entertaining sequel to War Under the Mango Tree, continuing the Gisawi Chronicles. The **espionage tradecraft and geopolitical setup are spot on**, leaving the reader to ponder where fact and fiction diverge. With **intriguing characters and addictive dialog**, Operation Hermes is **a must-read!**"

—Dave Edlund
USA Today bestselling author of *Valiant Savage*

"Voelz possesses **a wicked sense of humor that never disappoints**."

—Robert Bruce Adolph
author of *Surviving the United Nations: The Unexpected Challenge*

"What **a roller-coaster ride of international intrigue!** Glenn Voelz nailed this one as only someone 'in the know' could possibly do. Filled with intriguing characters, a **larger-than-life storyline, and back-stabbing politics**, Glenn has woven an engaging story that keeps one guessing as to 'who's going to do what next?' This was a great read, and once started, **hard to put down** - it has **all the elements of a Fredrick Forsyth piece of work**."

—Tom Wangler
author of *"Nigeria - An Ancient Secret Becomes the Adventure of a Lifetime.*

"Loaded with plenty of whiskey-tango-foxtrot moments, War Under the Mango Tree *is a thoroughly entertaining lampoon of the US military machine via a fictionalized mission in an equally fictional Central African country. Author Voelz delivers realistic characters and sharp, witty dialog that will leave you alternating between feeling genuinely sorry for the Army officers, who are constantly played by their third-world hosts, and hysterical fits of laughter. Not since Catch 22 has a novel this brilliant come along. Five cheeky stars!"*

—David Edlund,
USA Today bestselling author of *Guarding Savage*
(War Under the Mango Tree)

". . . a brilliant satire of the hypocrisy, bureaucracy, banality, and ineptitude of the military—as well as the sinister agendas and left-handed ways of the profit-hungry companies that work with them. Like the classic film Dr. Strangelove, War Under the Mango Tree *is scathingly funny and often feels absurd—yet other times, all too real."*

—David Aretha
editor of multiple award-winning military books
(War Under the Mango Tree)

OPERATION
HERMES

A NOVEL

GLENN VOELZ

Operation Hermes, *The Gisawi Chronicles, Book 2*
by Glenn Voelz

Published by

FSP First Steps Publishing
FIRST STEPS   PO Box 571
PUBLISHING   Gleneden Beach, OR 97388

Interior layout, cover design by Suzanne Parrott
Cover Art, Depositphotos.com
   © Roomyana / *The ancient Indian palace on the river bank*
   © Irusetka.yandex.ru / *Demonstration, protest*

Library of Congress Control Number: 2020944815
Genre: *dark humor, political satire, military fiction, war*

ISBN: 978-1-944072-06-3 (hb)
       978-1-944072-28-5 (pb/Amazon)
       978-1-944072-32-2 (pb)
       978-1-944072-29-2 (epub)

10 9 8 7 6 5 4 3 2 1

Printed in the
United States of America.

DEDICATION

For my parents

THE GISAWI CHRONICLES

War Under the Mango Tree

Operation Hermes

ACKNOWLEDGMENTS

Thank you to Lara M. and Laura G. for your careful editing and always insightful suggestions. And to Suzanne for your patience, support, and giving me a chance.

When elephants fight,
it's the grass that suffers.
–African proverb

CHAPTER ONE

———

Ambassador Claire Roberts glanced at the clock. It was past midnight, and most of her staff were still at work, waiting on hold with the White House Situation Room. A few people huddled in the corner, exchanging office gossip, waiting for the meeting to begin. Another group was gathered around the table, arguing over the wording of a draft cable. One young man, a new arrival on the staff, was slumped over in his chair, asleep and drooling on his tie.

Despite the late hour, Claire looked as sharp as when she had walked into the embassy early that morning: dressed in a charcoal pantsuit over a lilac blouse, wearing an ornate silver brooch that accentuated the gray streaks in her hair. The jewelry piece had been handmade for her by a local artisan. It was one of her favorites in a personal collection acquired over many years of working in obscure hot spots around the world.

Claire cleared her throat, calling for everyone's attention. "OK, team, I know it's been a long day. Hopefully, we're through the worst of this. The White House should be on the line any minute. Let's see what they have to say; then, we'll figure out where we go from here."

There were a few tired nods in response as everyone found their seats around the table. In the commotion, the sleeper had regained consciousness and was dabbing at the wet spot on his tie. Everyone else stared blankly at the video screen, waiting for something to happen.

On the other end of the teleconference line, they could see a windowless room about the size of a utility closet. Jammed inside were several pieces of faux mahogany office furniture, a computer terminal, and a bank of telephones. The only identifying feature in the room was the blue oval crest of the Situation Room hanging on the back wall.

Forty-five minutes after the meeting was scheduled to begin, Reid McCoy, the president's deputy national security advisor, appeared on the screen. He was balancing a thick stack of briefing papers and can of Diet Coke, struggling to squeeze into the seat without spilling the contents of either hand. Balding, portly, and dressed in a wrinkled off-the-rack suit, McCoy was the consummate government bureaucrat grinding his way to a pre-retirement heart attack.

"Sorry to keep you waiting, Claire," Reid said, settling in behind the camera. His voice echoed in the speakers, distorted by the satellites and thousands of miles of fiber-optic cable linking Washington to Africa.

"No problem, Reid," Claire said. "We appreciate you making the time. As you probably heard, we've had some excitement here today."

"So I gather. I caught some of the footage on the news. It didn't look good. The president has been briefed. He asked me to get with you for an update on the situation."

"My staff has been working all day to get on top of this," Claire replied. "We can go around the room and give you a rundown of what we know right now."

"Make it quick. I'm about to get jammed up against another meeting," Reid said, glancing at his watch to emphasize the point.

"In that case, we'll give you the abridged version. Yesterday evening, there was a small protest march downtown. Nothing out of the ordinary, but apparently, a scuffle broke out between some demonstrators and the police. According to eyewitnesses, things got out of hand, and a few of the marchers were roughed up and hauled off to jail. A bystander happened to capture it all on a cell phone camera. The video was posted to social media, then exploded overnight. By early this morning, crowds were gathering near where it happened, demanding that the government take disciplinary action against the policemen involved. Things escalated quickly from there. By late afternoon, riots were breaking out all over the capital. If you've watched the footage on TV, you have a good idea of how it looked out there today."

"Like a war zone," Reid said. "So you're telling me this was all because some cops roughed up a few kids?"

Claire shook her head, looking disappointed. "Hardly. Last night was just a spark thrown onto a pile of dry kindling. This has been a long time in the making."

"I'll be honest, Claire, this caught us by surprise. It's been a few years since we've paid much attention to the Democratic Republic of Gisawi. Do we have any idea why things suddenly came to a boil?"

"This was anything but sudden," Claire countered. "Our good friend President Namono has been running this country into the ground for the last thirty years, using it as a personal piggy bank. The regime is synonymous with corruption, nepotism, and oppression. If today was any indication, people are finally fed up with it."

"Well, I can tell you that POTUS wasn't happy about the surprise," Reid said, unable to conceal his frustration. "The intel community hasn't said a damn thing about DRoG since Operation Brushfire. He was under the impression that things were going OK since we nailed Odoki. How the hell did Namono manage to screw it up so quickly?"

"The same way every politician does. Overpromising, underdelivering, and blaming everyone else when it all goes to crap. It didn't take long for people to see Operation Brushfire for what it really was."

"A decisive military victory against a sociopathic warlord and his renegade militia?" Reid ventured.

"That's one version," Claire said with a defeated sigh. "Or a phony war concocted by President Namono and his cronies so they could sell off the country's mineral rights to foreign investors."

"I seem to recall that we briefed the first version back here," Reid clarified.

"Why am I not surprised?" Claire deadpanned into the camera. "In any case, after Operation Brushfire, Namono pitched a big development scheme, promising to jump-start the economy and bring in lots of new jobs. Naturally, none of that ever happened. No new schools, roads, or hospitals. Meanwhile, inflation has been running out of control, the store shelves are empty, and nobody can find work. That's the real reason people took to the streets today. The incident with the police was just the spark."

"Do the protesters think that burning the entire place down is going to make it better? How's that going to help anything?"

"I'm not trying to justify the rioting," Claire insisted. "But what we saw out there today has been thirty years in the making. I'm only surprised it took this long for things to finally blow up."

"Fair enough. But the president doesn't have much bandwidth for this right now. We're a few months away from midterms, and frankly, the voters don't want to hear about DRoG. As far as they're concerned, we fixed the damn place when we went in and killed Odoki. The last thing POTUS wants on the campaign trail is to be talking about DRoG again. So give me the bottom line. Are we going to see any blowback from this between now and midterms?"

"I can't promise you it won't turn ugly. President Namono has been around for so long that it's hard to imagine anyone else sitting in Green House. Nevertheless, we need to be prepared for that possibility. There's no telling how this could play out if the violence in the streets continues."

"How do we expect the regime to respond? What's the CIA's take on this?" Reid pressed.

Claire nodded to the man sitting next to her. "Let me turn it over to our station chief. He can give you the intel community's perspective."

The camera panned to a gaunt, leathery-skinned man sitting next to the ambassador. He had a gray, Caesar-style haircut and fingernails yellowed from years of chain-smoking. "Hey, Reid. Mike Jones here," the man said, nodding into the camera.

"Damn it, Mike! Good to see you. I didn't know you were over there. Why the hell did the agency send an old Russia hand over to DRoG?"

"I guess I must have pissed someone off back at Langley," Jones replied with a raspy chuckle. "But I won't be doing that for much longer. This is my last rodeo. I'm retiring next year."

"I guess you're going out with a bang."

"Seems that way. But it sure ain't like the good old days. I'd much rather be back sipping tea with the mujahideen and making life hard for Ivan. This just isn't the same."

"You're telling me," Reid said, shaking his head. "Anyway, what's your take on the situation over there? Do we need to be worried, or will this thing blow over?"

"You know the deal," Jones said. "Anyone who's bet against Namono over the last thirty years has ended up with a losing hand. But of course, this time could always be different. The guy is in his eighties, and my contacts inside Green House say that his health has gone to shit. We think Namono is looking to move on sooner rather than later. If things start getting dicey out in the streets, it may cause him to accelerate the timeline on the transition."

"If that happens, what's the risk for us?" Reid asked, jotting down a few notes on a legal pad.

"We've got to assume that Namono wants to keep things in the family. That narrows down the options to his third wife, Charity, or his son Fabrice."

"Do we care one way or another? They're both named Namono, right?" Reid asked. "I doubt anyone outside the Beltway will lose sleep over that headline."

"The name might be the same, but that's where the similarities end. We think both of them want the job, but Fabrice recently had a falling-out with his father," Jones revealed.

"The kid hasn't turned out to be dictator material?" Reid quipped.

"Let's just say he has other ambitions. The final straw was last year when he got piss drunk and crashed a vintage Lamborghini into a hotel swimming pool outside Monaco. The story didn't play well back home while people were staring at empty store shelves," Jones explained.

"So, is the playboy son out of the running?"

"Maybe, but the third wife isn't much better. She's a big fan of designer purses. According to one of my sources, she's got a huge collection of them stored in a two-thousand-square-foot walk-in vault somewhere inside the presidential mansion. We don't see much support for her out on the street, either."

"In that case, do we even have a dog in this fight?"

"We certainly do if we claim to care about good governance and democratic reform!" Claire interjected.

There was an awkward silence as the group digested this. The camera registered a hint of disgusted impatience on Reid's face as if he was sending a plate of undercooked fish back to the kitchen of an overpriced restaurant. "Well, obviously, Claire, the president is committed to that," Reid muttered in concession. "But we need to be realistic here. Mike, who's our best bet to keep things quiet if the place goes to shit before midterms?"

"Fabrice is our man," the grizzled spy said without hesitation. "We have reason to believe that President Namono has been cozying up to the Chinese. They've been pumping money into mining and infrastructure projects in the western region, trying to curry favor with the regime. We think Charity would likely follow suit if she moved into the top job. Fabrice isn't perfect, but at least he won't sell us out to Beijing. As long as he can keep his nose clean, he's our best option going forward."

Reid sipped his Diet Coke and weighed the options. "Any other concerns?"

Claire glanced across the table at Colonel Jeff Sawyer, signaling for him to enter the conversation. Sawyer nodded, his clean-shaven head glinting under the fluorescent lighting. He straightened his tie and tugged at the lapels of his business suit, not yet accustomed to the embassy's civilian dress code since arriving on the job.

"Sir, Colonel Sawyer here. I'm the defense attaché here at the embassy. There is one other issue we need to keep in mind. You may recall that after Operation Brushfire, DRoG was selected to host our regional counter-terrorism operating base. We've got a brand-new multimillion-dollar facility near the airport and several hundred American troops running operations from that base. It's the anchor point of our entire regional counter-terrorism strategy."

"So, your concern is that if DRoG goes down the tubes, our base goes with it?"

"Yes, sir. It wouldn't be an easy piece of real estate to replace overnight. Despite concerns about President Namono leaning toward China, our relationship with the Gisawian military remains solid. Defense Minister Mugaba Odongo has always been pro-American. As long as he stays in place, we should be able to maintain access to our operating base."

"Thank you, Colonel. That's good to keep in mind. What about the loyalty of the army? If Namono comes under pressure, does the military have his back?"

"That depends, sir. Mugaba has a tight hold on the generals. At the end of the day, they'll probably answer to him in the event of a crisis. If Mugaba is behind the president, then so is the army. But if he turns, it's hard to say what might happen."

"How is the army reacting to the protests?" Reid asked.

"So far, so good. The soldiers stayed in the barracks today and left the dirty work to the police. Frankly, we're not surprised by that. Mugaba is a canny player. He knows it's a losing hand to send his soldiers out into the streets against the protesters. He'd prefer to let the police take the bad press and keep the army on the side of the people."

"That sounds to me like the strategy of someone aspiring to greater things," Reid speculated.

Colonel Sawyer nodded. "As I said, Mugaba's a canny player. With him, I wouldn't rule anything out."

"Got it. But back to our immediate concern," Reid said, turning to the ambassador. "Claire, here's the bottom line. Our priority is keeping DRoG out of the headlines. Now is not the time to be rehashing Operation Brushfire or getting pulled into some petty family squabble over who's going to run the county. We can leave that shit to the UN. I don't want any disruption of our counter-terrorism operations at the base. We need to keep our soldiers focused on the mission. In case these riots worsen, what are we doing to mitigate potential threats to US citizens?"

"We've got a few thousand Americans in the country right now," the ambassador said, glancing at her notes. "But so far, we haven't heard any reports of foreigners getting caught up in the violence. Most of the frustration is being directed at the regime. But that could easily change if we make any missteps. We've been allied with President Namono since the Cold War. No matter what we do, there will always be a perception of guilt by association."

"We can't afford to take any risks right now. What's your recommendation?" Reid pressed, glancing at his watch.

"Given the potential for escalating violence, as a precaution, we propose evacuating all nonessential embassy personnel and family members. We'll also ask Consular Affairs in Washington to issue a travel advisory discouraging Americans from visiting DRoG until things settle down."

"That seems reasonable. I'll let the president know. So, in a nutshell, here's our plan. Get Americans out. Keep Namono in. And make sure DRoG doesn't show up on the front page. Are we all in agreement on the course of action?"

Everyone around the table nodded.

"Good work, Claire. I know your team is on top of this. Thanks for the update, and stay safe out there," Reid said, and then the video link went dead.

+++

Early the next morning, Lieutenant Colonel Lutalo "Louie" Bigombe walked into the Gisawian Ministry of Defense compound. The soldiers guarding the front gate recognized him from a distance. He was tall and thin, with the taut physique of a champion runner. His uniform was freshly pressed and fit like a glove, making him look as if he had been born to wear it. The guards straightened as he approached the gate, offering a smart salute as he passed by.

It was Louie's first trip to the ministry since the start of protests, and the compound was on edge. The roving security patrols outside the fence had been doubled, and the nearby roads closed off to traffic. The guards made a show of checking his identification, though everyone knew who he was and who he was there to see.

After passing through the gate, Louie entered the headquarters building and ascended a grand central staircase leading up the office of Minister Mugaba Odongo. Inside the reception area were two desks sitting side by side, one for the minister's secretary and the other for his long-suffering aide-de-camp, a perpetually tired-looking army colonel. That morning, both of them had wearied expressions, and neither made any effort to engage in small talk. Two straight days of rioting in the streets had left everyone humorless.

"The minister will see you right away," the secretary said before Louie had a chance to take a seat. He continued through the double doors into the minister's private office. Louie found the minister sitting behind a large executive desk, reading through a stack of reports, his bulky frame fitting snugly into the oversized chair. Louie was surprised to catch him without a cell phone affixed to his ear. The man appeared oddly serene, given the chaos out in the streets. Mugaba motioned Louie toward one of the leather chairs in front of his desk.

"Good morning, Lutalo," he said, addressing Louie by his given name.

"Good morning, Uncle," Louie replied, sitting down and pulling a notepad and pen out of his attaché case.

"How was the drive coming over from the base this morning?"

"Better than yesterday. Perhaps the demonstrators are resting after a late night," Louie said, trying lamely to lighten the mood. "I heard that there was fighting in the streets until early this morning."

Mugaba nodded and pushed aside the stack of papers. "Have you checked on your mother?"

"I called her this morning. She was frightened but fine. Fortunately, there weren't many demonstrations in her neighborhood. However, she was still close enough to smell the smoke from the fires. My brother saw the riots on the news back in the States. He called her last night and offered to send her a ticket. He said that she could stay with him in New Jersey if things got worse."

As Louie was speaking, his uncle's expression soured.

"That will not be necessary," Mugaba said firmly. "Your brothers and sister left her alone when they decided to make their lives overseas. Now they see a little something on the news and think they must rush back to save her? You can tell your brother not to trouble himself." He pointed his finger at Louie's chest. "I will send a car for my sister. She can stay with me until things return to normal. We can take care of our own business here without help from your brother."

"Uncle, you know that he didn't mean any disrespect," Louie insisted. "He's just worried about our mother. He's a good son and wanted to make sure that she was safe."

"I'm in charge of the entire army!" Mugaba exploded. "The generals answer to me! Yet somehow, your brother thinks that I can't protect my own sister? Who does he think he is?"

"No, Uncle, it's not like that," Louie stammered. "He was just disturbed by the pictures on TV. The whole world was watching what was happening yesterday. He only wanted to be sure that she was safe. That was all."

"Well, if your brother really cares about what goes on here, then perhaps he should move back home and do something about it. But the big New Jersey banker is too important for that. I suppose he only has enough time to ask his secretary to buy his mother a plane ticket."

Louie said nothing, knowing that there was no sense arguing when his uncle got into a mood. Instead, he gave Mugaba a moment to regain his composure, then tried steering the conversation to other matters. "Uncle, I'm worried there will be trouble again tonight. What do you hear from Green House? How does President Namono plan to respond?"

Mugaba took a deep breath and then exhaled as if venting his frustration over the matter of Louie's brother. "I haven't heard anything from Green House," he finally said. "The president seems satisfied to let the interior ministry handle the disturbance. I believe they are treating it as a police matter."

"He must know that isn't a solution," Louie said. "The people are angry. While I don't agree with their tactics, they have legitimate concerns. And some of the actions being taken by police are only making matters worse. Surely the president must see that fighting against the protesters won't solve the problem."

"The people must have patience," his uncle shot back. "They must give the reforms a chance to work."

"But Uncle," Louie said, revealing a hint of exasperation, "how many times have they been told to wait? Can't you understand their frustration?"

"Lutalo, do not forget where you are sitting right now," Mugaba warned him. "I may be your uncle, but I am also the minister of defense. And I am sworn to defend this country and uphold the authority of the presidency. I suggest that you watch your words when you sit before me in this office."

"I'm sorry, Uncle. I did not mean any disrespect," Louie murmured, chastened.

"And don't you forget who put you in this position," his uncle continued, gesturing the rank insignia pinned on Louie's shoulder. "After Operation Brushfire, the president called you out by name in front of the entire nation. He promoted you and gave you command of the elite counter-terrorism force. Out of all the officers in the army, he picked you."

"But that's exactly the point," Louie said. "I realize that I have benefitted from what happened during Operation Brushfire. And you know that I am grateful for the opportunity I was given. But those people out in streets, they're still waiting to see the fruits of that victory. After the army took back the land from Odoki's militia, the president promised jobs and development. It's been over two years since then, and nothing has changed. In fact, things have only gotten worse. That's the reason they're taking to the streets. They don't feel like they have any other option."

"Lutalo, you are a soldier. It is not your job to worry about such things. When soldiers become preoccupied with politics, it is then that we must worry over the fate of our nation."

"I understand this, Uncle, but I also love my country. How will we ever move forward if those in charge don't listen to the people?"

"I can assure you, President Namono is listening," his uncle said, clearly impatient to end the conversation. "He will do what is best for the people."

Louie nodded, sensing his uncle's exasperation, but he pressed on with a final question. "If the troubles in the street continue, is there a chance that the army will be called out?"

The big man sighed and shook his head. "These are difficult times. Nothing is assured. You know that I am loyal to the president; however, some lines should only be crossed as the last resort. I have advised Green House that the army should be kept in the barracks. For now, I believe the president will respect my request."

"But what if something changes? What if the president comes to believe that there are no other alternatives? Or that the people have turned against him?"

"We'll cross that bridge when we come to it. But if that happens, you must always remember that you are a soldier first, just like your father was. And a soldier must follow orders, even when their purpose may not be clear. You must trust that those above you are acting with good intent and in the nation's best interest."

"Yes, Uncle. Of course, I understand this. But is it really so simple?" Louie asked. "Yesterday, the police were following orders when they fought the protesters. Can you honestly say that that was best for the nation?"

Mugaba shrugged. "Lutalo, we can only hope that those above us act with wisdom as well as strength. It reminds me of an old saying from the village: One destined for power does not have to fight for it. We must pray that this is true."

Louie nodded and closed his notebook, sensing that the meeting had come to an end. His uncle had said all that he was going to say.

+++

After the meeting, Louie returned to the army base out near the airport. He tried focusing on work but found it impossible to go on with his routine and pretend that everything outside was normal. Between their duties, his soldiers kept sneaking away to listen to the radio or checking their cell phones, searching for information on what was happening in the streets. Louie tried to keep them on task but sympathized with their worry. Most of his soldiers had families or loved ones living in the city, which now felt as if it was under siege.

By late afternoon, Louie was resigned to the futility of the situation. He told the sergeant major to release the soldiers early so they could go home and check on their relatives. There was no use in keeping them confined to the camp when their minds were elsewhere.

As soon as the sergeant major made the announcement, the soldiers raced from the camp, under orders to report back no later than six o'clock the next morning. After the base had emptied, Louie heeded his advice and left the office early to check on things at home. He opted for the long route home, choosing a road far outside of the city to avoid getting caught up in the protests still raging downtown.

After an uneventful commute on mostly deserted roads, Louie pulled into his driveway. He turned off the ignition and sat there staring through the windshield, taking stock of his good fortune. By Gisawian standards, their home was more than comfortable, far exceeding the reasonable aspirations of most people in the county. They had several bedrooms, reliable plumbing, functioning air conditioning, a satellite dish, and a tidy garden for sitting outside in the evenings. The house was in a quiet middle-class neighborhood. Most of their neighbors were government bureaucrats, businesspeople, or other Gisawians of ability and ambition. A handful of expat families and staff from a few foreign embassies gave the neighborhood a cosmopolitan air.

Looking at the other houses, Louie wondered about the conversations going on behind closed doors. He guessed that some of his neighbors were sympathetic toward the protesters, yet they were reluctant to join in the marches. Like himself, they were likely ambivalent about the prospect of upending an imperfect system without knowing what might replace it.

Through the kitchen window, Louie saw his fiancé, Anna, making dinner. She was at the sink, still dressed in her work attire, wearing a simple skirt and blouse. Her shoulder-length, dirty-blonde hair was pulled back in a ponytail, a style—like most things in her life—intended to minimize time wasted on things she considered frivolous.

Anna glanced out the window and saw Louie sitting in the car. She smiled and waved, looking surprised to see him home early from work. Louie took his bags from the trunk and walked toward the door. The kitchen window was open, and he could hear BBC News on the radio. The announcer discussed some distant human tragedy that usually would have sparked his curiosity but seemed irrelevant during their own crisis.

When he walked through the door, Anna turned and smiled, glad to see him home. Louie met her by the sink and squeezed her arm, brushing his lips gently against her cheek.

"I didn't know if you'd be back tonight," she said, hugging him more tightly than usual.

"Me either. I was worried that they would keep us on the base overnight should things get worse in the city. I suppose it's a good sign that we were allowed to go home. Maybe someone in the government has reason to believe that things will quiet down."

Anna raised an eyebrow, skeptical of his optimism. "If anything, the protests were worse today than yesterday."

"How can you tell anything from the news?" Louie said, waving his hand dismissively at the radio. "They only report the worst thing happening at any moment. On TV, they were showing pictures of the police fighting with the protesters. But on my drive home, I didn't see anything out of the ordinary."

"How far outside the city did you drive?" Anna asked in a tone of mocking disbelief. "Trust me, it was a different story downtown. There were even some protests near the university."

"Were the police on campus?" Louie asked with surprise.

"No. They stayed outside the gates, but close enough that everyone knew they were in the area. I think they wanted to send a message, or at the very least, make the students think twice about joining the marchers out on the street."

"And was that message received?"

"That remains to be seen. So far, things have been quiet on campus—just a few meetings and speeches, all peaceful. For now, I think the students are more worried about finishing their classes than joining the protests. But that could change if things continue this way for much longer."

"Are your students sympathetic with the street?"

"You ask that as if you'd be surprised if they were."

"Perhaps a little. I wouldn't consider them natural revolutionaries."

"Really? They're students. It's their job to challenge the status quo," Anna argued.

"The status quo has been good to them," Louie shot back. "Most of those kids at the university owe their privilege to the system. You really think they're going to bite the hand that feeds them?"

"Louie, that's a bit cynical, isn't it?" Anna said. "I'm with those students every day. They're more idealistic than you give them credit for."

"I suppose we'll see their true colors once exams are over," Louie sniffed.

"You might be surprised. No offense, darling, but you did all your schooling in the UK and the States. That experience would leave anyone cynical about the seriousness of the average college student."

"You think I'm not giving them due credit?"

"No, I just think you're underestimating their desire for change. Soon, they'll be out there looking for jobs and trying to earn a living. And that's getting harder every day. Not everyone can go overseas and make a good life for themselves like your brothers and sister did. The students may have benefitted from the system, but that doesn't make them blind to its flaws."

"Now you're an expert on Gisawian politics?" Louie said, a hint of annoyance in his voice.

"No, of course not. But I listen to what they say. I think I understand the things they want from life."

"And what exactly would those be?"

"The same things that any reasonable person wants. Opportunity, stability, and more of a voice in their government."

"Yes, we all want those things," Louie said impatiently. "But when they grow up, they'll figure out that it's not so simple. There's more to it than just making a wish and waving a magic wand."

"Louie, don't be so patronizing! I think if you got to know them, you would admire their spirit. In fact, they remind me of you when we first met."

"What's that supposed to mean?" he asked, annoyed at the implication. "That was only a few years ago. Have I changed that much?"

Anna ignored the question and turned back to chopping vegetables next to the sink, avoiding his eyes. "A few of the students from my class asked me to join one of their meetings later in the week," she said.

"And you agreed to go?"

"Sure. Why not? I'm a faculty member. It's my job to be involved in their intellectual development. And that doesn't only happen in the classroom."

"Anna, you need to be careful about the things you become involved with. You can't simply show up to a student meeting when you don't know who will be there or even the topic they're discussing. There are implications."

"What do you mean, 'implications'?" she asked, taken aback by his tone. "It's a student government meeting, not a coup plot. It's no different than what goes on at every other campus in the world."

"No, Anna, there is something different. Not about them. About you. You're not like anyone else on that campus. You're an outsider. And a privileged outsider at that."

Anna's head snapped up from the cutting board, and she turned to look Louie straight in the eye. "I think I'm about to be offended by what you're implying."

"I'm not implying anything. I'm simply making a statement of fact. You are a white American woman teaching at an African university. On top of that, you're engaged to the nephew of the defense minister. Whether you like it or not, that puts you in an entirely different category than anyone else on that campus. For that reason, what you do and what you say have different implications for your students, yourself, and for me."

"So, you're telling me not to go to the student meeting?"

Louie sighed and shook his head. "No. I know better than to tell you what to do. It's just that I worry."

"About me? Or about your uncle?"

"Listen, Anna. You are about to become part of my family. Whether you like it or not, that comes with a certain amount of baggage. You knew that from the start. And it's going to be true for as long as we stay here. There's no escaping that fact."

"I guess I don't understand. Just tell me what you're worried about. That I'll embarrass you? That I'll shame your family name?"

"You know it's not that! It's because you're an American. Because you're white. Because you're a woman. Because of me. Because of my uncle. For all of those reasons and more, people will try to manipulate you. They will try to draw you into things that aren't what they seem."

"Are you speaking from experience?"

Louie's gaze dropped to the floor. He took a deep breath before looking back at Anna. "I just want you to be careful."

"Please don't worry. I can take care of myself. But it seems like something else is bothering you," she hinted.

Louie avoided her eyes, toying distractedly with his car keys. "I met with my uncle this morning," he revealed.

"Really! He called you over to the ministry?"

"Yes. Although I'm not sure why. We spoke for a while about the protests, and that was it."

Anna raised an eyebrow.

"I know you don't trust him!" Louie blurted out, knowing what she was thinking.

"And you do?" she shot back.

"Anna, we've been through this a million times. I'm not proud of what happened during Operation Brushfire: the drone strike on Odoki; any of it. Of course, it's easy to look back now and think about everything we could have done differently. But that doesn't change where we are right now. It is what it is."

"That's a cop-out, Louie, and you know it. You never confronted your uncle about any of it. Not the dodgy offshore bank accounts. Not the fact that Odoki was probably dead long before that drone strike ever happened. Not about where the money went from the government selling off those mineral rights. You never asked him about any of it. It's just been this big elephant in the room for the last two years."

"What am I supposed to ask him?" Louie said with exasperation. "Should I confront him with our wild speculation that he was at the center of some big conspiracy? The only evidence we had was a classified American intelligence report that I had to burn after reading, remember? We never had anything else to go on, no real proof that he was behind it all. Yet you still act as if I should simply walk into his office and accuse him of masterminding a phony war."

"No, Louie, that's not what I said," she said quietly, turning back to the cutting board.

"Anna, please, give me a little credit. Just because I couldn't prove my uncle's involvement doesn't mean that I trust him. But it also doesn't change the fact that he's my mother's brother. Or the minor issue that he happens to be in charge of the entire army. In case you forgot, I still wear a uniform when I go into work every day. As long as that's the case, I'm obligated to follow his orders. So if your idealistic students want a lesson in the complexities of real life, I'd be happy to join them for a little mentoring over coffee sometime."

"I'll be sure to pass along the offer," Anna said, putting down her knife and staring in dismay at the remains of the vegetables on the cutting board, minced beyond recognition in an unconscious fit of anger. Anna took a moment to regain her composure, then turned back to Louie. She reached for his hand, determined not to let the argument ruin their evening.

"I'm sorry. I know it's not easy," she said.

"I'm sorry too. We should have left here when we had the chance."

"When was that?" she asked with the hint of a smile.

"I don't remember," Louie said, shaking his head.

"Me either."

CHAPTER TWO

Claire, running late from another meeting, rushed into the conference room to find her staff waiting around the table. It was midafternoon, and she had consumed nothing but coffee, breath mints, and half of a stale croissant since waking up. Two weeks of rioting in the streets had pushed everyone to the point of exhaustion. Claire couldn't even remember waking up that morning and getting dressed. All of her essential survival functions had switched over to auto-pilot as the crisis wore on.

Hoping to get the day back on schedule, Claire took her seat at the head of the table, turning toward the embassy's security officer, Jake Baxter, the staffer responsible for overseeing the safety of the mission and its employees. Since the start of the protests, the former Marine led the briefing sequence, starting meetings with updates of the situation out in the streets.

"Let's get started," Claire said, dispensing with formalities. "By my count, we're now officially two weeks into the crisis. How are things looking out there today?"

Jake straightened in his chair. He was a wiry practitioner of jujitsu and an aficionado of exotic dietary supplements.

Though ten years out of the Marines, he wouldn't have looked out of place if he was suddenly thrown back into a set of fatigues rather than his business suit. "Ma'am, things were quieter yesterday after the violence last week. It seems that both sides were looking for an excuse to de-escalate. There were a few peaceful marches Sunday afternoon after the churches let out, but fortunately, no major confrontations with the police."

"That's good news. However, we shouldn't mistake a data point for a trend," Claire cautioned. "Still, it's better than another day of breathing in fumes from burning car tires. How are things going with the evacuation of our nonessential personnel?"

"Still on schedule, ma'am," Jake confirmed. "The last few family members went out on a charter flight over the weekend. Since we issued the travel warning, we've seen a drop-off in the number of American citizens entering the country."

"Good. What have you heard from your contacts over at Gisawian police headquarters? Do they see the situation stabilizing anytime soon?"

"It's hard to say. The government is still in spin mode, trying to pretend that everything is business as usual."

"I guess they haven't turned on the TV lately. The riots have been the lead story on all the international news channels for the last two weeks," Claire said.

"Denial is a strategy. My contacts at police headquarters said that their higher-ups were extremely upset when they heard about our travel advisory. The Ministry of Information issued a strongly worded response, denying any cause for concern and accusing us of contributing to 'irrational hysteria' over the riots," Jake said, adding air quotes for emphasis.

"Not surprising," Claire said. "The regime is reluctant to show any sign of weakness. Anything else?"

"No, ma'am. We're keeping a close eye on the street. I'll let you know if things start heating up out there today."

"All right, thanks, Jake. Let's go from the tactical to the strategic level. Stephen, what do you have for us?" Claire looked at the embassy's political officer.

The man was the perfect yin to the yang of the former Marine sitting next to him, with a well-padded physique, an unruly mop of hair, and the air of a frustrated academic. Inexplicably, he was also a devotee of three-piece suits, worn in stoic defiance of the sub-Saharan humidity.

"Madam Ambassador, we're almost done drafting a cable with some fresh analysis on the economic situation underlying the recent unrest," Stephen said.

"Good. That should be a useful primer for the folks back in Washington. What's the gist?"

"We're focusing on DRoG's long history of fiscal mismanagement and corruption, but particularly how these problems became acute following Operation Brushfire."

"At the time, I recall President Namono promising that the operation would create thousands of new jobs," Claire noted.

"Indeed. And in fact, the military campaign did turn out well for a select few. After the army neutralized Odoki's militias, the government quickly auctioned off a large block of new mineral concessions in the western region. But rather than saving the windfall for a rainy day, the regime treated the proceeds like a winning lottery ticket, setting off a wave of speculation and overspending. All based on wildly

35

ambitious assumptions concerning the revenue streams from the mining operations."

"And now comes time to pay the bill," Claire said, shaking her head.

"It appears that way," Stephen agreed. "Over the last few months, several infrastructure projects were abruptly canceled after the government defaulted on the loans. The central bank has been burning through foreign currency reserves to service debt and pay for critical imports. Meanwhile, they've been printing local currency at a record pace, exacerbating the already sky-high inflation."

"You don't need to be an economist to see that things are bad out there," Claire said. "I was down at the central market a few weeks ago and tried to pay for a set of earrings with some Gisawian notes, but the merchant refused to take them. He said dollars or euros only."

"Exactly. The people who are lucky enough to have relatives overseas can get by on remittances. But for everybody else, they can't carry enough local currency to do their daily shopping. And even if they could, the store shelves are empty."

"Obviously, it's painful out in the street, but are we seeing any signs that the regime is feeling the pinch?"

"Mostly anecdotal evidence," Stephen said. "A few weeks ago, the president's son Fabrice commandeered a plane from the national airline to shuttle his entourage to Ibiza for a bachelor party weekend. When the aircraft leasing company got wind of his little excursion, they called the Spanish government and had the jet grounded for overdue payments. The issue was mysteriously resolved a few days later amid rumors that some Chinese investors provided a bridge loan to keep the airline afloat and get Fabrice back home after the party."

Claire turned to the CIA station chief, who was sitting a few seats down the table. He had been pretending to take notes while surreptitiously working a sudoku puzzle.

"Mike, is this the same Fabrice that you recommended to the White House as our, quote-unquote, best bet to run the country?" Claire asked rhetorically.

Mike Jones glanced up from his puzzle and nodded thoughtfully before speaking. "'Do not judge by appearances, but judge with right judgment.' John 7:24," he said, before going back to doodling in the margins of the puzzle.

"Thank you for that insight. Let's move on," Claire said. "Stephen, please continue."

"In summary, Madam Ambassador, what we're seeing is a textbook case of the resource curse phenomenon: volatile revenue streams, high inflation, institutional corruption, and democratic backsliding. Unfortunately, we don't see much prospect for President Namono getting his house back in order anytime soon."

"Thank you, Stephen," Claire said. She turned back to the station chief. "Mike, what's the agency's take on the situation? Are the analysts back at Langley anticipating further destabilization?"

"Well, if you're talking about the likelihood of near-term regime collapse, that's an inherently tough call. I wouldn't want to get too far out ahead of this."

"But isn't that your job? Getting out ahead of major geopolitical risk?" she asked with mock incredulity.

"This isn't exactly the Yalta Conference," Jones smirked. "We're not dealing with rational actors here. No one has the slightest idea what President Namono is going to do when he wakes up tomorrow morning, including President Namono. The best I can offer you is a subjective assessment based on the sentiment out in the streets. And right now, that's not looking good."

"That seems somewhat self-evident based on two weeks of rioting," Claire shot back.

"Well, sure, superficially. But then again, what does it really mean when an angry mob sets fire to several city blocks?"

"Presumably, it suggests a profound dissatisfaction with the status quo," Claire sighed, quickly losing patience with the conversation.

"Yes, but I wouldn't call that a nuanced expression of political grievance. What I'm talking about is getting inside people's heads, figuring out what they think when they wake up and have that first cup of coffee. Are they going to grab their sack lunch and head off to work like a robot, or spend the day throwing Molotov cocktails at the police? That's the kind of thing I consider actionable intelligence."

"Fair enough. But how do you propose obtaining that kind of information? Maybe some opinion polling out on the street corner?"

"Hardly," Jones snorted. "We're beta testing a new social media exploitation platform. It's called the SMEAR program. Short for Social Media Entity Analysis and Reporting."

"And how does this SMEAR thing work?" Claire asked against her better judgment, glancing at her watch as she sensed the meeting slipping beyond her control.

"Because DRoG has a relatively high density of citizens active on social media, it's a particularly rich target environment for big-data analytics," Jones explained. "For the past six months, we've been scooping up thousands of tweets, photos, emails, and text messages, then using that data to create a real-time trending indicator of public opinion—sort of like a digital mood ring for the entire country."

"It sounds impressive, but what's that going to tell me that I can't already see out the window?"

"Based on the most recent data, we're still a long way from a tipping point. Plenty of folks are sitting on the fence, waiting to see which way the winds are blowing. At the moment, the protesters are trending slightly ahead of the government, but that could change instantly."

"And what does SMEAR say about what we should expect to see out in the streets over the next few days?" Claire said, her patience growing thin.

"In the near term, we expect the opposition to double down on their momentum and keep the pressure on the regime. Unfortunately, one thing that SMEAR can't predict is how the government will respond if backed into a corner."

"But you must have some idea what they're thinking inside Green House. What are you getting from your contacts?" Claire pressed.

Jones hesitated, darting suspicious glances at the rest of the staff. "If you don't mind, I would prefer that we discuss this one on one," he said under his breath.

Claire rolled her eyes and jerked her thumb at the door, dismissing everyone from the room. Once they were alone, she turned back to Jones, who had been sitting with his eyes closed in a self-hypnotic trance. "It's just us now, Mike. What have you got?"

Jones opened his eyes and glanced around the room, confirming that they were alone. "As I was saying, we have limited insight into President Namono's internal decision-making process. However, we assess that he is increasingly isolated from his staff and likely suffering from severe paranoia. He rarely leaves his bedroom in Green House and only eats imported freeze-dried food for fear of poisoning. Most of his trusted advisors are out of the loop, and he has cut off all communication with his son, Fabrice. The only person with regular contact is his wife, Charity. However, there are rumors that the relationship has descended into a pattern of domination and abuse."

"He's beating her!" Claire gasped in horror.

"What? No!" Jones said, shaking his head in confusion. "She's beating him."

"Jesus," Claire muttered. "What you're telling me is that the CIA doesn't have any idea about his next move?"

"President Namono is a hard target, almost impossible to penetrate."

"You don't have any reliable contacts around his inner circle?"

"It's not a matter of access. We have plenty of people on the inside. It's a matter of actual penetration into Namono's head. The guy is delusional. He probably doesn't have the slightest idea what's going on outside in the streets."

"If that's the case, then who's running the show?"

"That's the million-dollar question. Unfortunately, right now, all we're getting is a bunch of rumors and conflicting information."

"Is there anyone on the inside you can trust?"

"No way. The entire regime is nothing but a den of thieves. They're all busy jockeying for position and offshoring their bank accounts in case the entire thing come crashing down."

"You're telling me that there's no one who can give us an accurate picture of what's happening inside Green House?"

Jones hesitated, seemingly put out by the imposition of the question. "We have one asset who's got his finger on the pulse," he whispered conspiratorially across the table.

"You mean inside Green House?"

"Inside everywhere!" Jones said, his eyes wide. "This guy runs the deepest network in the county. He has people inside Green House, army headquarters, and police intelligence—even the university. Name the place, and he has someone working on the inside."

"And you trust him?" Claire asked skeptically.

"We don't have a choice. There's no one else with that kind of placement and access."

"What's his story?"

"You know I can't get into that," Jones said. "Those details are highly compartmented. If this asset gets compromised, then we've got nothing. All I can tell you is that he's proven highly reliable in the past and is open to tasking. More importantly, he's not afraid to get his hands dirty when necessary."

Claire leaned forward, looking Jones straight in the eye. "We're walking a fine line here. The Cold War's over, Mike. DRoG is not some pawn in a superpower chess match anymore. There's no presidential finding for any sort of covert action. Furthermore, our guidance from the White House is to minimize involvement and keep DRoG out of the headlines. I don't think playing games with their internal political process is part of that plan."

"I'm not talking about overthrowing the regime," Jones backpedaled. "But the reality is, if you want good information, you can't just sit back and expect it to fall into your lap. Sometimes you need to be proactive. Especially if you want to facilitate desirable outcomes."

"I don't need to remind you about the fallout from Operation Brushfire," Claire said. "We got ourselves involved in some pretty ugly stuff with that fiasco. We can't let that happen again. If changes are coming to DRoG, then we need to support that by enabling a legitimate democratic process. Otherwise, we risk losing what little credibility we still have left."

"Gee, that sounds great!" Jones said, dramatically throwing up his hands in mock surrender. "And I'm sure they're having the same conversation over in the Chinese embassy right now."

"Don't patronize me, Mike. I've been in this business as long as you have. What I'm saying is that there's more at stake here. We're potentially on the verge of a significant political transition in this country. We can't afford to be perceived as coming down on the wrong side of that process. Everyone is going to be looking at how we play this when the time comes."

"I think we both understand what's at stake," Jones said flatly. "You've got your job to do, and I've got mine. I'm sure, in the end, we're going to do what's right."

"I hope so, Mike. I really hope so," Claire said, getting up from her seat and leaving him alone.

+++

Later that day, when classes were over, Anna left her office at the university and headed to the SB Café, a popular student hangout a few blocks from campus. It was her first time there, but as soon as she entered the courtyard, she was hit with a powerful sense of déjà vu. The cheap plastic tables, the Christmas lights strung through the tree branches, and the shrubbery planted in mop buckets around the patio seemed familiar.

Wandering through the café, Anna spotted several artifacts that jogged her memory. A tattered American flag hung on the wall, looking as if it might have once flown over the sands of Iwo Jima. On the condiments table were several large bins of surplus plastic sporks sitting next to the creamer and sugar containers. Nailed to the wall next to the cash register was a faded newspaper clipping recounting the death of the infamous warlord Daniel Odoki. Finally, hanging above the bar was the final clue confirming her suspicions, a weathered wooden sign in bright, tropical colors reading "Sujah Bean Café."

Anna was startled from her nostalgic trance by the sound of a woman calling out her name. She spotted a group of students sitting together at a table across the courtyard. The young woman waving to her went by the nickname Nesi, and she had invited Anna to join them for coffee.

"Professor DeVore, I didn't think you'd make it," Nesi said as Anna joined them.

"Believe it or not, I don't get invited out often," Anna said. "I didn't want to miss the opportunity."

Nesi had long black hair woven into tight braids, elegantly bound in a swath of linen cloth. She was dressed in casual student attire, a loose-fitting, floral-patterned dress, and leather sandals. As Anna had gotten to know her, she had discovered an easygoing nature that was usually obscured by Nesi's intensity in the classroom.

"Ever been to SB Café before?" Nesi asked Anna. "It's the best coffee in town."

"Not exactly," Anna said. "At least, not in its current incarnation."

Nesi gave Anna a quizzical look before signaling the waitress, then calling for everyone around the table's attention. "For those of you who don't know her, this is Professor DeVore. I took her course last year, and now she's sitting on my thesis committee," Nesi announced.

The other students smiled and nodded politely. As the only white American woman on campus and a visiting professor, Anna rarely required an introduction. Even before she met new people, they had inevitably heard something about her and already formed an opinion about why she was there, occasionally to her advantage, but often not.

"So, how are classes going?" Anna asked as the other students resumed their conversations.

"Not as well as I would like," Nesi admitted. "Between working on my thesis and all the craziness happening off-campus, it's been hard to stay focused."

"I feel the same way," Anna said, nodding sympathetically.

"Honestly, I haven't even started thinking about exams. Over the last few weeks, all my free time has been with the student government committee. We've been going nonstop since the protests began."

"I know a few other students on the committee. It seems as if you've suddenly stepped into the spotlight, at least as far as the administration is concerned."

"So true," Nesi chuckled. "But I'm afraid the administration is not appreciative of our efforts. I think they would much rather have us go back to worrying about redecorating the student union or voting on snack selections in the vending machines. They don't seem quite as enamored with our new agenda."

As Nesi spoke, the waitress appeared at the table, delivering Anna a café latte with a dash of cinnamon and a single sugar cube set on the saucer.

"But she didn't even order yet," Nesi said, giving the waitress a confused look.

The young woman shrugged and nodded toward the bar. "The boss told me this was the order. He also said that the entire table is comped. No charge for anyone."

Dumbfounded, Nesi stared at the latte, then back at Anna. But by then, Anna had forgotten about the coffee. She was smiling at a man walking across the courtyard toward their table.

"Miss Anna, I didn't know you were still here in DRoG," the man said, arriving at the table with a giddy smile. He was a wiry local Gisawian dressed like a waiter, wearing white pants and a coffee-stained oxford shirt. "It is so good to see you again."

Anna stood up and gave him a long hug as the students around the table stopped their conversations and looked on in surprise.

"Sammy, it's good to see you, too," Anna said. "I would have come long ago if I had known this place was yours. You changed the name, but everything else looks the same."

"The coffee is much better now," Sammy assured her.

"I have no doubt about that. I hear it's the most popular place in town."

Sammy's eyes drifted modestly to the ground. "I have been lucky, Miss Anna. After the first Sujah Bean closed on the old American base, I started a new café at the airport. Since then, I've had no rest. I have ten cafés now and the concession for all the government offices."

"That's great, Sammy," Anna said. "I can't tell you how happy I am to hear this."

"And how is Colonel Lutalo?"

"He's well. Maybe you remember, after that business with Odoki, they made him the commander of the counter-terrorism force."

"Yes, Miss Anna, of course I remember. Please tell him I said hello. I will look for him the next time I visit my café out at the army base."

"I know he would love to see you, Sammy. So, I'm guessing you haven't heard the news that Louie and I are engaged."

"This is wonderful, Miss Anna," Sammy said, his eyes dancing with excitement. "I am so happy for you. Please let me know when you have the date. SB Café does catering, too! I will make a special price for my old friends."

"That sounds delightful, Sammy," Anna laughed. "You know we wouldn't want anyone else but you. It was good to see you again."

"You too, Miss Anna," he said before retreating behind the bar.

Anna turned back to the table with a smile on her face. She stirred her latte, thinking back to the old Sujah Bean Café and the table where she had first met Louie. When she awoke from her daydream, she found Nesi and the other students staring at her, still bewildered by the encounter.

"What?" Anna exclaimed when she realized she was the center of attention.

"How on earth do you know Sammy?" Nesi said, clearly in shock. "He's, like, famous. His cafés are the hottest thing in town."

"We're old friends from when I first came to DRoG, back before I got the job at the university," Anna explained. "Honestly, I didn't even realize that this place was his until I walked in and saw all the decorations. It looks exactly like his very first café."

Nesi squinted suspiciously at Anna. "I must say, Professor Devore, you are always full of surprises. First, I discovered that you were engaged to the nephew of the defense minister. And now I learn that you are old friends with the most successful entrepreneur in town. I think perhaps you lead a more exciting life than you let on." She gave Anna a teasing wink.

"Hardly. I wasn't kidding when I said that I don't get out often. Anyway, enough about my boring social life. Tell me about what you've been up to with the student government committee."

"Ahhh, it's been a crazy few weeks," Nesi said, shaking her head. "You know, for a long time, the committee had a reputation as a social club. It was all about planning parties and getting phone numbers. But ever since the protests started, something changed. I think seeing people out in the streets kind of woke everyone up. We're finally talking about things that matter: tuition fees, crowded classrooms, bad technology, the lack of funding from the government—all of it."

"It's hard to believe you never worried about those things before," Anna said with surprise.

"Well, it's not that we weren't aware of them. I suppose it was just easier to focus on solving nonproblems than real ones," Nesi said with a shrug. "I'm sure the administration preferred it that way as well. We could all agree to ignore the elephants in the room and spend our energy chasing after the mice instead. It was a matter of complacency. Honestly, I think most of the students didn't want to make trouble. Everyone just wanted to graduate and find a nice safe job with the government or go overseas to make money. In their defense, it takes a real act of courage to speak out against a club that you've been preparing all your life to join."

"But it wasn't always that way, was it?" Anna asked.

"Not at all! But we like to forget our history. This university was where it all began. The leaders of the independence movement sat in the same classrooms as us. They wrote the first draft of the constitution on the same tables where now we're arguing about which emojis to use on our Twitter feed."

"Don't be too hard on yourself," Anna reassured her. "You're in good company. Most students back in the States are far more concerned with social media than social justice. Apathy is a pandemic that knows no borders."

"Sad but true. Though I must say, since the start of the protests, at least some people are beginning to push for change. You remember Didier Kengo from class last year?"

"Of course, how could I forget? The two of you could have run the seminar by yourselves!"

"Certainly not," Nesi laughed. "But he's been leading a dissident faction on the committee, trying to shake things up. He's only the vice president, but he's getting all the attention at the meetings, talking about free speech on campus and ending government control over the curriculum and faculty appointments. It's probably more than most people want to hear, but he's starting to gain support—although he's attracting attention from the more conservative members of the committee as well. They're worried about getting on the wrong side of the administration."

"What do you think?"

"Both sides have a point," Nesi condeded. "Didier is right to push these issues on the agenda. We've waited too long for real reform. But the committee is also correct to be concerned about reprisal. The university still answers to the government. At the moment, with the protests going on, they have other things to worry about. But that may not be the case much longer."

"Why is that?"

"Because Didier is pushing for the committee to take a stand on issues beyond the university. At the meetings, he's been talking about things that could be perceived as critical of the regime."

"I'm sure that won't be taken lightly by the administration," Anna said.

"No, it won't. In fact, there are even rumors going around about informants keeping tabs on the committee. Some people are too scared to speak out during our meetings."

"But Didier is willing to take that risk? Does he have any chance of winning over those stuck in the middle?"

"Hard to say. But Didier can be very persuasive when he wants to be," Nesi said with a mischievous smile.

"Indeed. I seem to recall that the two of you were something of an item last year," Anna said with a wink of her own.

Nesi laughed and shook her head. "That's over now. A short-lived romance. It didn't take long before we both realized that we were better off as friends. We're both just too bull-headed to get on as a couple. But honestly, it's for the better. We're much closer now than before. It was a healthy change."

Anna smiled and nodded. "Well, with the two of you in charge, I'm sure it won't be long before the rest of the committee falls into line behind you."

"Oh yes," Nesi said with nervous laughter. "As we lead them off to the guillotine!"

+++

Later that evening, Anna arrived home to an empty house. She wasn't surprised to find Louie gone. Since the start of the protests, he had been coming home late each evening, sometimes only staying to catch a few hours of sleep and then returning to base before sunrise. But even when home, he was mostly silent about what was happening at work. When Anna inquired about his day, he would sigh in place of an answer, and turn on the TV to change the subject.

That evening, Anna was already in bed and reading a book when she heard Louie's car pull into the driveway. When he came into the bedroom, he looked tense and exhausted.

"How are you?" Anna asked.

Louie's back was turned as he took off his camouflage uniform and pulled on a pair of sweatpants and a T-shirt. "Fine. Just tired," he muttered, repeating the same words he had said to her nearly every day since the start of the protests.

"How was the drive home?"

"I took the long way around the city again. It was easier than stopping to show my identification at every police checkpoint around town."

"Were things bad again today?"

It was more a statement than a question since she already knew the answer from listening to the news on the radio.

"Mostly the same," Louie said, downplaying what they both knew to be true. "There are rumors about big marches planned for the weekend. We just received word that the ministry intends to keep all the army units on base through the weekend. They want us to be ready in case we're needed to reinforce the police."

"That sounds like a not-so-subtle warning to the marchers."

Louie shrugged.

"And I assume that your uncle was the one who decided this?"

"Well, he is the minister," Louie snapped. "Such decisions can't be made without him."

"I'm sorry. Louie. You know I'm not taking sides in this. It's none of my business. It's just that I worry about you. I only want things to return to normal and for you to be safe."

Louie nodded but seemed ready to drop the subject. "How was your day?" he finally asked.

"Good." She hesitated, then added, "Interesting."

"I'm surprised the students are still showing up for class," Louie said. "Haven't they demanded some kind of special holiday because of the inconvenience of the riots?"

"I don't think that's fair," Anna protested. "Some of them are taking it very seriously."

Louie sniffed as he began scrolling through messages on his phone.

"I met with a few of my old students today at a café off campus," Anna continued.

"And was that enlightening?" Louie mumbled, still reading his messages.

"I saw Sammy there. It was his café where we met. Apparently, he's doing rather well."

"So I gather," Louie said without enthusiasm.

"He's opened almost a dozen cafés around town."

"Yet another unlikely windfall from Operation Brushfire," Louie grumbled.

"You know, Louie, there are plenty of people who should feel guilty about what happened during Operation Brushfire. But Sammy's not one of them!" Anna snapped, surprised at her frustration.

"I suppose you're referring to me?" Louie said, putting down his phone and looking her in the eye for the first time that evening. "After all, I was the dupe, right? The one who pulled the trigger and became the big 'hero' of the story," he said, flashing air quotes with his fingers.

"You know I didn't mean you," she murmured.

"But still, you're implying that I should have known better."

"Louie, we've been over this so many times. None of us understood what was going on at the time. That's why it's called a conspiracy. And it certainly wasn't a coincidence that your uncle put you right in the middle of it all. You were the perfect one to play the part—the golden boy. The namesake of a famous soldier killed in battle, defending his country. The prodigal son returned home to serve his nation. Your uncle knew exactly what he was doing when he made you the center of attention. It was a magnificent bit of theater he was directing, a perfect story to divert everyone's attention from what was really going on."

"I don't want to talk about it," Louie said, shaking his head.

They were quiet for a time, and then Anna tried a different subject. "Some of the students invited me to a meeting next week," she said.

"What kind of meeting?"

"It's the student government committee. They're considering whether or not to make a statement of solidarity with the demonstrators. One of my old students is the vice president. Didier Kengo. He's pushing for the committee to become involved in the protest movement."

"Ah, a new hero in the making," Louie said, walking into their cramped bathroom and grabbing his toothbrush.

"He reminds me a lot of you," Anna called after him.

"Why? Because he's a sucker?"

"No. Because he believes in something."

"Then let me offer him some advice," Louie called back from the bathroom. "If your friend Didier really thinks that good intentions are enough to make a difference, then he has no idea what he's up against. I learned that the hard way. He will too." Louie said, staring into the mirror.

Anna was about to speak, then changed her mind. She rolled over and turned off the bedside lamp while Louie finished brushing his teeth.

CHAPTER THREE

———

A few days later, Mike Jones left work early, informing his secretary that he wouldn't be back in the office until morning. She knew better than to ask for details as he disappeared out the door. He left the embassy through the service entrance, donning a windbreaker, sunglasses, and a floppy hat when he stepped outside. Instead of taking his government vehicle, he left the compound behind the wheel of a beat-up Hyundai Sonata, blending in perfectly with the other cars on the road.

A few blocks from the embassy, Jones began a series of erratic maneuvers, racing through back alleyways and making several quick turns the wrong way down one-way streets. He completed two full circuits through a parking garage, then pulled over at a gas station and got out of the car. While hunched over, Jones pretended to check the tire pressure while glancing over his shoulder, trying to spot surveillance. The old habits from his Moscow days were hard to shake, now as ingrained into his routine as his midmorning cigarette break.

After a few more minutes of evasive driving, Jones turned the Sonata toward the city's expat district, a leafy enclave of hip cafés, artists' shacks, and dive bars that felt like a cocoon of tranquility amid the bustling chaos of the capital. He pulled over on a crowded residential street where the availability of parking spots was limited only by a driver's imagination and dexterity. Jones slipped out of the car and glanced over his shoulder, confirming that he was alone.

When satisfied the coast was clear, he took off on foot along a dirt path running parallel to the road. With dusk falling, he finally stopped outside the gate of an old Victorian mansion, a once-grand colonial residence now fallen into disrepair. The house was partially concealed behind an overgrown garden, but from the sidewalk, passersby could hear the sound of music and laughter coming from inside. A string of Chinese lanterns woven through the tree branches illuminated a path through the undergrowth to the entrance.

Jones opened the gate and pushed his way through the bushes to the front door. Once inside, he paused in the foyer, letting his eyes adjust to the light. The main room of the mansion had been turned into a speakeasy, with several adjoining alcoves reserved for more intimate gatherings. The clientele was an improbable assortment of races and nationalities, resembling a seedy version of a UN general assembly meeting. At one of the tables, two scantily clad Eastern European women were chatting up a delegation of Arab businessmen. Near the bar, some dusty roustabouts played a round of darts, kicking off a weekend furlough from one of the mining operations out west.

Jones walked through the bar, surreptitiously glancing into the private alcoves off the main room. In one, he spotted some Chinese businessmen having cocktails with a well-dressed Gisawian. Jones assumed he was a minor local official, perhaps a stamp-holding member of the permitting raj, angling for a bit of baksheesh. In the next room, a gang of thuggish-looking Russians was lounging on a sofa, watching a soccer match and guzzling cans of the local lager that smelled of formaldehyde.

Jones took off his hat and windbreaker, then gave the bartender a familiar nod as he walked through the room. The barkeep was a local Gisawian who had a lucrative side business keeping tabs on everyone who came through the door, then knowing who might find such information useful. As Jones crossed the room, he spotted his contact sitting alone at a table in a window bay. The man was staring into the garden, smoking a cigarette and nursing a tumbler of scotch. Jones joined him, taking a seat in one of the leather chairs. The man didn't seem surprised to have company and casually tossed a pack of Gauloises onto the coffee table between them.

"Thanks," Jones said, taking a cigarette from the pack and lighting it with some matches from his pocket.

"Yeah, man. Anything for my good friend from the CI of A," the man said with a heavy Gisawian accent, flashing an irreverent grin.

"Cut the shit, Fabrice," Jones snapped. "I don't think either one of us needs any extra attention right now."

"Oh, come on, Mr. Jones. Don't worry. We're among friends here," he said, nodding at the criminals, misfits, and ne'er-do-wells occupying the tables around them. "Anyway, what's so important that we had to meet tonight? You know, I had to cancel my plans with a very nice lady friend."

Jones took a drag on his cigarette, squinting at Fabrice through a cloud of smoke. The man possessed the roguish good looks and muscular physique of a professional soccer player a few years past his prime. He wore expensive leather shoes and a matching belt, with pressed linen slacks and a baby blue silk shirt unbuttoned halfway to his navel. Perched on his head was a pair of designer sunglasses, ready for a blitz of paparazzi, should it appear.

"Your lady friend can wait," Jones said. "We've got bigger things to worry about right now."

"Oh, Mr. Jones, you CIA people are always worrying about something," Fabrice said, chuckling and shaking his head. "The sun will come up tomorrow, and life will go on. I can promise you this. But if you really want to talk serious, then let's have a little drink. Scotch?"

Jones nodded impatiently as Fabrice waved to one of the Bulgarian hostesses loitering around the bar.

"Glenfiddich twenty-one," Fabrice yelled across the room. The woman nodded and disappeared behind the bar. Fabrice turned back to Jones. "What's so important that I had to cancel my date?"

"Listen, Fabrice, I don't know where you've been hanging out for the last two weeks, but maybe you noticed that things have been a little crazy around town?"

Fabrice glanced around the bar as if answering the question of where he had been spending his time. "Everything looks fine to me, boss," he said with a casual shrug.

"Really? In that case, let me give you a little tip. If you happen to wander outside and see a parade of people marching through the streets, chanting your father's name and setting cars on fire, they're not part of his reelection committee."

"That's none of my business," Fabrice said, reaching over and grabbing another cigarette.

"It damn well should be!" Jones hissed. "Do you really think that just because Daddy kicked you out of Green House, you've suddenly become a man of the people? Believe me, they'd happily run your ass out of town along with him if they had half the chance."

For an instant, Fabrice seemed to lose a bit of his swagger, perhaps weighing the likelihood of such an encounter with the hoi polloi. "What do you want from me?" he said defensively.

"I need information. What's going on inside Green House?"

"Why do you think I know? I haven't been there in months. You know that."

"But you still talk to people on the inside," Jones insisted. "What about your stepmother, Charity? What's going on with her?"

"Ahhh, that insufferable snake!" Fabrice moaned in mock pain. "If you want to know what's going on at Green House, she's the one you should be talking to."

"Well, if I could do that, do you think I'd be wasting my time sitting here with you in this shithole bar? Besides, from what I hear, Charity's only talking to the Chinese these days. What do you know about that?"

"Yeah, it's true. The stinking Chinese are everywhere," Fabrice said, spitting in the general direction of the alcove where the Beijing businessmen were enjoying some bonhomie with one of the Bulgarian barflies.

"You think Charity is in tight with them?" Jones asked.

"I know she's got a lot of business going on. I heard the Chinese gave her some money to get things started. But that's all I know. She doesn't tell me anything. Whenever I try to call my father, she makes sure I don't get through."

"You think she's the one running the show inside Green House?"

"Yeah, man. I told you, the snake is in charge!" Fabrice blurted out, again becoming agitated.

The barkeep appeared beside their table. "Gentlemen, I'm sorry to disturb you," he said, bowing slightly. "However, there seems to be a small problem with the drink order."

"Don't tell me you're out of scotch," Fabrice said, throwing up his hands in disgust.

"No, sir. We have the twenty-one. However, the manager insisted that we settle a small matter before fulfilling the order."

"Not this again!" Fabrice exploded. "He knows my credit's good. If he's worried about it, just tell him to send the bill over to Green House. Someone there will take care of it."

The man smiled awkwardly. "I'm sorry, sir. The manager tried that the last time, and the bill was returned unpaid. I'm afraid we must settle the account before we can bring out the bottle."

Fabrice shot to his feet, on the verge of violence, when Jones stepped in to de-escalate the situation. "What's the tab?" he asked the bartender, putting a hand on Fabrice's shoulder and pressing him back into his seat.

"Four thousand, one hundred and eighty-six dollars, sir. That includes the Glenfiddich."

"Jesus," Jones muttered, looking at Fabrice in disbelief. "OK, I'll take care of it," he told the barkeep. Fabrice and the bartender watched in silence as he pulled a fat billfold from a hidden pocket of his windbreaker, then proceeded to peel off fifty hundred-dollar bills from the large stack.

"There's a little extra in there for your trouble," Jones said, handing the wad over to the bartender.

"Thank you, sir," the man murmured. "I'll bring the Glenfiddich straight away," he added before scurrying off behind the bar.

He returned a minute later with the bottle and two clean glasses, then disappeared again without a word. Fabrice poured them each a drink and settled back into his chair, apparently having already forgotten the matter of the tab.

"Here's to you, boss," he said, tipping his glass at Jones before taking a long sip.

Jones, unamused, left his tumbler on the table but helped himself to another Gauloises. "So, Fabrice, I don't want to pry into your business, but I get the sense that you're having some cash flow problems. Am I correct in that assumption?"

"The snake cut me off," Fabrice spat out, spilling scotch on his shirt. "I know she talked my father into it. Right after that thing in Ibiza."

"Ah, yes. I think I heard something about your little excursion with the boys. Not exactly great timing, given the food crisis and all."

Fabrice shrugged and then finished off his drink in a single gulp.

"From what you're telling me, Charity is calling the shots now over at Green House. Let's say, hypothetically, that your father's health took a sudden turn for the worse. If he were forced to step down, how would Charity respond?"

"How the hell do you think she's gonna respond? She's already in charge, man. That's what I've been telling you. All she's waiting for is the chance to make it real. Don't you see what's happening? She's taking everything that's mine!" Fabrice said, manically waving an unlit cigarette in the air.

Jones reached across the table and poured Fabrice another glass of scotch. "Let's just take it easy," he said, handing over the glass. "We're not going to solve any problems by losing our heads."

"Yeah, that's easy for you to say, mister CIA! You're walking around town with pockets full of cash and no cares in the world."

"That's where you're wrong, Fabrice. I do care what happens to DRoG. I care a great deal. That's why we need to come up with a plan. A good plan. One that ensures that Charity doesn't get the chance to take over Green House."

"I think you're a little late for that, boss," Fabrice sniffed.

"Maybe. Maybe not. Give me a little time to brainstorm. In the meantime, go easy on the sauce," Jones said, nodding at the bottle. "And try to be someplace where I can find you. Got it?"

Fabrice nodded and glanced around the bar, signaling that he was already at that location. "Sure boss, you got it," he said, tossing off an irreverent two-fingered salute for good measure.

Jones rose and straightened his tie, then walked toward the door, leaving his tumbler of scotch untouched on the table.

The next day, the embassy staff assembled in the conference room again. The mood around the table was subdued as
they waited for Washington to come on the line. Three weeks
of long hours and little sleep had taken its toll, and everyone
struggled to stay awake. Finally, Reid McCoy appeared on
the screen, dialing in from the White House Situation Room.

"Good morning. Or afternoon. Or whatever the hell
time it is over there," Reid said.

"Good evening, Reid," Ambassador Roberts clarified.
"I've got my primary staff here in the room. Of course you
know Mike, our station chief. I also have Stephen, our political advisor, and Colonel Sawyer, the defense attaché."

"All right. Good," Reid said. "I've only got a few minutes.
What's the latest on the situation over there?"

"Simmering but under control," Clair explained. "We
still have some sporadic protests, but there have been fewer
incidents of violence over the last few days."

"That's a good sign. Are we trending in the right direction?" Reid asked.

"Too soon to tell. Unfortunately, there's not much im-
provement in the underlying issues. The currency is still in
free fall, and the government just announced a new round
of austerity measures. Last week, the treasury implemented
exchange controls making it illegal to use foreign currency
for domestic transactions. Yesterday, the police were out conducting raids in the local markets, shutting down merchants
doing business in dollars or euros. As you can imagine, they
aren't winning many hearts and minds."

"On the bright side, none of that is making it into the headlines back here," Reid observed. "By the way, nice job pulling off that evacuation with minimal drama. POTUS was pleased with how things went down. He even mentioned it during the National Rice Pudding Day event on the South Lawn. Good work making that happen without a lot of hoopla."

"Thanks, Reid," Claire said. "We got the press release, along with several cases of rice pudding. It was really gratifying."

"Great. I only wish our colleagues over on the Hill were half as professional. I'm assuming you saw the interview yesterday with Congressman Burke?"

"Yes. In fact, it just started hitting news over here," Claire said. "We're expecting to see some pushback from all sides. I can tell you that his comments aren't going to play well inside Green House or out on the street. Amazingly, he's managed to piss off almost everyone in the country."

"You don't say?" Reid said sarcastically. "That little shit is throwing us all under the bus, accusing POTUS of giving DRoG over to the Chinese. Burke has all but called for regime change over there."

"You know, Reid, the kid may have a point," Mike Jones interjected. "POTUS can pretend that Namono is on our side, but that doesn't change the facts on the ground. He's selling us out to Beijing. No doubt about it. He—"

"Listen, Mike," Reid said, cutting him off, "I know you're worried about China's footprint over there, but that's not what this is about. It's about Burke trying to save his own ass at the expense of our bilateral relations."

"I don't understand," Claire said, inserting herself back into the conversation. "Why does a junior congressman from Pennsylvania care about US policy toward DRoG?"

"Because Operation Brushfire got him elected," Reid said. "He was still in uniform and over there when we took down Odoki. He made it the centerpiece of his campaign."

"Right. Now it's coming back to me," Claire recalled. "But why is he bringing it up now? What's he got to gain by attacking the administration on some wonky foreign policy issue that no one really cares about?"

"It's a red herring. Burke doesn't care about DRoG. He's in hot water with the voters back home and decided that his best strategy is creating a diversion. The only reason he's flogging POTUS on our DRoG policy is to distract the attention away from his legal problems."

"Dare I even ask what he did?"

"Having an undocumented nanny, sous chef, and pool boy on his personal payroll after running as an anti-immigrant hardliner. Now he's talking about DRoG any chance he gets to keep people distracted. We don't expect him to let up until after midterms."

"How do you plan to respond?" Claire asked.

"POTUS gave him a smackdown this morning by announcing a bipartisan three-hundred-sixty-degree strategic posture review of US policy toward DRoG."

"Who's in charge of that?"

"Does it matter?" Reid asked rhetorically. "The point is that it will keep our DRoG policy out of the headlines for the next few months by putting everyone to sleep. Burke can stick that in his ass and figure out some other way of salvaging his pathetic campaign."

"That's all well and good, but what should I tell the Gisawians when they ask about our response to Burke's call for Namono's ouster?" Claire asked. "They're going to see this as yet another example of Uncle Sam sticking his nose into their business."

"Right, because they only want us sticking our nose into their business when it happens to be convenient for them," Reid said, rolling his eyes. "Just tell them that Burke is a nitwit, and there's no change to US policy or our steadfast support for President Namono."

"Fine, I'll have our press office draft something," Claire said, eager to end the conversation. "Anything else we need to know?"

"Just some usual nonsense going on over at the UN. We're expecting to see a draft resolution proposing an arms embargo on DRoG in response to the government's crackdown against the protesters."

"Ha! Arms embargo my ass," Jones blurted. "Game on!"

"Listen here, Mike," Reid said, pointing his finger into the camera. "For the next two months, the only game we're playing is keeping DRoG out of the headlines. I don't want any funny business over there. I don't give a shit what Burke, the UN, or anybody else is doing. Our measure of success is me not having to waste any more of the president's time worrying about DRoG. Are we clear on that?"

"Got it, Reid," Claire said, glaring across the table at Jones. "We'll do our best to keep things quiet on this end."

"Good. Then I hope this will be our last conversation for a while. I'm about to hit another meeting. Do you have anything else?"

"No. I think we understand your guidance," Claire reassured him.

"OK. Then good luck," he said before dropping off the line.

+++

Early the next morning, Colonel Sawyer made his way across town to the joint counter-terrorism training center near the airport. At the front gate, he flashed his identification card to the guards, explaining that he was there to meet with the unit commander. The guards waved him through security, toward the headquarters building of the Gisawian counter-terrorism force.

Sawyer had been in DRoG over a year but still found the place confounding. However, his occasional visits to the army camp provided a dose of the familiar. Walking onto the base felt like coming home to the small midwestern town where he'd grown up. Everything was in its place, and people behaved precisely as expected. He found comfort in seeing soldiers marching back and forth across the yard, white lines painted in the dirt for no apparent reason, and the perfectly cut grass of the parade field.

On his way over to the headquarters, Sawyer stopped at the edge of the parade field, watching with warm satisfaction as a gruff old Gisawian NCO barked out orders at some new recruits. When the drill sergeant finished his corrections, the young soldiers scattered in all directions like frightened cats. Sawyer chuckled to himself, finding it reassuring that some things were the same in every army. Then he continued toward the headquarters building.

He was early for his appointment with Lieutenant Colonel Bigombe, so he took a seat in the outer office. Sawyer was reading the newspaper and drinking a cup of milky tea when Louie stuck his head out of the office door.

"Jeff, good morning. Sorry to keep you waiting. Please come in," Louie said, waving him inside. "I hope you weren't out there too long," he said as they sat down.

"Nope, just reading the paper and enjoying a cup of tea."

"Any good news today?" Louie asked, nodding at the paper.

"I suppose that depends on which side you're rooting for. These days, the headlines read like the sports page. Each morning, I wake up looking to see who won in the streets the night before."

"I suppose that's one way of looking at it," Louie sighed. "Although I'm afraid this is a game where everyone loses."

"Probably true. I think that's why my government has been reluctant to take sides on this. I'm sure you can appreciate that we're in a difficult situation, particularly given some of the tactics being used out in the street."

"I assume you mean by the police?"

Sawyer nodded. "Some of the stuff on TV looks pretty bad. The police are playing hardball out there with the protesters. As an outsider looking in, it doesn't seem like a fair fight."

Louie took a deep breath, carefully considering his words before speaking. "Jeff, I think you know me well enough to guess how I feel about what's going on out there. But we're also both soldiers. For that reason, you can understand my dilemma. Our job is to follow orders. And we don't always have the luxury of speaking our minds, at least, not publicly."

"I understand that, Louie. That's why I came here to see you. So we could speak in confidence."

"Of course. You know we can talk freely here. Nothing leaves this room. You have my word on that," Louie assured him.

"I appreciate that. And because I trust you, I'm going to be straight with you. I think you know that because of our military presence here, what happens in DRoG gets extra attention from the politicians back at home. We've got hundreds of American soldiers here running operations from our base. Our entire regional counter-terrorism strategy is based on the assumption of uninterrupted access to that facility. But we're getting some tough questions from members of Congress about our support of your government, especially given some of the stuff that's been on TV the last few weeks."

"I'm aware of how your system works," Louie reminded him. "Don't forget, I lived in Washington for a few years during grad school."

"Right, then you know that optics are everything. People back home are looking at these protests and wondering how it's going to end."

"Jeff, what exactly are you trying to tell me?"

"Off the record, right?" Sawyer cautioned.

"Naturally."

"Between you and me, we're under a lot of pressure not to get pulled into this thing. This is coming all the way from the top. Given the uncertainty, the White House wants us to keep a low profile and avoid getting caught in the middle between the protesters and your government. However, at the same time, we can't afford any disruptions to our counter-terrorism operations. That's the number one priority right now."

"So far, I'm not surprised by anything you've told me," Louie said.

"But you also need to understand that we have some red lines."

"Such as?"

"The Gisawian army needs to stay on the sidelines of what's happening out in the streets. If, for some reason, that was to change, it could force us to re-evaluate our relationship with President Namono, not to mention our support for the Gisawian army."

"Jeff, I can assure you that my uncle is fully aware of the implications of deploying the army against the protesters. Believe me, we don't want that any more than you do. That's why I'm sitting here in my office right now and not out in the streets. We understand the risks and don't want to cross that line."

Sawyer nodded and reached into his briefcase. He pulled out a file and pushed it across the table to Louie. "Have you seen this?" he asked. "It's an urgent request that we received from your defense ministry asking us to transfer some excess US military equipment to your army."

Louie quickly scanned through the first few pages of the requisition, then looked up at Sawyer and shrugged. "I'm the commander of the counter-terrorism unit. Acquisitions are not part of my job description. If you have questions about this, you'll need to take it up directly with someone over at the ministry."

"Well, ordinarily, I would, except that all of the equipment on that list was specifically earmarked for your unit. If you look at the last page, your name is even listed as the receiving agent. That's why I thought it would be best if I came to you first."

Louie took a closer look at the requisition order, his eyes widening as he got down to the itemized list of equipment and his name on the final page.

"Louie, I don't need to tell you that this is not the kind of equipment typically used by a counter-terrorism unit. It's all riot gear: plexiglass shields, batons, body armor, stun grenades, tear gas launchers, and ten thousand rounds of rubber bullets. There's even a request for a vehicle-mounted water cannon. And it's all supposed to be delivered to your unit."

"I didn't know anything about this," Louie insisted.

"I believe you. I'm not saying that you did. But your uncle signed off on the request, so clearly, he knew all the details of the order. We received the paperwork a few days after the protests started."

Louie nodded but said nothing.

"The only reason I bring this up is that we've always had a good relationship with your army, even when things weren't so good on the political side. That's why this request raised some eyebrows back at the embassy. We're just trying to understand what your uncle plans to do with this equipment. Have you received any guidance about why he wants this?"

"No, in fact, just last week, he reassured me that the army was not going to get involved with the protests. I know he feels strongly about it and has informed Green House accordingly."

"Well, that's good to hear. You know that we've always viewed your uncle as a stabilizing factor. Someone we could trust. I hope that's still the case."

"I know that he values the relationship with your country…" Louie said, his voice trailing off, as if he wanted to say more but thought better.

Sawyer nodded, then was quiet for a moment before continuing. "There is one other issue I wanted to discuss, if you don't mind." When Louie gave a nod of his own, Sawyer asked, "What about the Chinese? Does your uncle have any kind of relationship there?"

"Jeff, I don't speak for the minister. Just because he's my uncle doesn't mean that I know everything that is happening in his office. If you have specific questions about policy matters, you'll need to take that up directly with him."

"Sure, I get that, Louie. I didn't mean to put you on the spot. I just wanted to ask. As you can imagine, people are going a little crazy right now back at our embassy. We're all trying to figure out what's what and who we can trust."

Louie handed the equipment requisition back to Sawyer. "I'm assuming from your question that you have some concerns about the Chinese?"

"Yes, among other issues," Sawyer confirmed.

"I suppose that explains the news this morning. I saw something about one of your congressmen accusing the Chinese of trying to take over our country."

"I can assure you, Congressman Burke doesn't speak for the administration. That's just the way our system works. Congressmen can say whatever they want, no matter how ridiculous."

"Yes, I'm familiar with how it works."

"Right. I keep forgetting that you lived in the States," Sawyer said.

"But this particular individual, Congressman Burke. You're aware that he has some history in my country?"

"So I've heard. But that was long before my time here."

"I knew him, in fact," Louie continued. "Our paths crossed a few times during Operation Brushfire."

"No kidding! You should have gotten his autograph before he became famous."

"As I recall, he was something of a wanker."

"Not surprising. You could say that about most of our politicians. In our system, the worst ones have a way of rising to the top."

"Well, I suppose our countries have that in common," Louie agreed.

"That's all the more reason for us soldiers to stick together. We can always be straight with each other. Let me know if you need anything," Sawyer said, rising and offering Louie his hand.

"Of course," Louie said, shaking his hand. "You do the same."

CHAPTER FOUR

————

The next morning, Claire worked in her office when her secretary unexpectedly buzzed her on the intercom. "Madam Ambassador, Jake Baxter is here to see you," said the voice through the speaker.

Claire glanced at her calendar.

"It's not on the schedule," the secretary added as if reading Claire's mind. "But he says it's urgent."

"Very well. Send him in," Claire said, pushing aside the pile of reports she had been reviewing.

The former Marine burst into the office, out of breath, appearing agitated. "Madam Ambassador, I'm sorry for interrupting, but there's something you need to see outside the front gate."

Claire knew him well enough to trust that whatever had brought him to her office, he wasn't overreacting. She got up and followed him down the hallway toward the front entrance of the building. When they walked out the door, it was immediately apparent why he had brought her here. Just beyond the security fence, several dozen young Gisawians were marching in a circle, chanting and carrying signs, blocking the entrance to the embassy.

"When did this start?" Claire asked.

"About fifteen minutes ago. I just got a call from our military base out at the airport. There's another group protesting over there. So far, it's been a peaceful demonstration. But apparently, some of them have chained themselves to the front gate and blocked traffic into the base."

"Have you talked to the Gisawian police?"

"Yes, ma'am. They said students from National University organized the protest. They've already dispatched a unit of riot police to each location."

As he spoke, several armored vehicles sped down the road and skidded to a halt, forming a semicircular perimeter around the students. Two squads of police outfitted in riot gear burst from the troop carriers, looking like gladiators entering the Coliseum. A water cannon atop one of the trucks sprayed a jet of water into the air, creating the odd effect of a rainbow arching over the skirmish. As the mist settled and the illusion faded, a phalanx of police charged head-on into the line of protesters. The impact of the human battering ram sent the students scattering in all directions as they tried to escape the blows of the police batons.

"Get everyone in the conference room now," the ambassador said, already on her way back inside the building. "This is about to get ugly."

By the time the staff had assembled for the impromptu meeting, everyone was aware of the bloody melee taking place outside the front gate. They watched in horror from the windows as the scene unfolded. Sitting at the head of the table, Claire pressed the button on the speakerphone, asking the State Department operations center to call Reid McCoy's home phone. After a few rings, they heard a groggy "Hello?" on the other end of the line.

"Reid, it's Claire Roberts calling from DRoG. Sorry to bother you in the middle of the night, but we've got a situation developing outside the embassy."

"Dammit, Claire. This better be good," Reid said, suddenly wide awake. "Didn't we just talk less than fifteen hours ago?"

Claire glanced at the clock. "Give or take a few minutes."

"And during that conversation, didn't we agree that our goal was not have any more conversations?"

"Trust me, I wouldn't reach out unless it was important. This isn't the kind of thing you'll want to hear about for the first time on TV."

"All right," he sighed. "What's going on now?"

"We have several hundred Gisawian university students protesting outside the embassy gate and at our military facility out by the airport. Apparently, some of them are chained to the front gate there."

"A bit melodramatic, isn't it?" Reid said. "I hope you brought them out some Kool-Aid and cookies."

"Reid, I realize that you think I'm overreacting; however, right now, the Gisawian riot police are in the process of beating them all to a pulp. The local news channels are covering the story. Some clips have already started hitting social media."

"Claire, if someone woke me up every time there was an anti-American protest outside one of our embassies, I'd never get any sleep. They've been rioting there for weeks. Why are you suddenly getting worked up about this?"

"Because this is the first protest specifically directed against us. Actually, it's not exactly us."

"What do you mean?"

"They're furious about the statements yesterday from Congressman Burke and his calls to oust President Namono."

"That fucking little twit," Reid muttered. "POTUS is going to go through the roof when he hears about this. But why the hell are they so upset? I thought they hated Namono."

"It appears that the one thing they hate more than him is the idea of an obscure American politician threatening to meddle in their domestic politics," Claire said. "Burke's comments were way out of line. He's jeopardizing our credibility at a time when we need to be seen as a stabilizing influence."

"Well, at least we can all agree that Burke is an idiot," Reid interjected. "But the protesters want it both ways. When POTUS comes out and says we're neutral on Namono, they don't like it. Then when Burke says that we should dump Namono, they don't like that either. What the hell do they want from us?"

"I think they don't want us involved at all," Claire suggested. "It appears to be a principled call for non-interference in their domestic affairs."

"Oh, well, in that case, please go outside and tell them that the United States is profoundly moved by their youthful idealism and has decided to relinquish all claims to global hegemony. We'll be immediately withdrawing all combat troops from around the globe and replacing them with magical unicorns that shoot rainbows out of their asses."

There was a moment of silence on the line before Claire responded. "Are you finished yet?"

"Claire, it's three-thirty in the morning! Do you expect me to conduct coherent foreign policy in my pajamas, hungover from a mind-numbing state dinner with the Slovenian prime minister?"

"It's called public service for a reason, Reid."

"Right, thanks for reminding me. So, clearly, there's not much I can do about any of the nonsense coming out of Burke's mouth. Unfortunately, unlike in DRoG, we can't arbitrarily imprison members of the political opposition. As long as Burke is in hot water over Nannygate, he's not going to let up on this DRoG thing. The best we can do is damage control on your end."

"We've already put out a press release reiterating the president's desire for a peaceful resolution to the protests and stabilization of DRoG's economy," Claire reminded him.

"I guess the students didn't get the memo. Here's what I want you to do. Get over to the university ASAP and tell those spoiled brats that we have no interest in micromanaging their pathetic little country."

"But isn't that what we've been doing for the last thirty years?" Claire countered.

"Claire, this isn't a grad school debate. Just tell them that the United States has complete respect for DRoG's sovereignty and is committed to a policy of noninterference in their internal political process."

"So basically, you want me to lie."

"You're a diplomat. That should be easy."

"OK, Reid. Thanks for the help. We'll do our best to tamp things down on our end and hope this blows over."

"Please do. And next time, unless Namono has been abducted by aliens, wait until morning to call."

The air inside the auditorium was stifling, with hundreds of students and faculty packed into the room. A lucky few had arrived early enough to claim a small supply of plastic chairs. Everyone else was standing in the heat, frustrated by the unexplained delay. A rotation of speakers was taking the mike, keeping the crowd entertained with public service announcements, improvised oratory, and even a brief a capella number.

Anna was standing in the audience, waiting for the event to begin. She was half-listening to the presentations while chatting with students and occasionally waving at a colleague or friend across the room. As more people pressed into the auditorium, Anna was surprised to find that she had butterflies in her stomach, not on her account, but for Nesi and Didier. She hoped that things would go well for them. She caught a glimpse of them standing together offstage. They were engaged in a tense conversation, presumably discussing a strategy for keeping the crowd pacified until the arrival of the keynote speaker.

Then Didier emerged from behind the curtains and moved to center stage. The crowd was hushed with anticipation as he fiddled with the microphone. By now, everyone on campus was aware that he and Nesi had been the masterminds behind the demonstrations outside the American embassy and army base. What was intended to be a quiet protest had thrust them into the spotlight, turning them into minor celebrities on campus.

Under the stage lights, Anna saw bruises and stitches on Didier's forehead, the result from his encounter with the wrong end of a police baton outside the embassy gate. As Didier took the stage, he attempted to transform from student provocateur to statesman by welcoming the adversary into their midst.

"Ladies and gentlemen," Didier said, tapping on the microphone, "I'm very sorry for the delay and happy to announce that we are ready to commence with our guest speaker. As you are all aware, this week, the student government committee took the unprecedented step of signing a declaration of grievance in response to an American lawmaker advocating direct interference in our political system. While the committee has taken no formal position for or against the Namono administration, the body was unanimous in our agreement that no outside powers, whether friend or foe, have the right to threaten our self-determination.

"But in the interest of open and balanced dialogue, the committee extended an invitation to the American ambassador so that we may hear firsthand their rebuttal. We are pleased that Ambassador Roberts has honored our request and offered to personally clarify the American position. Please join me in giving her a respectful welcome to National University."

Claire stood at the edge of the stage listening to a round of polite but lukewarm applause. Her security detail was posted just behind the curtains, looking nervously into the crowded auditorium. When she took the podium, Didier ceded the microphone, then disappeared into the wings.

"Thank you, Mr. Kengo," Claire began, looking out into the stern-faced crowd. "I would like to offer my sincere appreciation to the students and faculty of National University for extending this invitation. In times of crisis, the wise build bridges, while the foolish build dams. In that spirit, I hope that my presence here today will lay the foundation for a strong and durable bridge between our two countries.

"As you are aware, the United States has been a close partner of DRoG since the tense days of the Cold War and through the tumultuous decades that followed. During that time, we have weathered many storms together. There have been times of friendly disagreement and misunderstanding, but also of mutual support and progress.

"I am here because this week, outside our embassy, we heard your voices. We heard you, and we understand your grievances. Furthermore, we share your desire for a bilateral relationship based on trust, transparency, and mutual respect. And we fully intend to deal with DRoG on those terms.

"I can assure you that the United States does not seek to meddle, uninvited, in the affairs of our friends. I want to reiterate our commitment to a peaceful resolution of the current crisis. I also believe that we share your aspirations for an orderly transition to a stable and enduring democratic system. And on that note, I will conclude my remarks and open the floor to any questions or comments."

An hour later, Claire finally escaped the stage after a thorough grilling by the students. She was passing through the foyer with her security detail, heading for her car, when Anna spotted her. Before she escaped through the door, Anna introduced herself.

"Madam Ambassador, my name is Anna Devore," she said, reaching out to shake Claire's hand. "I want to thank you for coming today. I can't imagine it was the most enjoyable way to spend an afternoon."

"To be honest, I didn't really know what to expect. But it went better than I would have guessed. The questions were tough but fair."

"Even though it may not seem like it, I know the students appreciated the gesture. Just the fact that you were willing to meet them face to face says a lot."

"I'm guessing from your accent that you're an American," Claire said. "Do you work here at the university?"

"Yes, at least for now. I'm a visiting professor on a two-year contract. However, I'm guessing it won't be renewed. And in the interest of full disclosure, I should tell you that two of my former students were responsible for organizing the protest outside the embassy this week."

"In that case, you must be teaching them something useful," Claire said, giving Anna a conspiratorial wink.

"Believe me, they don't need my help."

"In any case, I admire their passion, even when it's directed against me. So, how did you find your way to DRoG? It's somewhat off the beaten path for an American academic, isn't it?"

"It's a long story. But the short version is that I came here for work and stayed for other reasons."

The ambassador nodded, encouraging Anna to continue.

"My fiancé is Gisawian," Anna explained. "We stayed here for his work."

"And what does he do?"

"He's in the Gisawian army."

"Hmmm, I'm intrigued," Claire said. "How did the two of you meet?"

"I came here as a civilian advisor during Operation Brushfire. At the time, he was working on the American base as a liaison officer for the Gisawian ministry of defense."

"Well, that is surprising. I think it's the first time I've ever heard about something positive coming out of Operation Brushfire," Claire said with a sigh. "What does your fiancé do for the army?"

"He's the commander of the counter-terrorism force."

"How interesting," Claire nodded with curiostiy. "Your fiancé doesn't happen to be the nephew of the defense minister, by chance?"

"Yes, in fact, he is. Lutalo Bigombe. You've met him?

"No, but I remember the headlines about his role in the hunt for Daniel Odoki. And of course, I've known his uncle for a long time."

Anna nodded, trying—and failing—to keep her expression neutral.

"Judging by your reaction, I'll assume that we share a similar opinion of the minister," Claire speculated.

"Did my face give it away?" Anna chuckled. "I suppose since I'm joining the family, I'll need to do a better job of hiding my feelings when people mention his name. In any case, I know him well enough to be wary."

"That would certainly be my recommendation," Claire said as her car pulled up outside the door. "It was nice meeting you, Anna. I wish you the best of luck, and to your fiancé as well. I fear that we may all be in for some trying times ahead. Please be careful."

Anna waved awkwardly as the ambassador walked out the door, ducked into the sedan, and sped off toward the embassy.

+++

The next day, before lunch, Mike Jones returned to the old Victorian mansion. The clientele was virtually indistinguishable from his last visit—as if time inside the bar had somehow stopped. Fabrice was sitting in his usual spot by the bay window, smoking a Gauloises and nursing a tumbler of Glenfiddich as a late breakfast.

Jones sat down in the chair opposite Fabrice and helped himself to a cigarette from the pack lying on the table. While he searched his pockets for matches, Fabrice tossed a copy of the local morning paper in front of him.

"Did you see this?" Fabrice spat, pointing at the headline. The picture above the fold showed Ambassador Roberts addressing the crowd of students at National University.

"I wouldn't worry about it," Jones shrugged. "She's just throwing out a few bones to keep them happy."

"Really? Your idea of keeping them happy is encouraging a revolution? For the last thirty years, you Americans never bothered saying the word 'democracy.' Now, all of a sudden, you change your mind and decide that we're gonna turn the place into Sweden?" Fabrice said, shaking his head in disgust. "That's like one of those girls at the bar waking up tomorrow and deciding she's going to be a virgin."

"Listen, there's no need to get worked up about this. Believe it or not, Claire Roberts doesn't work for me. I can't control what she says in front of a bunch of college students.

But what I can do is help get you ready for the day when this entire house of cards comes tumbling down. And the way things are going, that's not too far off. Don't forget, I'm on your side."

"Yeah, just like you used to be on my father's side."

"Well, Fabrice, for your information, that situation changed for a reason," Jones said. "I don't like this any more than you do. However, your father is no longer holding up his end of the bargain."

"And what exactly was that bargain?" Fabrice asked, eyes narrowing with suspicion.

"Basically, keep DRoG stable and don't get too friendly with the Russians."

"And what's the deal now?"

"Same as before, except replace the Russians with Chinese."

"So, is that what you want from me?"

"What I want from you is the same thing we wanted from your father: status quo. Someone who isn't going to rock the boat. We need continued access to our counter-terrorism operating base, and we need to keep DRoG out of the headlines. It's that simple."

"If that's the deal, then what's in it for me?"

Jones chuckled as he stubbed out his half-smoked cigarette in the ashtray. "No offense, Fabrice, but you're not exactly in a strong negotiating position here. I'm paying your damn bar tabs, for god's sake! Meanwhile, your stepmother is a heart attack away from taking over Green House. How do you think things are going to play out for you when that happens? For starters, I'm guessing it means no more weekend party trips to Ibiza with the boys."

Fabrice flicked his cigarette onto the floor and stared out the window into the garden. After a few minutes of pouting, he turned back to Jones. "OK, then what's the plan?"

"For right now, we need to focus on maximizing our optionality. That means being prepared to move when the situation ripens. With things like this, timing is everything. If we play our hand too soon, it gives people time to react. But if we play it too late, then the game is over before we get our chance."

"What do you have in mind?"

"We need to start organizing ASAP. Let's call it the Citizens Action Committee. You'll need to start gathering up some people you can trust. And I'm not talking about your party-boy posse. We need guys who know how to play rough, people with some street cred who can organize a mob on short notice."

"Then what?"

"Then we'll need a place to train. Somewhere out of the way where we won't attract much attention. You got any ideas?"

Fabrice rubbed his chin, gazing up at the ceiling as he considered the options. "Maybe," he answered. "There's an old presidential hunting retreat about two hours north of the city. Charity hates it, and my father hasn't been out there in years. I hosted a friend's bachelor party there a few months back. It's in good shape, with plenty of open space. No one will ever know we're out there."

"Perfect," Jones said, wheels spinning in his head. "Next, we'll need a shopping list: uniforms, guns, ammo, trucks, the whole deal. Just let me know what you think you'll need."

Fabrice simply shrugged, unable to provide an answer.

"Jesus," Jones muttered, shaking his head. "Don't worry about it. We'll just go with a standard coup starter package until we have a better idea of what we're looking at. While I'm working the logistics, I want you to get the training site up and running. Then we start gathering your team. Let me know when you're ready for the first shipment. The way things are going, I don't think we've got much time."

Fabrice straightened in his chair, starting to feel comfortable in his new role as the Citizens Action Committee's commander. He lit a fresh cigarette and tossed the match onto the floor, looking at Jones through a cloud of smoke. "Before we get too far, tell me why I should trust you. How do you even know this plan will work?"

"Kid, I've been running operations like this since you were in diapers. The important thing is that you listen to everything I'm telling you. I don't want any bullshit. The only way this works is if there's no daylight between us. Is that clear?"

"But how do I know you're not going to turn on me, just like you did to my old man?"

"For Christ's sake, Fabrice! It wasn't us who did the turning! It was your father who went looking for a better deal." Jones didn't bother to hide his disgust. "We gave him everything he needed for Operation Brushfire. Then he went and pulled a fast one on us by selling off half the damn country to the Chinese. He invited the fox right into the henhouse. All I'm asking from you is a little bit of loyalty in exchange for our support. I don't think that's an unreasonable expectation."

"OK. I get it. But I still don't see how this Citizens Action Committee is going to change anything."

"You leave that part to me. Your job is to be ready when I call. Now, if you can handle that, then I think we have the basis for a working partnership."

Fabrice smiled and reached for the bottle of Glenfiddich, nodding at the empty glass on the table.

"It's fucking ten-thirty in the morning," Jones said, unamused.

"Just celebrating our new partnership," Fabrice explained, refilling his glass and raising it in a solitary toast. "To a new beginning."

"Yeah, let's hope so. I'll be in touch soon," Jones said. He got up and left the bar.

CHAPTER FIVE

─────

A week later, the embassy staff gathered in the conference room for a working lunch. The large video screen on the wall was tuned to Gisawian state television, with the volume muted. The news was broadcasting live footage from Independence Square, only a few miles away from the embassy compound. The camera panned back and forth across a narrow slice of the grandstand that was suspiciously packed with eager, flag-waving supporters. In the foreground was a large parade field, previously a colonial-era polo pitch, now filled with a phalanx of Gisawian soldiers.

A reviewing stand behind an empty podium was filled with the nation's officialdom, waiting patiently for the ceremony to begin. To the right of the dais were several rows filled with various cabinet ministers and generals decked out in full regalia. Seated to the left was first lady Charity Namono, hidden behind sunglasses and surrounded by a coterie of lackeys and local celebrities waving at the camera. In her lap, she was cradling an elegant cobalt blue calfskin shoulder bag with a palladium swivel clasp.

Ambassador Roberts entered the conference room carrying a plastic clamshell of wilted salad from the staff canteen.

"Has it started yet?" she asked, slipping into her seat at the head of the table.

"Not yet," Mike Jones said between bites of a hoagie. "They're probably just doing a quick refill of Namono's embalming fluid."

Claire shot him an annoyed glance and pushed aside her salad, having lost her appetite. "OK, team. Any idea what we expect to hear in the speech? Let's go around the table," she said, looking over to Jake Baxter to begin.

"We don't expect him to mention the recent chaos in the streets. Given the audience, he's going to want to project an image of stability. He'll likely ignore the protests and pretend that everything's going fine," the security officer said.

"What's the situation out in the streets today?" Claire asked.

"The police are out in full force. They've got the entire city on lockdown. There's a tight security cordon stretching the entire route between Green House and Independence Square. Anyone riding in the presidential motorcade wouldn't have the slightest hint that anything was wrong out in the streets."

"Nice bit of whitewash," Claire said, then nodded at the television. "And it looks like state TV is dishing out a similar version of the Potemkin village. It's all pomp and circumstance, and nothing at all about the protests."

"I do have one bit of good news to report," Jake continued. "It seems that your trip last week to the university helped cool things down with the students. We haven't had any more demonstrations outside the gate since your visit."

Jones rolled his eyes as he continued chewing on the hoagie.

"Stephen, you're next," Claire said, turning the political officer. "Are we expecting anything interesting on the political-economic side?"

"Based on our contacts at the ministry of finance, we believe that Namono is going to unveil a new five-year economic plan," Stephen said.

"Any idea what that's going to look like?"

"Probably a cosmetic repackaging of every other five-year plan for the last thirty years. It will mostly be dog-whistle messaging intended to reassure investors and keep them from pulling their money out of the country."

"What are his chances of pulling it off?"

"Namono's in a tough spot, given the situation. However, he's managed to bumble his way through similar crises in the past. If he can convince people that he's still in charge and get a few good weeks without DRoG leading the headlines, he's got a decent chance to ride out the storm."

"Good. Who's next?" Claire asked, looking around the table. "Colonel Sawyer, are we expecting to hear anything on the military side?"

"Yes, ma'am. Our contacts at MoD are hinting that Namono plans to announce a major military spending package as part of an economic stimulus program."

"Stimulus package? He just announced an austerity plan last month. How does that work?"

"It doesn't. All the money going to the army is coming from cuts to other programs. We're expecting him to outline several new procurement contracts and a pay raise for the troops."

"That sounds to me more like an insurance policy," Claire said, shaking her head.

"The timing would be right," Sawyer agreed. "When your approval rating slips into the low teens, it's always good to keep the people with the guns happy. If nothing else, it will remind the generals who signs their paychecks. One other thing we need to be watching for is any details about the new procurement programs."

"Why is that?"

"We've heard rumors that the budget may include some high-tech equipment for the counter-terrorism force, possibly including some Chinese surveillance technology."

"I wasn't aware that DRoG is facing a new terrorist threat," Claire said.

"It's not unless the regime plans on expanding its definition of terrorism."

"Such as, including street protesters and political opposition groups?" Claire hinted.

Colonel Sawyer nodded. "It hasn't gone that way yet, but that could always change."

"Is Mugaba coming under pressure from Green House to bring the army out of barracks in response to the riots?"

"We don't believe so. But Namono may be waiting to see how the situation plays out. If he starts feeling cornered, there's no telling how he might respond."

"Mike, do you have anything to add?" Claire asked, turning the station chief.

"Not really. But I did just get the latest readout of our social media exploitation data before coming in."

"And?"

"Public opinion is still trending against Namono. However, he did get a spike of sympathetic support when the students were protesting outside our front gate. But the bounce didn't last long."

"Does the data suggest that we're anywhere near a tipping point?"

"Probably not. As long as his inner circle and the army are still behind him, we think that Namono can continue to manage the pressure from the street."

As Jones spoke, the news broadcast cut away to a video of the presidential motorcade racing into Independence Square. Five identical Mercedes S-Class sedans rolled to a stop in front of the reviewing stand's VIP section. The crowd rose to its feet, cheering wildly when they spotted Namono's silhouette through the tinted windows. The car doors opened with choreographed precision as his security detail fanned out to secure the perimeter. Meanwhile, two burly bodyguards plucked the feeble sovereign from the sedan's back seat and placed him on the dais like a plastic mannequin.

"Here we go," Claire said. "Can somebody please take it off mute?"

With the volume turned on, they could hear the military band striking up the Gisawian national anthem while President Namono stood at the podium. With one hand, he steadied himself against the lectern. With the other, he offered a frail wave to the cheering crowd. When the applause finally faded, the president pulled some speaking notes from his jacket and cleared his throat into the microphone.

The camera panned across the VIP section, where the dignitaries were settling in for an extended oration. At the center of the first row, Defense Minister Mugaba Odongo stared off into the distance, appearing distracted as Namono warmed up the crowd with staples of his routine from earlier days.

Back in the conference room, the staff was finishing up lunch, having lost interest in the speech. A few people passed the time by making a list of Namono's favored clichés from thirty years of presidential oratory. Others were scrolling through text messages or exchanging office gossip. Someone had brought in a tray of homemade baklava that was working its way around the table. Colonel Sawyer helped himself to a piece of pastry then froze in his seat, staring slack-jawed at the television.

Everyone else in the room looked up just in time to see President Namono's face contorted in fear. His arms curled defensively around his head, as if he was protecting himself from imminent danger. There was a blinding flash of light followed by a thundering explosion. The camera shook violently, momentarily losing focus as a blast echoed across the stadium. When the picture returned, they could see the toppled podium through a cloud of smoke and debris. Along the dais's bottom edge was a sooty black scab where something had impacted with great force.

The television camera zoomed wide, revealing the chaotic aftermath of whatever had just happened. The VIP section was in utter pandemonium, chairs overturned, people rushing down the aisles. Scores of bodies lay scattered on the ground. In the corner of the picture, several members of the presidential guard could be seen picking up Charity Namono from the debris and carrying her limp body toward one of the armored sedans.

Out on the parade field, the phalanx of soldiers had broken ranks, scattering in all directions. Military discipline gave way to mass confusion and hysteria. Some soldiers lay on the ground in the prone position, aiming empty rifles in the air at an unseen enemy. Others rushed for the gates in fear. A voice boomed over the public address system pleading for calm as spectators in the stands began pouring over the stadium walls like rioting soccer fans.

Back in the embassy conference room, the staff was speechless, watching in disbelief as the drama unfolded. When the camera panned back to the VIP section, they could see at least a dozen bodies lying amid the overturned chairs. Medics were attending to some of the wounded while soldiers helped other, less seriously injured victims limp to safety. Several presidential bodyguards were digging madly through the remains of the plywood dais. One of them began waving frantically to the others for help.

When the bodyguards lifted a limp figure from the rubble, the reality of what had just happened dawned on everyone watching. An instant later, the live broadcast was cut off and replaced by a prerecorded image of a Gisawian flag waving gently in the wind, accompanied by a scratchy recording of the national anthem.

The conference room was in a state of shocked silence, hypnotized by the image of the waving flag. Finally, Ambassador Roberts awoke from the trance and leaned over to her assistant.

"Get me the White House on the line, now!" she said.

+++

Louie was working in his office, half-listening to the speech on the radio, when he heard what sounded like an explosion, followed by the panicked cries of the radio announcer. Louie raced from his office, trying to figure out what had happened. By the time he got to a TV, the state broadcasting channel had already switched over to the canned clip of the Gisawian flag flapping in the wind.

An hour later, after watching a shaky, bootleg video uploaded from an attendee's cell phone camera, Louie fully grasped the significance of what had happened. Despite the media blackout, someone had sent the video to an international news network. Now that footage was replaying on an endless loop across every news channel in the world.

Within a few hours of the attack, Louie received a phone call from the defense ministry, issuing an order for all army units to return to their bases. The alert came with vague instructions to pack their kit and await orders for deployment. Meanwhile, the ministry of information issued a gag order to all TV and radio channels forbidding any discussion of the attack or replaying footage while the investigation was underway.

In the absence of information, the radio call-in shows quickly filled the void with conspiracy theories ranging from the mildly preposterous to the somewhat plausible. Most early callers bent toward garden-variety jingoism, declaring the attack an act of war perpetrated by any number of DRoG's real or imagined rivals. Other callers demanded a full military mobilization along the borders, with threats of reprisal against unnamed perpetrators.

Of all the theories making rounds, perhaps the most creative involved the resurrection of the warlord Daniel Odoki, somehow returned from the grave to exact revenge on President Namono for his role in Operation Brushfire. The ministry of information seemed determined to thicken the atmosphere of irresponsible speculation by refusing to confirm or deny rumors about President Namono's condition or whether Charity Namono was somewhere outside the city limits, being held in a secure, undisclosed location.

As the reality of the situation sank in, Louie struggled to keep his soldiers on task. He did what he could to maintain a semblance of routine, refusing to cancel meetings or alter the training plan. However, that wasn't enough to stop his soldiers from sneaking off to listen to the radio or checking their cell phones, searching in vain for updates on the president's condition. Any pretense of normality abruptly ended when Louie received a text message from his uncle's aide-de-camp ordering him to report immediately to the ministry headquarters.

Louie drove out the front gate of the camp and found the streets deserted. Without traffic, it took him only a few minutes to cover the distance to the ministry. When he arrived there, the place looked like a fortress under siege. Extra security patrols were out along the perimeter, accompanied by several lethargic-looking guard dogs suffering in the equatorial heat.

At the security checkpoint, the guards exchanged none of the usual friendly banter, even demanding that Louie empty all his pockets for inspection before entering the compound. After thoroughly patting him down, the guards waved some sort of magic detecting wand over his entire body and searched his briefcase. After finally passing inspection, Louie passed through the gate and on to his uncle's office.

As soon as he walked through the door, his uncle's secretary waved him into the main office. Mugaba was sitting at his desk, talking on one of his three cell phones. He was listening intently to whoever was speaking while waving for Louie to take a seat.

"I came as soon as I was able," Louie said as soon as his uncle finished the call.

"Of course," Mugaba said, dismissing the apology. "I know that you needed to attend to your soldiers."

"How are you, Uncle? Were you there when it happened?"

"Yes. And I'm lucky to be alive. If I had been a few feet in either direction, I might not be sitting here with you now. The minister of agriculture was two seats away from me and was killed. The trade minister, sitting next to him, lost an arm, but with God's grace, he will recover."

"As soon as I realized what happened, I called the military intelligence section, but they didn't know anything more than the wild rumors on the radio," Louie explained.

"Police intelligence has begun an investigation," Mugaba said. "However, I think it will take some time before they can say anything definitively. They will want to be cautious about releasing information if they believe that the perpetrators are still at large."

"The international news reports that it was some kind of improvised explosive device attached to a drone. Is that true?"

"That much I can confirm," Mugaba said. "I saw it with my own eyes, Lutalo, just before it hit the stage. It's a miracle that the president survived. The initial reports say that the explosive didn't fully detonate. If it had, it could have taken out our entire government. We were all sitting there right behind the president."

"Do they know anything more about the drone?"

"Yes." Mugaba drew in a deep breath and shook his head. "That is why I needed to speak with you right away. Please, look at these," he said, sliding a stack of photos across the table to his nephew.

Louie sifted through the pile of black and white pictures.

"The bomb disposal unit took those photos right after the attack," Mugaba explained. "Those pieces are what was left of the drone that delivered the explosive."

Louie's eyes widened in astonishment. "It's an American model," he said. "I recognize some of the parts from the fuselage. It's the same version they sold to our army last year."

"Yes," Mugaba said. "But there is more. Police intelligence believes that a serial number recovered from the debris matches one of the devices from our inventory."

"Uncle, are you saying that the drone came from our army?" Louie said, astonished at the news.

Mugaba nodded. "But not just that. It must have come from the counter-terrorism force. Your unit is the only one in the entire army with that kind of equipment."

Louie slumped down in his chair. His heart was racing, and his chest felt tight.

"When was the last time you inventoried your drones?" his uncle asked.

"I can't remember exactly," Louie muttered, his voice trembling. "Maybe a few weeks ago. We haven't used them for training since the protests began."

"Is it possible that one could have gone missing and you didn't know about it?"

"Of course it's possible, but I don't see how it could have happened. Only a few people have access to our storage facility, and none of them would ever do something like this. It can't be true!"

"Lutalo, now is not the time to panic," his uncle said soothingly. "The pictures I've shown you are restricted information. Only a few senior people at police intelligence are even aware of this right now."

"But if you're telling me about it, then they must already have suspicions. If they confirmed that the drone came from our inventory, then my unit must be the focus of their investigation."

"I cannot speak to that," Mugaba said. "I have no authority over the investigation. Everything is being run through police intelligence. However, I expect that at some point, they will need to ask you some questions. Of course, it doesn't mean they're looking at you, Lutalo. Pieces of a broken drone won't tell them who was behind the attack. You know the old village saying: A knife does not recognize its owner."

"I don't understand any of this," Louie said, shaking his head and staring down at his hands. "How could this be happening?"

"I know this comes as a shock for all of us. But for now, all you can do is go on with your duties, however difficult this may be. Let me deal with police intelligence. You must focus on your soldiers and be ready to lead them when the time comes. Who knows, perhaps when this is all over, some good will come of it."

"What are you saying? How could anything good come from this?" Louie asked, his voice cracking with emotion.

"You saw it for yourself. The streets were empty when you drove over here. Today is the first day in over a month without protesters marching in the streets. Perhaps this tragedy will give us time to reflect, a chance to heal our wounds, and bring the nation back together."

"I'm sorry, Uncle, but I'm finding it hard to share your optimism."

"Until we see what happens, all we can do is remain vigilant. The days ahead will be difficult for everyone. There is no telling how we may be tested. But the nation is counting on us. And I am counting on you, Lutalo. If the time comes and we are forced to act, I must know that you will be ready. Do you understand me?"

Louie nodded without fully understanding what his uncle was implying. His mind was reeling from the news as he tried to process everything that had happened over the last few hours. He rose unsteadily, feeling lightheaded.

"Lutalo," Mugaba continued, "I know you're concerned about what I've told you, but please, trust me. When your father died, I promised your mother that I would always protect you. That promise still holds true. When a family stays together, no evil can harm them. Do not forget that, Lutalo."

As Mugaba spoke, one of the three cell phones on his desk began ringing. He glanced down at the number, then back at Louie. "I'm sorry, I must take this," he said, implying that it was a private matter. Louie nodded and turned toward the door, leaving his uncle to his call.

When he arrived back at his car, Louie fumbled with his keys, struggling to turn them in the ignition with his shaking hands. He had been so consumed with the revelations that he had entirely forgotten to ask his uncle about the shipment of riot gear. The equipment had arrived at the camp just before the attack and was still sitting in the shipping containers. Suddenly, it seemed like a trivial matter, so he decided to wait until their next meeting to bring it up.

Louie put the car in gear, then stopped, having to think about where he was going. He knew that his soldiers were waiting for him back at the base, most likely sitting around the radio, trying to figure out what was happening. At the least, he owed them some kind of explanation. But Louie wasn't even sure what he was allowed to tell them—presumably not the fact that they were all under investigation for the attempted assassination of President Namono.

On the short drive back to the camp, Louie's mind was blank. When he arrived at the front gate, the guard waved him straight through. But instead of going to his office, Louie turned the other direction, toward his unit's warehouse. Before facing his soldiers, he needed to see what was there and what might be missing.

+++

Anna was in the middle of teaching her morning class when everyone's phones began buzzing. Her first thought was that it was an end-of-semester prank; all of her students were aware of her intolerance for the sound of electronic devices going off during lectures. But when her phone joined in the chorus, that theory seemed less likely. Anna gave in to the disruption, pausing her lecture and granting everyone permission to check their messages. Meanwhile, she dug down into the bottom of her purse, searching for her phone.

The classroom was silent as everyone stared at their screens, trying to comprehend what was happening. Gradually, it dawned on them that their entire world had been thrown into uncertainty. Anna looked at her students, realizing that not a single one of them was old enough to have known any other occupant of Green House than President Namono. Now, it appeared as if he was being rushed to the hospital and might already be dead.

Once reports of the attack were confirmed, the university canceled classes for the rest of the day. Anna was relieved that she was no longer responsible for keeping her class focused on her lecture as if nothing had happened. As soon as they escaped the classroom, the students rushed to find a television or radio, hoping to find out more about the fate of the president.

Anna made her way to the faculty lounge, joining a few other staff members who were doing the same as the students. She felt out of place as the only foreigner in the room, like an interloper thrust into the midst of a private family tragedy. After lingering uncomfortably in the margins, she slipped away to her office, leaving the others to process the news on their own terms.

Later, it became clear that nothing new was being reported on the radio. Anna turned it off and tried to catch up on grading papers. Once done, she moved on to organizing her files and cleaning out her desk drawers for the first time since occupying the office a year before. Anna briefly considered returning to the faculty lounge. Instead, she packed her things to leave. She assumed that Louie wouldn't be home that evening but couldn't bear to stay in her office any longer.

As she was gathering up her things, her phone buzzed with an incoming text. Anna grabbed it, hoping it might be Louie. Instead, it was a message from Nesi inviting her over to Sammy's café for coffee. Anna was about to send her regrets, then reconsidered, finding the prospect of sitting home alone too depressing.

She locked the office door and made her way to the café. When she arrived, the place was surprisingly busy, but without the usual buzz of lighthearted socializing. Nesi and Didier sat together at a table in the corner of the garden, slouched in their chairs, staring blankly into empty coffee cups. Nesi's face brightened somewhat when she looked up and saw Anna walking toward their table.

"I was just heading home when I got your message," Anna said, taking one of the empty chairs.

"I'm glad you changed your mind," Nesi said. "It's been such a crazy day. I wanted to make sure you were OK."

"I'm fine, just shocked about what happened. How about you guys?"

They both shrugged in response.

"Have you heard anything from Louie?" Nesi asked.

"No. He hasn't been answering his texts," Anna explained. "But I know that he wasn't at the stadium when the attack happened. I guess that's one advantage of being in an elite counter-terrorism unit: They don't make them stand in parades. Although I suppose things will get busy for him soon enough."

"That might be true, once the government settles on its terminology," Didier said, nodding at the television. "First, they were calling it an accident. Then it became an incident. They were briefly calling it an assassination attempt, but the censors quickly corrected that. Now, it seems that they've all agreed to call it a terrorist attack. That designation puts it firmly into your fiancé's wheelhouse."

"I haven't seen the news in a few hours," Anna said. "What's the latest?"

"Who knows?" Nesi said. "State television isn't putting out any new information, and the radio programs are filled with people calling in to discuss crazy conspiracy theories."

"Like what?" Anna asked.

"Everything under the sun," Didier said, shaking his head in disgust. "Some people are saying that your government is behind it. Others are pointing the finger at the Chinese, even the UN. Then, of course, there are the rumors that the Gisawian Liberation Army has come back to take their revenge for the killing of Odoki. I'm sure there are a few others that I've already forgotten."

"Which sounds right to you?" Anna asked, curious about what Didier and Nesi thought about everything that had happened.

"Take your pick. It doesn't really matter," Didier said, almost mockingly.

"Please, Didier, be serious," Anna insisted.

"I am serious. The truth doesn't matter. In the end, the government will give us whatever story best suits their needs. That will become the official truth."

"Isn't that just another version of a conspiracy theory?" Anna pressed.

"Is it really?" he shot back. "Here is the only truth that matters: The government just announced a state of emergency. They've imposed a nighttime curfew and ban on all public gatherings. Don't you see what's going on? The attack has become an excuse to shut down everything they don't like. There's even a rumor that the university isn't going to reopen tomorrow."

"I hadn't heard that," Anna said. "Will the administration push back?"

Didier glanced across the table at Nesi, deferring the question to her.

"We don't think they'll openly challenge the government," Nesi answered for him. "But if it does shut down, we're not going to sit by and let it happen. We've called for a meeting tomorrow of the student government committee."

"Why? What could the committee possibly do if the administration refuses to reopen the university?"

"We don't know yet, but we're not going to give them a chance. Holding classes is not a threat to national security. There's no way they can justify shutting it down. We'll march on Green House if we have to. We've got to do something."

"While I don't disagree in principle, are you sure this is the right time to press the issue? Given everything else going on?" Anna asked, becoming worried about her friends.

"Now is exactly the time!" Didier jumped in. "If we stand by and let them push through all these measures, there's no going back. I can assure you, it won't stop there."

Anna was quiet, thinking about Didier's prediction. "Whatever happens, promise me that you'll both be careful," she finally said.

"Don't worry," Nesi said. "We won't do anything rash. But for now, can we have a coffee and talk about something else? I need a few minutes to think about anything besides all this bad news."

"Agreed," Anna said, spotting a waitress and waving her over.

+++

Anna woke up when she heard Louie's car pulling into the driveway. She glanced at the clock and saw that it was after midnight. She got up and went into the kitchen to put on a kettle for tea. When Louie came through the door, she could see that he was exhausted. He dropped his bag on the floor and walked over to her.

"I didn't think you'd be home tonight," Anna said, reaching for his hand.

"I just came to pick up some extra uniforms. I need to go straight back."

Anna nodded, disappointed, but not surprised. "Do you have orders?"

"No, not yet. But the entire army has been recalled. We're on standby until they figure out what's going on."

"What does that even mean? Standby for what? Who are you supposed to fight?"

Louie shook his head. "They're still trying to gather information. Police intelligence is investigating into the attack. I expect we'll hear something soon."

"On the news, they're calling it an act of terrorism. Is that why your unit is on alert?"

"It's complicated," Louie said, his gaze fixed on the kettle as it began to boil.

"That's what you always say when you don't want to talk about something. Please, just tell me what it is."

Louie began searching the cabinet for mugs. "My uncle called me over to his office this afternoon. He told me that police intelligence thinks the attack may have been planned from the inside."

"What do you mean, the inside?"

"Someone from the government," he clarified.

"Then why are they calling it terrorism? Wouldn't that be assassination?"

"I'm not sure it matters what they call it."

"Funny. That's what Didier said too. Did your uncle tell you anything else?"

"There was one other thing," Louie said, putting two tea bags into the mugs, still avoiding her eyes. "There was a discrepancy found during an equipment inventory of our warehouse. Apparently, my unit is missing a small, unmanned drone."

"Do they think it's related to the attack on Namono?"

Louie nodded. "It was a drone that delivered the explosives to the stadium," he explained as he poured hot water into the mugs. "Only a few people have access to our warehouse."

"I'm assuming you're on that list?" Anna said.

"Yes, among a few others. But not many."

"Louie, are you trying to tell me that police intelligence thinks you or someone in your unit was involved with the attack? That's crazy! Who would ever believe that you had anything do with a plot to kill the president?"

"That's not what they're saying. At least not yet. They're just following the evidence from the attack site. In the debris, they found a serial number matching an aircraft from our inventory. I don't know how to explain it, but it's true. I saw the pictures myself in my uncle's office. Then I went straight to our warehouse and confirmed it. The serial number of the missing aircraft was the same as from the pictures."

"Don't you see what's happening?" Anna pleaded. "Somehow, these things always come back to your uncle. He's setting you up as a fall guy."

"Maybe," Louie said. "Or maybe he's just letting me know that he's the only one who can save me."

"Save you from what? From something that you didn't even do? Listen to yourself, Louie. This entire conversation is completely insane! It's like we're in the middle of a Kafka novel. You can't just wait for them to come and take you away. You need to do something!"

"I know, I know," he sighed, finally turning and looking her in the eyes, as if accepting the reality of the situation. "I called my old friend over in police intelligence, the same guy who helped me get those interrogation reports during Operation Brushfire."

"Are you sure that was a good idea? Can you trust him?"

"What choice do I have? Otherwise, the only information I can get is what my uncle decides to tell me. If I'm going to find out the truth, there's no other way. I need someone on the inside."

"There is one other way."

Louie shook his head in confusion.

"We could leave here and forget about all this," Anna said. "We can move up the wedding. Once we're married, you can apply for a visa. We can start in the States. Or somewhere else. Anywhere else. I don't even care, as long as you're safe."

"No," Louie said adamantly, not even stopping to consider her suggestion. "If I run, all it will do is prove their suspicions."

"Are you sure? We could leave tomorrow. Nothing is keeping us here."

"How can you possibly say that, Anna? My job is here. My mother is here. I can't just run away from this."

Anna closed her eyes and pulled him close.

"If you want to leave, I understand," he whispered to her. "You can go home for a while, then come back once this is over."

"No. Absolutely not. I'm staying with you," she said, giving him no chance to argue.

He squeezed her tight, then glanced at his watch. "I'm sorry. I need to get back to the camp."

Anna reluctantly let go of him. Without another word, Louie turned and went back to their bedroom to search for his uniforms. Anna stood alone in the kitchen, lost in thought, staring blankly at the untouched mugs of tea on the counter.

Claire and Mike Jones were sitting in her office, staring at the speakerphone on her desk. They had been on hold with the White House for twenty-five minutes and had long since exhausted their shallow reservoir of small talk. Finally, a voice on the speaker broke the awkward silence.

"Ambassador Roberts?"

"Yes, I'm here."

"Madam Ambassador, we've got the deputy national security advisor on a secure line. He'll be with you in a moment."

"Claire, what the hell is going on over there?" Reid McCoy's voice blared through the speaker.

"Hello, Reid. I've got Mike Jones here with me. We've been scrambling all day trying to get some—"

"Is Namono still alive?" he said, cutting her off midsentence.

"As far as we know. After the attack, he was taken to the hospital in critical condition."

"And the assumption is that this was some kind of drone attack?"

"That's the best we know based on limited information. The television footage was pretty grainy, so it's been difficult to do any kind of technical analysis from the video clips. However, we believe that it was an unmanned aerial vehicle carrying some kind of small explosive charge."

"Hey, Reid. Mike Jones here," the station chief interrupted. "Officially, the government isn't saying anything about the attack. But we've been able to get some information from intercepts of police intelligence internal communications."

"Have they been talking about suspects?"

"Not specifically, but we did pick up some interesting tidbits," Jones continued. "Apparently, there was some excitement over at the counter-terrorism training center this afternoon."

"What kind of excitement?"

"Police intelligence conducted an impromptu inventory of a warehouse used by the Gisawian counter-terrorism unit."

"What do you make of that?" Reid asked. "It seems strange that they would waste resources for an inventory just a few hours after someone tried to kill the president."

"It is strange," Jones said, "except when you consider that the warehouse is probably the only place in the country where you could find a UAV big enough to carry explosives for that kind of attack."

"Are you saying the drone that hit Namono belonged to the Gisawian army? How do we know they have something like that?"

"Because we sold it to them," Jones confirmed.

"So you think this was an inside job?"

"It's too soon to say, but we did pick up one other interesting piece of information. After the attack, we went back and reviewed all our intercepts of high-level government communications from the last few days. We were trying to see if we missed any obvious hints."

"Anything interesting?"

"Not much, except one strange phone call a few days ago between the president's wife, Charity, and someone with links to the Chinese government. During the conversation, they kept referring to something they called 'the prototype.'

They were discussing plans to unveil it during the presidential speech."

"Holy shit!" Reid said. "But that doesn't add up. Why would the Chinese be involved in a plot to knock off Namono? You said that he's already in their pocket. If that's true, then why bother trying to kill him?"

"Because the Chinese are playing the long game," Jones insisted. "They're already two or three steps ahead of us. It's not Namono they care about, but who comes next."

There was a brief silence on the other end of the line, followed by the sound of crumpling foil. "How long has Charity been working with the Chinese?" Reid asked through a mouthful of corn chips.

"Probably as long as she's been living at Green House."

"Damn," Reid said. "POTUS isn't going to like this. But he won't risk dumping Namono just a few months before the midterms. We don't need the headache right now, especially with that nitwit Burke making a big stink about DRoG and the Chinese. We'd only be validating everything he's been saying."

Jones slapped his hand on the desk in frustration. "Reid, listen to what I'm telling you. We're making a big fucking mistake here. Even if Namono survives, he's not going to be around forever. We've got a rare opportunity to set the course for a generation. It's not too late to keep DRoG from slipping away. I guarantee you that the Chinese aren't sitting around right now, twiddling their thumbs, waiting to see how this plays out. They're doing everything they can to turn this into a win for their side. And if that happens, it's not going to look good for POTUS. We're talking legacy stuff here."

"Come on, Mike. This isn't the Cuban missile crisis. We're talking about DRoG. POTUS doesn't have the bandwidth for this right now. So what I need from the two of you is to handle the situation on your end. My guidance hasn't changed. We need to maintain the status quo until after the midterms. Is that clear?"

"Reid, it's Claire again," the ambassador cut in. "We understand the president's priorities, but it's not just the Chinese we need to be worried about. We're already seeing indications that the government is overreaching. They've declared a state of emergency. They're using the attack as a pretext for a major crackdown against the protesters. They've banned public protests, suspended classes at the university, and started detaining members of the political opposition."

"Claire, let's not forget that their president was almost killed in a drone attack less than fifteen hours ago," Reid reminded her. "At least for the time being, we need to give them the benefit of the doubt. Of course, we should encourage them to respect the rule of law, but we can't just walk in there and start lecturing them about how they should be handling a major domestic security crisis."

"If we look the other way, we could be enabling egregious violations of basic human rights," she countered.

"There's no need to be overly dramatic about this," Reid argued. "Listen, I'm about to bump up against another meeting and need to cut this short. However, there's one last thing you need to know before we get off the line. And you're not going to like it."

"Dare I even ask?"

"Congressman Burke is coming over for a little visit."

"Are you kidding me?" Claire exclaimed. "Why is this the first we've heard about it?"

"Because he just announced it a few hours ago. He saw an opportunity for a little grandstanding and jumped on it. We considered trying to scuttle the trip, but the optics of POTUS shutting him down would have been worse than letting him come over."

"Reid, with everything going on right now, this is not a good time for us to be hosting some congressional boondoggle. Can't we put it off for a few weeks until things settle down over here?"

"Nope. He's getting on a plane now and lands first thing in the morning. Can you make sure that someone's over at the airport to pick him up?"

"Sure. We'd be thrilled," Claire said dryly. "Any other good news from Washington?"

"Hmmm. Nothing off the top of my head. I guess the Nationals are tied for first in the division, if that counts for anything."

"Not really. We'll pick up Congressman Burke in the morning. Anything else?"

"Nope. That's it! Thanks, Claire. I knew you'd be able to handle it. Good luck," Reid added before hanging up.

CHAPTER SIX

The next day, Claire was in the conference room, reading through a briefing book with the day's agenda. She was sitting at the head of the table. On either side of her were empty chairs with name tags designating the seating arrangement for the meeting, one for Mike Jones and the other for their special guest, Congressman Burke.

The staff filled in the remaining seats around the table, waiting for the congressman to arrive. Several of them were killing time, thumbing through text messages or doodling in the margins of their notepads. At the far end of the room, several other staffers were discreetly reconnoitering a pastry tray in the middle of the table, sealed in a protective layer of cellophane. A quick visual survey revealed a troubling imbalance between the coveted cinnamon scones and the notoriously inedible banana-nut muffins, a discrepancy that assured a tense standoff among the staff once the VIPs took their pick of the offerings.

Someone poked their head through the door and announced the congressman's arrival at the embassy compound. Claire got up from the table, positioning herself by the door while the remainder of the staff dutifully queued up behind her, looking like a poorly dressed cotillion receiving line.

Mike Jones appeared in the doorway with the congressman in tow. After some awkward introductions, everyone took their seats around the table. Congressman Burke immediately seized on the pastry tray, helping himself to three of the four cinnamon scones before pushing the rest of the pastries back to the center of the table.

The unexpected move left everyone momentarily stunned and pondering the reputational costs of a preemptive play for the remaining cinnamon scone. However, the moral dilemma was soon resolved during a brief distraction caused by a technical glitch with the PowerPoint slides. Taking advantage of the diversion, Jones deftly extracted the remaining scone from the tray unobserved, as if plucking a dead drop from a hollow tree trunk in a Moscow city park.

"Congressman Burke, I want to say again how pleased we are to have you here," Claire began, utterly unaware of the expert bit of tradecraft that had just transpired under her nose. "We don't have many delegations visiting from Washington, especially on such short notice."

"When America's national security is at stake, my constituents expect immediate action," Burke said through a mouthful of scone.

"Indeed. I had no idea that DRoG was such a high priority for the citizens of northwestern Pennsylvania," Claire observed.

"A very high priority, I can assure you. In fact, one of the towns in my district is a sister city of a local village around here. As you can imagine, we take an exceptional interest in DRoG's future. That's why, as soon as I heard about the attack, I needed to get over here ASAP. I had to see for myself what was going on."

"Well, I hope the visit will prove helpful," Claire said, forcing a smile. "Unfortunately, due to the security situation, we weren't able to arrange the usual round of meet-and-greets with our local counterparts. Obviously, things have been a bit chaotic since the attack, and the government is still trying to find its footing."

"No problem," Burke said, waving away the apology. "I'm not interested in having smoke blown up my ass by a bunch of local mafiosi. I don't need them telling me what's what."

"Naturally. So, I understand that you're already something of an expert on DRoG."

"Let's just say I know my way around," Burke assured her. "Before running for office, I was deployed here during Operation Brushfire."

"Then, given your experience, I'm sure you can appreciate the complexities of what we're dealing with regarding the bilateral relationship."

"Madam Ambassador, there's no need to beat around the bush here," Burke interrupted, tossing his napkin decisively onto the remnants of the scones. "We all know that POTUS has been asleep at the wheel on our DRoG policy. Meanwhile, our adversaries are gaining the upper hand, taking advantage of our indecisiveness."

"On the contrary, I believe that the president has been quite explicit about our policy. We're actively engaging key stakeholders and trying to facilitate a peaceful resolution to the unrest. At the same time, we've been discreetly urging a policy of restraint by government security forces in their handling of the protests. So far, I think we've been moderately successful at helping to avoid a major escalation of the crisis."

"But you're still standing by Namono," Burke said, pointing accusingly at the ambassador.

"Congressman Burke, that's not my position, that's our government's stated policy. And yes, we continue to support a mutually beneficial relationship with our longtime ally President Namono. Furthermore, we will do what we can to enable an orderly political transition so that the Gisawian people are free to choose their leadership through a transparent democratic process without external interference."

"In other words, we're going to hand this entire thing over to the Chinese and let them run the show from now on."

"That's not what I'm saying at all. I think perhaps you're oversimplifying what's really going on here."

"Well, that's your opinion," Burke said before turning to Jones, who had been sitting quietly, sipping a cup of coffee. "I'd be interested to hear what the CIA thinks about your assessment, Madam Ambassador."

Jones glanced at Claire, then stared at the congressman. "What exactly was the question?"

"Has Namono gone red? Is he in bed with the Chinese or not?" Burke asked impatiently.

Jones cleared his throat, collecting his thoughts. "I'm sure the ambassador would agree that China has growing ambitions here in DRoG. They're looking to expand their economic reach and gain political influence through a wide range of bilateral projects and strategic investments."

"But what about the reports I've been reading saying that the Chinese have penetrated the regime?" Burke pressed.

"We've seen some indications of Chinese influence inside Namono's inner circle," Jones admitted, "possibly including attempts to co-opt senior officials and perhaps even members of the president's immediate family. However, it's not yet clear whether these efforts have produced actionable results."

"By the time you confirm that, it'll already be too late," Burke blustered. "By then, Namono's paymasters in Beijing will be calling the shots and booting us out of the country. This entire discussion is absurd. We're sitting around here twiddling our thumbs when we should be laying the groundwork for the post-Namono transition. That's the only way we're going to protect America's interests and ensure access to our base."

Jones was about to speak when Claire said, "Congressman Burke, with all due respect, the president's national security team has been explicit in their guidance that we remain neutral on the matter of regime succession. It's not our fight. We may not like the outcome, but we need to respect the process."

Burke shook his head, unable to conceal his disgust. "Namono could kick off any minute. If that happens, then what?"

Claire nodded at Jones, letting him respond.

"At the moment, we don't have high confidence in our assessment for that particular scenario," Jones said. "Namono has been tight-lipped about his plans for succession. We've always assumed that his son Fabrice was first in line for the job; however, they've had a bit of a falling-out since the old man remarried. Now, the smart money seems to be on his new wife, Charity. Our contacts say, she's got him under her thumb and may already be calling the shots over at Green House."

"But she's in with the Chinese too," Burke protested.

"Presumably, but she doesn't have much of a track record; therefore, it's difficult to know for sure," Jones said.

"So, who are the wild card candidates if Namono doesn't walk out of the hospital alive?"

"Defense Minister Mugaba Odongo would certainly be high on that list," Jones said. "We've always assumed he had ambitions, not to mention the support of the generals. Besides him, the head of police intelligence could be a player. He knows where all the bodies are buried and could pull some strings behind the scenes. There might also be some members of the opposition flying under the radar. But most of them are in jail right now, so they're out of play unless there's a full-scale reshuffling of the deck."

Burke jotted down a few lines in his notebook. "Who on that list is going to be our most reliable partner?" he asked.

"Congressman Burke," Claire interjected, "I hope you appreciate the sensitivity of such discussions, especially while President Namono is lying in a hospital bed in critical condition. We can't afford to be perceived as picking favorites, even in private conversation. We're potentially entering a critical transition phase for Gisawian democracy after thirty years of one-party rule. Even the perception of the United States weighing in at this juncture would risk tainting everything that we claim to stand for."

"Madam Ambassador, hope is not a method," Burke said indignantly. "We can't just cross our fingers and pray that everything turns out OK."

"Congressman, perhaps you're aware that the last time you publicly commented on this matter, we had hundreds of angry students protesting outside our front gate, denouncing American meddling with Gisawian internal affairs. We most certainly do not need a repeat of that fiasco."

"I had no choice. The president has been derelict in his duty of protecting the American people and our national interests. How do you expect me to look my constituents in the eye when, one morning, they wake up and discover that our sister village has turned red? How could I ever face them knowing that I stood by and let that happen? That's not diplomacy, it's cowardice. We need to stop DRoG from sliding toward Beijing. It's now or never!"

"With all due respect, I sense that we're not going to re-solve this over coffee and scones," Claire said. "Nevertheless, as a professional courtesy, may I ask that you refrain from making any public statements on this matter while you're here on the ground? Given the current situation, we don't need to add to the uncertainty."

"Keeping quiet in the face of injustice is not part of my DNA," Burke said, puffing up in his chair.

"Be that as it may, out of respect for hosts, we owe them the opportunity to work through this crisis on their own terms, without our interference," Claire insisted.

"Very well, but I've heard nothing so far that has changed my mind about any of this. I can assure you that I'll be taking up this issue with the White House the minute

I return to Washington. I owe nothing less to the citizens of Pennsylvania's Fourth District, who care deeply about the fate of DRoG and its people."

"That's wonderful, congressman," Claire said, forcing a smile. "Then perhaps we can transition right into the first of many exciting briefings on today's agenda. First up, we'll be reviewing some new results from a US-funded project looking at the effects of microfinance partnerships on the installation of drip irrigation technology for Gisawian smallholder groundnut farms. I think you'll find the initiative fascinating." She flipped to the first slide of the presentation.

+++

After a full day of briefings, Mike Jones left the embassy compound behind the wheel of the battered Hyundai Sonata. He was running late and dispensed with the evasive maneuvers, making his way directly to the Palm Hotel. When he turned onto the street in front of the hotel, he drove slowly past the valet parking area. Then, in the next block, he pulled over and parked under a broken streetlight where he could observe the hotel entrance without being seen.

Pulling a pair of high-powered binoculars out of the glove compartment, Jones did a quick surveillance of the building, looking for anything out of the ordinary. There were a few bored-looking parking attendants and a bellboy standing around the valet station. At the far end of the street, a couple of taxi drivers were sitting on the hoods of their cars, enjoying the evening air, waiting for customers to emerge from the hotel. A young woman in a sequined miniskirt and towering heels was chatting with the taxi drivers, also keeping an eye out for potential clients wandering out of the hotel bar.

Once Jones was satisfied that the scene was safe, he shot off a text message, then sat back and waited. A few minutes later, he spotted a man leaving the hotel lobby and walking down the street. Jones kept an eye on the front door through the binoculars, ensuring that the man wasn't being followed. When the man reached the end of the road, he glanced nervously over his shoulder, then turned down the alleyway. As soon as the man disappeared from view, Jones made his move. He revved the engine and gunned the car out of the parking spot, driving quickly with the headlights off. He followed the man down the alleyway and pulled up beside him.

"Get in!" Jones hissed out the window, slowing down just enough so the man could leap into the passenger seat. "Did you leave your cell phone in the room?" he asked once his passenger was safely inside the car.

"Yeah, just like you told me," Congressman Burke answered. "Don't you think that's a little paranoid?"

"I won't tell you how to do your job, so you don't tell me how to do mine. And in case you've forgotten, this meeting is totally off the record. It didn't happen. You got that?"

"Sure, I got it."

"Good. Did anyone ask where you were going?" Jones asked, keeping his eyes fixed on the road, still driving without headlights.

"No, I told my assistant that I was going for a drink in the hotel bar before bed. Don't worry, he gets paid not to ask questions."

Jones rolled his eyes. They drove for twenty minutes through the city, and then Jones pulled the car over on a darkened side street. "We're walking from here," he announced.

"Stay close, and don't talk to anyone unless I tell you to. Got it?"

The congressman nodded. They got out of the car, and Burke followed Jones down a dirt path. They passed several dimly lit shacks selling street food and sundry items. Eventually, they came to a residential neighborhood, where they stopped at the gate of the old Victorian mansion. Jones led Burke through the overgrown garden and into the hidden nightclub. Inside, the bar was hopping with a happy hour crowd, no one even noticing their arrival. Jones and Burke made their way across the room to the window bay, where Fabrice Namono was entertaining two scantily clad Bulgarian servers.

Jones cleared his throat to get their attention. When the women saw him, they quickly got up and excused themselves, heading back to the bar.

"Fabrice, this is the friend I wanted you to meet," Jones said once the women were out of earshot.

"Good to meet you," Burke said, holding out a hand.

Fabrice ignored the congressman's gesture and nodded for them to take a seat. "So, you're the guy from Washington who's going to help us?" he asked, pouring scotch for his guests and refilling his empty tumbler.

"Let's not get ahead of ourselves," Jones said before Burke had a chance to reply. "Our friend is just here for a little chat. I've told him about your Citizens Action Committee, and he is intrigued by the initiative. If things move in a favorable direction, it could be helpful to have some knowledgeable friends back on Capitol Hill."

"Mr. Jones has told me quite a bit about you, Fabrice," Burke said. "I think we have some things in common."

"Really?" Fabrice said, shaking his head and chuckling to himself as he reached for a cigarette.

"Indeed. Our fathers were in the same line of work. Mine served in Congress for almost as long as yours has been in Green House. I guess you could say that we've both inherited our family's interest in politics."

Fabrice lit his cigarette and squinted at Burke through a cloud of smoke. "But not exactly the same," he said. "Your old man gave you his job, but mine is trying to keep me out of his."

"Oh, no. It doesn't work quite that way in our system," Burke backpedaled. "Of course, I had to win an election first. The point is, I appreciate the value of maintaining family tradition. That's why when Mr. Jones told me about your project, I was very interested in meeting with you. Perhaps at some point, I may even be in a position to help."

"Maybe you can start by talking some sense into your lady ambassador."

"Easy, Fabrice," Jones warned. "I told you not to worry about her. You take care of things on your end, and I'll take care of things on mine. Are we still good with that?"

Fabrice ignored the warning, turning back to Congressman Burke.

"So, Mr. Fabrice," Burke continued, "you're probably aware that I've made some public statements that have been critical of your father. I want you to know that it's nothing personal. I realize that he was a good friend to the United States for many, many years. But recently, we've had some concerns about the nature of his relationship with the Chinese."

"Man, you're looking in the wrong place!" Fabrice burst out. "It's all Charity. She's the one who's turning him. She's the one!"

Jones put a steadying hand on the congressman's arm, indicating that it was time for him to step into the conversation. "Listen, Fabrice. We know all about what's going on with Charity. That's the reason we're here to talk. With your father in the hospital, we're concerned that she may try to exploit the situation. I don't need to tell you that we're getting dangerously close to a tipping point out in the street. God forbid that something happens to your father. Nevertheless, we need to be prepared for that eventuality. That means moving full speed ahead with the Citizens Action Committee. I was hoping that you could provide the congressman with an update on your progress."

"Yeah. Everything's going fine," Fabrice declared, waving his cigarette in the air and taking a quick sip of his scotch.

"You're up and running out at the training area?" Jones pressed.

"Yeah, yeah. Everything's good. We got the first shipment of equipment, but we need more."

"More?" Jones asked, surprised by the request. "Exactly how many men are you training out at the camp?"

"Hmmm, we've got a lot out there," Fabrice said vaguely.

"That initial shipment should have been more than enough to field a full battalion of irregulars. Are you sure you still need more?"

"Yeah, that's what I said," Fabrice insisted, becoming agitated. "You told me to get men. That's what I'm doing. But if you can't hold up your end of the deal, I can't promise you they'll stay on. They want to be part of a professional organization, not some jungle militia."

"Right. OK," Jones said. "Give me a few days. I'll see what I can do about getting some additional supplies. Otherwise, how is the training going?"

"Good. No problems at all."

Jones nodded, then turned to the congressman. "For the time being, we're considering the Citizens Action Committee a contingency force. This is all off the books. We'll brief the appropriate committees when the time comes, but until then, we need to keep things close-hold. It should go without saying that our success here depends on maintaining the element of surprise. Any leaks could place the entire plan in jeopardy."

"Is anyone else at the embassy read in on the plan?" Burke asked.

"No way. That place is a total sieve. We can't risk the exposure. For now, this stays between us."

"And the other issue we discussed? Regarding the ambassador," Burke prompted.

"That's an unrelated initiative. I'll leave that part to your judgment," Jones said before turning back to Fabrice. "One last thing. I'm starting to work on the operational plan. For now, your men don't need to know about the target. The most important thing is tactical proficiency. I want you drilling them on all the basics: marksmanship, raids, ambushes, convoy operations, close-quarters combat, and hostage rescue. If we're going to have a chance of pulling this thing off, all that stuff has got to be second nature. We're not going up against a bunch of amateurs. You understand?"

"Sure, boss, no problem," Fabrice said, stubbing out his cigarette in the ashtray.

"I need to get the congressman back to the hotel," Jones said, glancing at his watch. "Just remember, this meeting never happened. Does everyone understand?"

Jones waited until he received an affirmative nod from both Fabrice and Burke, feeling like an overworked nanny. "OK, Fabrice, you keep making things happen out at the training center. I'll work on getting you that second shipment of equipment. I'll be in touch once I have a timeline for delivery."

Fabrice offered a faux salute with the fresh cigarette dangling between his fingers. Jones and Burke got up and made their way across the bar. As they were leaving, Jones saw the two Bulgarian hostesses rejoin Fabrice on the couch and watched, shaking his head, as the commander of the Citizens Action Committee poured a fresh round of drinks for the table. Then Jones pushed open the door and led the congressman back to the Sonata.

+++

The next morning, Anna awoke early to began her regular routine—except for the fact that she hadn't see Louie in several days and all classes at the university were suspended.

After coffee, she read through her email, then started doing laundry. When Anna pondered her next chore—deicing the freezer or turning the compost pile in the backyard— she realized she couldn't spend another day puttering around an empty house. She decided to go to her office at the university and see what was happening on campus, maybe even do some research for a journal article. She texted Louie to let him know that she was heading into the city, then took off, relieved to escape the house.

On her way to campus, Anna was surprised to find the streets mostly empty. It felt almost like an early Sunday morning except for the conspicuous presence of armored police vehicles and concrete barricades situated every few blocks. The street protests had been muted since the attack on President Namono. However, she could still feel the pressure beneath the calm, like floodwaters rising behind a dam, ready to burst forth in a violent torrent.

When she arrived on campus, Anna found her building empty. Even the cleaning and maintenance crews were apparently on mandatory furlough. She had been working for several hours when she heard a knock at the door. She looked up and saw Nesi and Didier standing there, poking their heads in from the hallway.

"You're here!" Nesi said, squealing with delight. "Can we come in?"

"Please do. Have a seat," Anna said, happy to see familiar faces after days of living like an exile. "I've been going stir crazy at home, so I decided to come in and get some work done. But why on earth are the two of you here?"

"We're having an emergency meeting of the student government committee," Didier explained.

"Really!" Anna said. "About the suspension of classes?"

Nesi nodded. "It's been over a week, and the government still hasn't said anything about when classes might resume. We petitioned the ministry of education for details, but they won't tell us anything. Even the university administration declined to give us a specific reason for the closure or say how much longer it will last."

"So, what happens now?" Anna asked.

"The committee has been meeting all morning trying to agree on a plan of action," Didier said. "It hasn't been easy, but I think we're finally coming to a consensus."

"And?" she prompted.

"We've decided to call for a sit-in as a protest against the closure," Nesi said. "Starting tomorrow, here on campus. We're still working through the details, but we've got an agreement from the committee on a basic plan of action. We'll notify everyone on social media, then organize at the student union. Once everyone assembles, we'll issue a statement demanding that the government reopen the university."

"Is the administration aware of what you're doing?" Anna asked.

"Hmmm, sort of," Didier hedged. "We've had some conversations with a few faculty members. Privately, they've expressed support. However, they also warned us that there's no way the administration will endorse the action. But at the least, we're hoping they won't stand in our way."

"Wow, this is big," Anna said. "I'm proud of you two. I'm embarrassed to think about what I was doing when I was your age. It certainly wasn't anything like this."

"Well, maybe you can have your chance now," Nesi hinted.

"What do you mean?"

"You can join us for the sit-in."

"Will there be any other faculty members there?"

Nesi and Didier looked at one another, each waiting for the other to speak. "You need to understand their situation,"

Didier finally said. "I think most of them would support us, but the risks for them are too great. They all work for the government. They have families to consider. If they came out and joined us in the protest, it would mean the end of their careers. I know in their hearts they are with us, but it's just too much to ask."

"But I'm somehow different?" Anna said.

Nesi jumped in. "Of course, you understand that the risks are different for you. If you had to leave tomorrow and start over somewhere else, you could. That's not true for any of the other faculty here. You can't blame them for putting their families first."

"No, of course not," Anna said, straining to offer a smile. "I don't blame them. It's not the same for me. So, when do you plan to kick things off?" she asked, hoping to change the subject.

"Tomorrow morning," Didier said.

"And you're sure about this? Anna asked. "You've thought through all the potential consequences?"

"The consequences of not acting are far worse," Didier insisted with a hint of false bravado.

Anna thought for a moment before answering. "OK, then I'll be there."

"Thank you," Didier said. He gave Nesi a wink, then got up and moved toward the door. "I need to get back to the committee meeting so we can start working on the announcement."

"Go on," Nesi said. "I'll catch up with you in a minute."

Didier nodded and disappeared out the door.

"He seems excited," Anna said once he was gone.

"I think he feels like our moment has finally come. We've been pushing for so long to make the student committee into something more relevant. Today was a big step forward."

"This definitely won't go unnoticed. Won't the government be forced to respond?" Anna asked.

"I guess that's the intent, isn't it? Otherwise, we're nothing more than a tree falling in an empty forest."

"True. I hope the government is willing to meet you halfway with some kind of reasonable compromise. However, given everything that's going on right now, there's no telling what might happen. Most of all, I just want you and Didier to be safe."

"It's nice that you're worried about us. But still, don't you find this a little bit interesting?"

"Interesting? What do you mean?" Anna asked, taken aback by the suggestion.

"I mean from an intellectual perspective. Wasn't your dissertation on something having to do with organized political violence?"

"Yes, it was, but I guess I haven't been thinking about this as a scholar," Anna said. "I suppose most researchers would be eager to have a case study fall into their lap, but it's hard to be objective when your friends and family are caught in the middle."

"Since you're an expert on these things, do you have any thoughts about what might happen?" Nesi asked. "Does this situation have the right ingredients to blow up?"

Anna shrugged. "My research wasn't meant to provide a predictive model for why political violence happens in some cases and not in others. I must have read a hundred different theories about why humans fight one another, and I'm still not sure I could give you a useful explanation of its causes."

"Maybe it's just in our nature. That's a depressing thought," Nesi mused.

"Perhaps, but who knows?" Anna speculated. "I guess Edward O. Wilson would agree with you that it's somehow rooted in our biological impulses. But then for Clausewitz, it's all about politics. For Thucydides, it's a sociological phenomenon. For Marx, it's materialism. For Weber, it's institutional dynamics; and for Geertz, cultural myths and symbolism. I could go on and on, but you get the drift. We're complex creatures. We can find a million ways to rationalize our cruelty to each other."

"You aren't convinced by any of those explanations?"

"Oh, I suppose each provides a piece of the puzzle, but not a complete picture. I think the important thing is asking the right questions and not worrying so much about finding a perfect answer."

"Are you giving me that advice as a friend or as my thesis advisor?"

"Ha! Good question. Don't worry, Nesi. I'm confident you'll find the answers you're looking for."

"I'm actually curious about what you think is going to happen," Nesi said, pressing for an answer.

"You mean with the sit-in?"

"Sure. Are we being naïve and wasting our time?"

"That depends on the stakes, what each side stands to gain or lose. So far, it doesn't seem like the government is interested in negotiation. I think they're convinced that they're playing a strong hand and don't have a reason to fold."

"And what about our side?"

Anna paused for a moment. "I'm hesitant to go too far down that path."

"What do you mean?"

"I mean giving you an opinion," Anna clarified. "I'm an outsider. This isn't my country. It's not my place to judge what's going on here."

"Sometimes it's helpful to have an outsider's opinion," Nesi insisted. "Why do Americans still read de Tocqueville? He was an outsider who explained America to Americans."

"You're comparing me to de Tocqueville?" Anna laughed. "That's flattering, but I can assure you, we're not in the same category."

"Don't worry. No pressure," Nesi said, giving Anna a mischievous wink. "But seriously, I want to know what you think."

Anna considered the question. "I'm not certain what you mean when you say 'our side.'"

Nesi seemed confused, as if the answer should have been obvious. "When I say 'our side,' I'm talking about all of it: the protests, the marches, the student committee—everything that we're demanding from the government."

"That's what I'm getting at," Anna explained. "The people who started marching in the streets last month were doing it because they couldn't afford to buy food. For them, the protests were about empty store shelves and shopkeepers who wouldn't take their money. But the things you and Didier are worried about are very different. You aren't talking about putting food on the table. Of course, that doesn't make your concerns any less legitimate, but it feels like we're talking apples and oranges. Right now, the only thing you have in common with the people in the street is wanting to see the end of the regime. But once that's done, then what's the common denominator? What's brings it all together?"

Nesi nodded, her expression thoughtful.

"I hope I haven't overstepped," Anna said. "It's only an opinion. I won't be offended if you think it's rubbish."

"No, it's OK," Nesi reassured her. "I'm sure there's something to what you're saying. I know we live in our own little bubble here on campus. Sometimes it's easy to forget that the world doesn't revolve around us and our problems."

"I couldn't agree with you more. But please, don't let that stop you. Remember, all good revolutionaries live in bubbles. Otherwise, they wouldn't be able to do what they do."

Nesi smiled and stood up. "Thanks for the chat. I hope we'll see you at the sit-in tomorrow."

"You bet," Anna said. "And good luck!"

CHAPTER SEVEN

———

Several days later, the embassy staff gathered in the conference room, awaiting the broadcast of a special announcement from the Gisawian ministry of information. On the television, one side of a split-screen view showed live footage of riot police battling a group of rock-throwing youths somewhere in the city. On the other half of the screen, a reporter from Gisawian state television was standing in a tranquil courtyard outside the main hospital where President Namono had been recovering. Just a few miles apart, the two images made for a jarring juxtaposition of life in the city.

The staff was engrossed in the macabre spectacle of baton-wielding riot police smashing through a thin line of protesters. The head-on assault sent a group of marchers retreating into a cloud of tear gas. Everyone was so absorbed in the unfolding drama on TV that no one noticed Ambassador Roberts slipping into her seat.

"Can someone please tell me what we're all looking at?" Claire said. Everyone turned to stare at her, each waiting for someone else to answer.

"How about the picture on the left?" she encouraged. "Does anyone want to take a crack at that one?"

Jake Baxter glanced around the table. Seeing no one else responding, he straightened in his chair and nodded at the TV. "Madam Ambassador, it's a live shot of a protest about two blocks from Independence Square."

"It looks bad."

"It is. The violence has been getting worse for the last two days. But this is the worst we've seen since the start of the protests. The police aren't holding back anymore."

The television showed a wave of police reinforcements arriving on the scene. As they entered the fray, the police quickly seized the momentum and shifted the battle in the government's favor. The police line pressed forward against the retreating marchers, delivering a series of high, arching blows with their batons. Several protesters fell helplessly to the ground, taking the full brunt of the counterattack.

The second wave of officers stormed into the melee, advancing behind their transparent plexiglass shields. They smashed through the remaining protesters like a battering ram, leaving them dazed and confused. The television camera zoomed in for a tight shot of the police line, so close that the lettering on their shields and helmets was visible. Stenciled in bold block letters across all the police gear were the words "PROUDLY MADE IN THE USA."

Claire groaned as she read the words on the equipment. "Jesus. This not what we need right now," she muttered. "Colonel Sawyer! Where the hell did the Gisawians get that equipment from?"

Sawyer closed his eyes and shook his head. "A few weeks ago, it was issued to the Gisawian army as part of a counter-terrorism assistance package. The transfer was legit, except the equipment wasn't supposed to be used by the police. Only for external defense, not domestic crowd control."

"What else did we give them besides shields and helmets?"

"Rubber bullets, tear gas grenades, and some vehicle-mounted water cannons," Sawyer answered.

Claire closed her eyes and took a deep breath, trying to regain some semblance of composure. "Get over to the counter-terrorism base ASAP. You tell the Gisawians that I better not see a single piece of US-supplied equipment used against the protesters. Do you understand?"

"Yes, ma'am."

"Then go!" she yelled.

Sawyer leaped to his feet and sprinted for the door as Claire turned back to the television. "Now, what the hell is going on over at the hospital?" she asked, nodding toward the state television channel broadcast.

"I got this one," Mike Jones volunteered. "I just got off the phone with one of my contacts over at Green House. It seems that President Namono's condition has improved. Apparently, he's now conscious and responsive."

"So, what's this special announcement about?"

"We're not entirely sure. Since the drone attack, the government has been in panic mode. Nobody's saying anything, and everyone's watching their backs. From what I hear, it's total chaos inside Green House. I assume they're trying to show that Namono is still alive and kicking. Reassuring people that the ship of state isn't adrift in stormy seas."

On TV, a Gisawian news reporter was standing in the hospital courtyard with a finger pressed to his earpiece, looking confused. He was about to speak when the camera cut away to a remote feed inside the hospital. The next image was from inside a sunny recovery suite. President Namono was propped up in a hospital bed, surrounded by a gaggle of smiling doctors and nurses. The medical paraphernalia had been pushed off to the side, making the room look more like a Scandinavian spa than an intensive care unit.

The camera revealed hints of burgundy-hued bruises around President Namono's neck and a thin line of sutures stretching across his forehead. An IV tube ran along the length of his bony forearm, and a nasal cannula provided supplemental oxygen.

The news anchor outside in the courtyard provided an impromptu play-by-play as the president said a few words to his medical team. Namono offered a weak handshake to each of the doctors and nurses as they filed past his gurney like a mobile receiving line. Meanwhile, Charity Namono sat on the edge of her husband's bed, stone-faced and silent, as the procession continued. Over her shoulder was a suede, monogram print tote with an elegant, gold chain strap, and a matching closure.

After the medical team left the room, a presidential aide placed a black leather binder on Namono's lap. The president made a dramatic show of opening it, leafing through the documents, pausing briefly, and pretending to read through some pages. When he reached the end, Charity took a silver pen out of her purse and handed it to her husband.

The president struggled awkwardly to remove the pen's cap when Charity reached over and offered her assistance. With her hand resting firmly on his shoulder, President Namono signed the last page of the document, then handed it back to his aide. The video ended as he slumped back into the pillows, smiling feebly, appearing spent by the effort.

The next shot cut back to the news reporter in the courtyard. For a moment, he seemed befuddled, uncertain what was happening. Then someone from off-camera reached into the frame and handed him a sheet of paper. The reporter quickly scanned the document, trying to process what he had just been given, then began reading directly from a summary of the presidential decree.

> Immediate and indefinite institution of emergency martial law...authorization for the deployment of regular army troops for the purpose of internal defense...mandatory pre-registration of all political gatherings and public demonstrations...restrictions on the use of any nonapproved social media platforms...

When the reporter finished reading the statement, Claire turned to Mike Jones. "What do you make of it?"

"It's a Hail Mary pass. Namono's trying to prove that he's still in charge."

"Agreed. But why the hospital bed theatrics? I didn't find that particularly convincing. It made him look weak, not strong," she said.

"Maybe that was the intention."

Claire gave Jones a puzzled look.

"Think about it," he continued. "Namono barely survives an assassination attempt. The streets are in chaos. Investors are pulling their money out of the country, and the currency is in free fall. If I were sitting at home and watching this on TV, I'd be thinking this guy's done for. He's lost his grip, and he's not getting it back. But who else do I see in that picture?"

"Charity?" the ambassador ventured.

"Exactly. I'd be willing to bet that she talked him into the entire dog and pony show, knowing that he'd come across looking like a doddering old fool. Meanwhile, she's sitting there cool as a cucumber, even helping the old man take the damn cap off his ballpoint pen. Everybody is already saying that she's the real power behind the throne. She just proved it."

"OK, then what comes next?" Claire asked. "If we're to believe this so-called decree, this country is about to turn into a police state. Is this what finally pushes us past the tipping point?"

"That's the million-dollar question. Unfortunately, since Namono just turned off the pipe on all social media, that makes our exploitation program somewhat useless."

"Any other options?"

"Maybe," Jones said. "We've been beta testing a new program for passive open-source data collection during the street protests."

"What does that gather?"

"Anything that can be seen with the naked eye or transmitted over the cellular network: time, place, size, activity, participants—all of it. We call it Group Affiliation and Identity Tracking, or GAIT for short."

"You mean you've been tracking every single demonstrator out on the streets?"

"More or less. We've got a network of distributed sensors gathering live footage, cell phone data, even selfies; basically, any digital data that we can scoop up. Then we cross-reference all the biometric signatures with known digital identities that have been cataloged from years of social media activity."

"And what does that tell you?"

"Once the computers do their magic, we get a complete demographic profile and link analysis of the entire protest movement. From that, we can infer trend lines, like whether people are getting friends and family to join them in the street. It's a perfect leading indicator for predicting social contagion and mass hysteria."

"I don't know whether to be amazed or horrified," Claire said. "So, based on what this GAIT thing is telling you, what's your assessment of the situation?"

"That the trouble for President Namono is just getting started."

+++

An hour later, Colonel Sawyer was standing outside the joint counter-terrorism training camp, trying to convince a skeptical guard to let him through the gate.

"Listen, I realize that the appointment is not on the books, but I must see Lieutenant Colonel Bigombe immediately. This is urgent," Sawyer pleaded with the sergeant-in-charge.

"I'm sorry, sir, but you're not on the list."

"Please, just call Colonel Bigombe. Let him know that I'm here and that I'm not leaving until I see him."

The guard sensed that Sawyer would not be deterred and retreated into his shack. After a lengthy phone conversation, he returned to the gate and waved Sawyer into the compound. By the time he arrived at the headquarters building, Louie was standing outside his office, waiting for him.

"Sorry about the hassle at the gate," Louie said, reaching out to shake Sawyer's hand. "I didn't know you were coming over; otherwise, I would have told them to wave you straight through. Even since the attack, the place has turned into a high-security prison."

"No problem. Thanks for seeing me on short notice. I didn't want to talk over the phone," Sawyer explained.

Louie nodded and led him into the office. They sat down at the coffee table while a sergeant served a tray of tea and biscuits, then disappeared without a word.

"We haven't spoken since the attack on President Namono," Sawyer said. "How have you been?"

Louie shrugged as he poured them each a cup of tea. "I've been better. We've been stuck here at the camp since it happened. They've told us to be ready to deploy, but so far, we haven't gone anywhere beyond the front gate."

"Maybe that's about to change," Sawyer hinted. "I assume you saw the announcement on TV about the new presidential decree? It sounds like President Namono has authorized the use of the army against the protesters."

"I'm aware of it, but so far we've not received orders. Is that what you came over here to talk about? The presidential decree? Because if that's the case, I honestly don't know any more about it than you do."

"Yeah, that's part of it," Sawyer confirmed. "But there's another thing. You remember that shipment of surplus gear that we discussed a few weeks ago?"

Louie nodded, sensing where the conversation was going.

"Well, today on TV, we saw the riot police using it against the protesters. Ambassador Roberts went through the roof. That equipment was provided to support counter-terrorism operations, not to suppress domestic protests. That's a red line for us, Louie. It can't happen again."

"Believe me, I understand," Louie insisted. "But the police came and took it from our warehouse. I didn't have the power to stop them."

"I bet your uncle could. He's the minister. He could put a stop to all of this right now if he wanted to."

"Be reasonable, Jeff. No one even knows who's in charge of the county right now. We're on the verge of a total breakdown of social order. My uncle can't just wave a magic wand and bring it all back together."

"I'm not expecting the police and protesters to join hands and start singing 'Kumbaya.' But we also can't have pictures on the television of riot police cracking heads with American-made equipment. I'm telling you, there are going to be repercussions if it happens again."

"I'll let my uncle know," Louie said, feeling powerless to offer anything more than empty promises. "But you need to remember, the police don't work for him. They report to the minister of the interior. Even if my uncle wanted to, I don't think there's much he can do."

"I get that. But please, do your best. That's all I'm asking. The ambassador wasn't kidding around."

"I'll pass along the message," Louie assured him. "And since you're here, there is something I need to ask you about."

"Sure. What's up?"

"I assume you're aware of the ongoing investigation?"

"You mean into the attack against the president?"

"Yes. The one being led by police intelligence," Louie clarified.

"We've been trying to find out what's going on. Unfortunately, your government hasn't been forthcoming with details," Sawyer explained.

"Don't feel bad. You're not the only one in the dark. The only reason I know anything is because I have an old friend who works for police intelligence. His office is conducting the investigation, and he's keeping me in the loop." Louie paused and glanced at the door, making sure that they were alone before continuing. "I'm assuming you've heard the rumors that the explosives used in the attack were delivered by one of the drones your government sold us."

"Yes, we're aware of that," Sawyer said. "And we also know that the drones were assigned to your unit and stored here on this base."

"In that case, you probably understand why my unit hasn't been allowed to leave the camp since the attack. Officially, we've been told it's due to the state of emergency, but no one here believes that. We're basically under house arrest. They don't want us going anywhere until the investigation is over."

"I assumed as much," Sawyer said. "Unfortunately, that's an internal matter with your government. I don't think there's anything I can do to help you out with that."

"Don't be so sure. How much do you know about the model of the drone used in the attack?"

"I'm not an expert, but I'm familiar with it," Sawyer said.

"Then you probably know that they're controlled from a small ground station that receives all the flight data and surveillance feeds."

"Yeah, I've trained with that model a few times."

"Well, the ground station control box for the drone used in the attack was never found."

"That makes sense," Sawyer said. "I'm sure whoever was at the controls didn't want to leave any incriminating clues around. It's probably at the bottom of a lake somewhere."

"Maybe," Louie said. "But because the explosives on the drone didn't fully detonate, there was a considerable amount of intact debris recovered from the attack site, including the drone's onboard memory card."

"I think I see where you're going with this," Sawyer said, nodding slowly. "If I recall how that model works, the memory card keeps a temporary digital backup of the latest mission data should the aircraft lose its communications link during the flight. Theoretically, all the telemetry data, full-motion video, and GPS tracking from the final flight should still be on that memory card. Do you think police intelligence knows that?"

"I'm guessing not. They don't use drones," Louie explained. "In fact, we rarely even bother with the memory card either. It's a failsafe measure in case something goes wrong in flight. Besides, the card is encrypted. Even if they knew it was there, I doubt they could download and read the data."

"That all makes sense, but I still don't see how I can help."

"What if I could get you that memory card?" Louie asked. "Could you find someone who could download the data and get it back to me? I can't take the chance of giving it to anyone here. I don't know who I can trust anymore."

"Yeah, I suppose I could do it. But how are you going to get the card?"

"Don't worry about that," Louie reassured him. "My friend at police intelligence has agreed to help me out. He's got access to the evidence room where they're storing the debris from the bombing. If the card is there, he'll be able to get it. I'm guessing that they won't even know it's missing. I'll send you a text once I get ahold of it."

"OK, Louie. You know I'll help you if I can," Sawyer offered. "But please watch your back. I've got a bad feeling that someone may be trying to set you up."

"I'm sort of feeling that way myself. That's why I need to see what's on that memory card as soon as possible. And I hope this goes without saying, but we need to keep this between you and me."

"Yeah, no problem. Let me know when you get your hands on the card. I'll take care of the rest."

+++

That evening, Mike Jones lingered in the office long after everyone else had left for the day. He was sitting at his desk, deep within the secure inner sanctum of the embassy reserved for classified information. In his windowless office, Jones killed time surfing the internet, checking out baseball scores, and the returns on his mutual funds. He had just glanced at his watch, annoyed to still be at work, when the red light on his secure telephone began flashing. He let it ring a dozen times before finally picking up.

"Jones here," he barked into the receiver.

"This is Congressman Burke. Where were you? I almost hung up."

"I'm a little busy over here," he replied curtly.

"Apparently so. What's the latest? I saw on the news that Namono pulled some kind of stunt today from his hospital bed."

"All he did was confirm what everybody already knows: Charity's in charge now. I doubt the old man has the slightest idea what's going on out in the streets."

"How could he not know? From what I see on TV, the riots are completely out of control. It's even worse than before the attack."

"He's living in a bubble. The police have the entire neighborhood around the hospital cordoned off. He might as well be sitting in downtown Oslo. Meanwhile, Charity is getting ready to make her move."

"How do you know that?" Burke asked. "I thought you said that you weren't getting any good intel out of Green House."

"I'm not. Green House is a circus. Nobody knows anything. But I've got one deep-cover asset who's still in the game. We're getting some good reporting from him, and it confirms all our suspicions. Charity has been meeting with her Chinese contacts. She's had multiple communications since the attack."

"What are they talking about?"

"More conversations about the 'prototype' and plans to move forward with production. It's the same stuff she was talking about on the day before the attack."

"Do you know any more about what she might be up to?" Burke asked.

"I'm still trying to figure that out. But I'm tracking every move she makes."

"How?"

"Did you happen to download the UGo2 app while you were here?"

"No, what the hell is it?"

"Only the most popular multitasking app in DRoG. It's got everything: online dating, rideshare, e-shopping, check-ins, restaurant reviews—the works."

"Are you saying that the CIA hacked it?"

"No, we built it, then marketed it through a local front company," Jones said smugly. "And Charity happens to love it. So long as she's got the app on her cell phone, we've got complete visibility of all her movements. I've got a surveillance team tailing her twenty-four seven. It's just a matter of time before we figure out her game."

"Then what?"

"Then we throw a wrench in whatever she has planned. That's where Fabrice and the Citizens Action Committee comes into play. If Namono kicks the bucket—which, based on how he looked this morning, could be any minute—we'll be ready to move with the CAC."

"Do you really think Fabrice is cut out for this?" Burke asked. "I didn't come away from our meeting with a lot of confidence."

"At this point, we don't have much choice. We're not dealing with the major league draft over here. Sometimes you gotta make do with what you've got, and right now, that's Fabrice."

"How soon until he's ready?"

"No idea. I'm going to take a little drive out to his training camp later this week and see how things are going. I'll let you know what I find out."

"Sounds good. Any developments regarding our other little problem?"

"You mean the ambassador?" Jones asked.

"Yeah, is she still going on about pushing for elections?"

"Don't worry about her. I've got her contained. If she wants to keep coddling the kids over at the university, that's fine. We'll let her keep on rambling nonsense. The fact is, nobody's paying any attention. It's complete chaos out there, and the government is about to come down hard on the protesters. I don't see the protests lasting much longer. The only question is, when the music stops, who's going to be sitting in Green House, Charity or Fabrice?"

"Right. Let me know if there's anything I can do on this end," Burke said.

"For the time being, the best thing you can do is keep your mouth shut about getting rid of Namono," Jones advised. "We don't want to be forced into action before Fabrice is ready to go with the CAC. After this morning's performance at the hospital, Charity probably thinks she's on her way to Green House. Let's let her believe that for now. It will buy us a little more time to get our shit together."

"But once that happens, then I'll be able to talk about it on TV, right?"

"What? No! Of course not. You can't talk about any of this. That's not how it works. There's a reason we call them clandestine operations."

"I was just asking," Burke said defensively. "Listen, I'm taking a big chance here by supporting your little scheme. I can't afford to have this blow up in my face before midterms. I've got enough problems as it is."

"Don't worry. I've got it under control," Jones assured him. "I'm not going to let things fall apart. Fabrice knows who's looking out for him. Once we get him into Green House, he won't forget who put him there."

"I should hope not," Burke said. "Anything else?"

"No. I'll let you know how the visit to the training camp goes."

"OK. We'll talk after that."

CHAPTER EIGHT

Two days later, Colonel Sawyer was working in his office when his cell phone began buzzing. He recognized Louie's number on the caller ID and closed the door before answering. "What's up?"

"Did you hear what's going on?" Louie asked, sounding panicked.

"Let me guess, another day of rioting?" Sawyer quipped.

"No, I mean out here at the airport."

"Louie, I have no idea what you're talking about. I haven't heard about anything happening at the airport."

"The Chinese just landed a transport plane filled with troops. They're offloading equipment into a compound next to our base."

"What the fuck? Are you serious?" Sawyer blurted out, now sharing Louie's alarm.

"Why would I make this up?"

"Can you see them now?" Sawyer asked. "How do you know they're Chinese?"

"For god's sake, Jeff, I know what Chinese people look like! They just landed a giant transport plane. It looks like one of yours, except for a big red flag with five stars on it. What else do you need to know?"

"Holy crap!" Sawyer said. "Can you take a few pictures and text them to me right away?"

"Yeah, sure. They don't seem to be trying to hide. If you want, I can walk out to the airfield and ask what they're doing. I'd be happy to give it a try."

"You're kidding, right?" Sawyer asked in disbelief.

"Why not? It isn't every day that a rising global superpower recolonizes your country. It almost feels like some kind of space alien movie."

"Louie, listen to me. Whatever you do, don't go out there," Sawyer urged. "Just take some pictures of the plane and text them to me ASAP. Give me a few minutes to find the ambassador, then I'll call you right back."

"Got it," Louie said before hanging up.

Sawyer leaped up from his chair and took off at a dead sprint down the hallway. After bounding up several flights of stairs, he arrived at the ambassador's office, gasping for breath.

"I need to see Ambassador Roberts right away," he said to the secretary, bent over his knees and struggling for air while checking his phone.

"I think she's on a call with Washington," her assistant said. "Can you wait a few minutes?"

"No! I need to see her right now!"

The assistant got up and stuck her head into the ambassador's office. She whispered something through the door, then waved Colonel Sawyer inside. Claire was sitting at her desk with her notorious red pen in hand, editing draft diplomatic cables. "OK, Jeff, what's so urgent that it couldn't wait?"

Sawyer passed his smartphone across the desk. On the screen were the photos that Louie had texted from the airport.

"Can you please tell me what I'm looking at?" Claire asked as she studied the photos. "I see a large gray plane and some soldiers in camouflage uniforms walking out of the back."

"Look at the flag on the tail fin," Sawyer said. "The Chinese just landed a transport plane at the airport. They're offloading combat troops and equipment."

Claire examined the picture more closely. "Who sent you these?"

"Lieutenant Colonel Bigombe. He's the commander of the Gisawian counter-terrorism unit at the training base."

"The defense minister's nephew?"

Sawyer nodded. "He called me and said that Chinese troops are moving into an empty compound between our base and the Gisawian counter-terrorism training center."

"Does he know why they're here?"

"No. Just said they landed about an hour ago and started offloading equipment."

"Well, someone must know what's going on. A foreign military plane doesn't just land without somebody authorizing it."

The secretary stuck her head through the door, interrupting the conversation. "Madam Ambassador, I think you should turn on the TV. The local networks are getting ready to broadcast some kind of special announcement."

Claire reached for the remote control and turned on the television mounted on the wall of her office. On the news, they saw a gaggle of local reporters crowding around a podium where the Gisawian finance minister was calling for quiet. Once everyone settled down, the minister began reading from a prepared statement.

> ...Chinese Development Bank is extending a temporary emergency line of credit to meet short-term obligations covering state salaries and military pensions...immediate phase-out of all Gisawian banknotes and mandatory exchange for a new sovereign currency...selection of a new minister for the State Mineral Authority...a twenty-five-year base-leasing agreement granted to the Chinese People's Liberation Army, providing advisory assistance and logistical support to DRoG forces for peacekeeping and stability operations...

Once the minister finished reading the statement, the scrum of reporters rushed the podium and began peppering him with questions. The minister smiled and waved dismissively before leaving without answering any of them. When it became apparent that the press conference had ended, Claire hit the mute button and turned to Colonel Sawyer.

"That explains why a Chinese plane is sitting at the airport," she said. "President Namono has found someone willing to bail him out."

"But he's a sinking ship," Sawyer said. "Why would the Chinese go to all the trouble of keeping him afloat now?"

"I'm assuming they view it as an insurance policy. They've sunk a lot of money into the mining sector over the last few years. They don't want to lose that investment should a disorderly transition of power occur."

"I guess that means we're getting some new next-door neighbors out at the airport."

"It appears that way," Claire said. "So, here's what needs to happen. We'll prepare a flash cable to let the folks back in Washington know what's going on, at least as we understand it. The Chinese aren't trying to keep their arrival a secret, but that doesn't mean we won't see some kind of reaction on the street. The opposition was already accusing Namono of selling out to the Chinese. This will only confirm their suspicions and put more pressure on the regime."

Sawyer nodded. "What do you want me to do?"

"See if you can get a meeting with Defense Minister Odongo. Find out what he knows about all this. Beyond that, we'll need to wait for guidance from Washington and see how they want to handle it. At this point, there's nothing to be gained by overreacting. We need to get a better idea of what's really going on. Any questions?"

"No, ma'am," Sawyer said.

"Good. Let me know what you find out after you speak with Mugaba."

+++

Early the next morning, Colonel Sawyer arrived at the Gisawian Ministry of Defense for a meeting with Minister Mugaba Odongo. He waited in the reception area for nearly an hour before the secretary escorted him into the minister's office. Sawyer had been inside the office a few times as a notetaker for high-level meetings, but this was his first solo audience. When he entered the room, Mugaba rose from his chair and came around the desk to greet him.

"Minister Odongo. Thank you for seeing me on such short notice," Sawyer said.

"It's my pleasure," Mugaba said, taking Sawyer's hand in a viselike grip, leading him to a set of leather chairs. "I always make time for our American friends. Can I offer you a coffee?"

"No, thank you, sir. I know you're busy, so I hope you don't mind if we get straight to business."

"As you wish," Mugaba said with a relaxed smile.

"I imagine you know why I asked to meet so urgently."

Mugaba nodded thoughtfully.

"Given yesterday's events out at the airfield, Ambassador Roberts asked me to see you as soon as possible. It goes without saying that we were surprised by the arrival of the Chinese plane, as well as the announcement about the new base-leasing agreement."

"As was I," Mugaba said. "The first I heard of it was from my nephew Lutalo. I understand that he called you as well."

"Yes, he did. So, Minister Odongo, just to be clear: Are you saying that you had no advance warning about the arrival of the Chinese plane or the new leasing agreement?"

"I can assure you, none whatsoever," Mugaba insisted.

Sawyer stared blankly at the minister, uncertain what to say next.

"You seem surprised," Mugaba observed.

"Well, yes. I suppose I am. A twenty-five-year base-leasing agreement with the PLA seems like a major policy decision.

To be honest, I'm a little shocked to hear that you were left out of the loop."

"I agree, Colonel Sawyer. There is no good explanation. All I can say is that we are living in extraordinary times. Many things are happening that I no longer have control over or even awareness of. Surely you've heard the rumors about what's happening inside Green House?"

"We hear many rumors, but it's hard to know what to believe."

"Tell me what you are hearing. Perhaps I can confirm or deny this information. That's why the ambassador sent you, isn't it? To find out what's going on?"

Sawyer shifted in his chair, taken aback by the minister's bluntness. "Yes," he finally said. "She sent me to get the truth."

Mugaba chuckled as if Sawyer had just told a good joke. "You know, we have an old saying here: A lie travels halfway around the world while the truth is still putting on its shoes."

Sawyer smiled, familiar with Mugaba's reputation for quoting old village proverbs. "What lesson I should take from that?" he asked.

"Be cautious about believing first reports," Mugaba explained.

"Minister, with all due respect, yesterday a PLA plane landed at the airport with combat troops on board. Then your finance minister described it as a semipermanent military presence. People are saying that President Namono is moving closer to Beijing. Everything that we saw yesterday at the airport seems to confirm that suspicion. How else should we interpret this?"

"What you are saying is a reasonable conclusion, but only if you believe that President Namono is still in charge at Green House."

"Are you suggesting that someone else made that deal with the Chinese? I assume that you're talking about Charity."

"Perhaps," Mugaba said with a shrug. "Your guess is as good as mine. I was not exaggerating when I said that I was not consulted on the decision. Since the attack, I've had no contact with anyone inside Green House. Someone must be running the government, but I cannot say exactly who that is, though I've heard that Charity has been busy while her husband is in hospital. But of course, you Americans have your own ways of figuring these things out. Perhaps you can tell me what she's been up to?"

Sawyer ignored the leading question and pushed back with his own. "So what you're telling me is that Charity Namono was behind the deal with the Chinese? That she's the one pulling strings inside Green House?"

"I believe that what happened yesterday at the airport speaks for itself. It reminds me of another old saying from the village: One who is accused of stealing goats shouldn't entertain their guests with goat stew. Yesterday, we were all fed a large helping of goat stew."

"Minister Odongo, may I be frank with you?"

"Of course."

"Given the uncertainty inside Green House, there has been some concern about the long-term viability of our counter-terrorism operating base. As you're aware, the United States has invested considerable resources in developing that asset. It's a critical hub for implementing our regional strategy."

"Colonel Sawyer, you know that I was closely involved in the negotiations that enabled your county to use that base. I can assure you that, at the time, the deal was made in good faith. Our two nations have enjoyed a long and mutually beneficial alliance. We all hoped that the base would represent an enduring symbol of that partnership. However, I fear that things may have changed since then. Whoever is now making decisions inside Green House may have different priorities."

"Based on what we are seeing, that appears to be true," Sawyer said. "But can I ask you a hypothetical question? Confidentially, of course."

"Please, go ahead."

"If President Namono were to leave Green House unexpectedly, in your opinion, could such a scenario jeopardize our access to the base?"

"That is a difficult question," Mugaba said, rubbing his chin and leaning back in his chair. "I wish I could offer you a definitive answer, but of course, it depends on who is sitting in Green House after he's gone. Until that matter is decided, nothing can be guaranteed."

"In that case, may I ask your position on the matter?"

"All l can say is that as long as I am minister, I will do everything in my power to ensure that the American base remains open. I give you my word on that."

"Minister Odongo, that's very reassuring to hear. May I pass along that message directly on to the ambassador?"

"By all means. And please give Ambassador Roberts my best regards," Mugaba said, rising and offering Sawyer his hand.

The next day, after lunch, Mike Jones grabbed a khaki safari jacket and a small backpack from a hook behind his door. He locked the office and told his secretary that he'd be out for the rest of the day. In the parking lot, he walked past the battered Hyundai Sonata and climbed into an old Toyota Hilux pickup truck that was usually driven by the embassy's maintenance crew. Jones pulled a small GPS from his backpack and entered a set of coordinates from a scrap of paper. On the screen, the endpoint of his journey appeared, somewhere in the vast emptiness several hours outside the capital.

Jones started the engine, checked that the gas tank was full, and then pulled out into the busy street. Once he was beyond the city limits, traffic thinned to almost nothing. Occasionally, he passed a hitchhiker or a truck filled with farm animals on its way into the city. After an hour or so of driving, the GPS instructed him to turn off the paved highway onto an unmarked dirt road. Looking up ahead, he could see the path disappearing in the distance over a gently rising bluff.

Jones followed the rutted path until he reached the top of the hill, then pulled over to the side of the road. Through the windshield, he had a panoramic view overlooking a flat plateau that looked similar to a sprawling West Texas ranch. As far as the eye could see, rocky scrubland and clumps of low trees dotted the terrain.

Jones pulled a pair of binoculars out of his backpack and followed the road's thin line off into the distance. It dead-ended at what looked like a country estate, surrounded

by pastures, a small pond, and what appeared to be an old dressage arena. Behind a row of overgrown privacy shrubs was a small-scale recreation of a nineteenth-century English manor house. Adjacent to the residence was a tennis court, its surface cracked and dotted with weeds, a tattered net blowing in the wind. In front of the house was a circular gravel driveway where a dozen luxury SUVs were parked end to end.

Jones put the binoculars back into his backpack and took a SIG Sauer compact semiautomatic pistol from one of the zippered compartments. He calmly chambered a round and slipped the weapon into a shoulder holster hidden beneath his safari jacket. Jones glanced over his shoulder, making sure that no one had followed him from the highway. Then he eased the truck back onto the dirt road.

After a few more minutes of driving, he came to a makeshift roadblock constructed from several rusted oil drums and industrial piping sections. Jones brought the truck to a halt when he saw someone emerge from a small guard shack hidden in the bushes. The man wore a pair of aviator-style sunglasses, camouflage cargo pants, a soiled T-shirt, and rubber flip-flops. An antique AK-47 was strapped across his chest, and he appeared to have just woken up from a midafternoon siesta.

Jones rolled down the window and nodded as the man approached the truck. "I'm here to see Fabrice," he announced.

The man shrugged and shook his head as if he had no idea who Jones was talking about.

"Listen, friend. I'm not here to play games. I'm from the American embassy, and I'm here to see Fabrice," he said, flashing a fake identification badge listing one of several assumed identities.

When the man showed no intention of opening the gate, Jones calmly reached over and took a signaling mirror out of the glove compartment. He stuck the mirror out the window, catching the sunlight and reflecting it skyward several times. He glanced up and waved into the air before putting the mirror back in the glove compartment. Then Jones looked the guard directly in the eyes while making the universal sign for a gun with his thumb and forefinger, aiming it playfully at the man's head.

"You've got thirty seconds to let me through that gate or my friends up there are going to be a little upset," Jones said, winking suggestively up into the empty sky.

For a second, the man seemed to be weighing the likelihood of a bluff. Then, without a word, he stepped back from the truck and moved toward the gate. He leaned hard on a cinderblock counterweight that lifted the flimsy barrier. With the road clear, Jones gave the guard a friendly salute as he maneuvered the Hilux through the obstacle. In the rearview mirror, he watched as the guard beat a hasty retreat back into the scrub brush.

"Ha! I can't believe that still works," Jones chuckled to himself as he sped off in the direction of the manor house.

A few minutes later, he pulled into the gravel roundabout, parking the truck behind the line of black SUVs. The house appeared deserted, but he could hear the faint beat of Afro-pop music from the backyard. When he stepped out of the truck, the music was suddenly punctuated by several staccato bursts of automatic gunfire, followed by the sound of men laughing.

Jones ducked for cover behind the truck and drew the SIG from its holster. He advanced quickly along the side of the house, tucked in a combat crouch, scanning the horizon for danger. Jones peeked around the corner, his finger hovering over the trigger. Then he stopped dead in his tracks, slowly stood up, and holstered his weapon.

Behind the house was a perfectly manicured lawn dotted with a bizarre assortment of animal-themed topiaries. In the middle of the jade carpet was a kidney-shaped swimming pool filled with inflatable beach toys. Next to the pool was a partially collapsed badminton net and an assortment of broken croquet mallets that appeared to be covered in blood. Wafting through the air was the scent of barbequed meat and marijuana.

Jones made a beeline toward the pool as another volley of gunfire rang out, followed by boisterous laughter. In the adjacent field, a group of men gathered at one end of a makeshift rifle range. At the far end was a line of tree stumps topped with an assortment of bottles, gourds, and melons. One of the men clumsily dropped his beer to the ground, then aimed at a papaya set downrange. With a burst of automatic fire, the fruit exploded into a pinkish mist, followed by an eruption of cheers and drunken high-fives from the other men.

Jones spotted several large shipping containers behind the firing line that had been pried open with a crowbar, the packaging littering the yard. Stenciled in block letters across one of the crates were the words "Express Beauty Supply Company Ltd., Abu Dhabi UAE." Inside the containers were dozens of brand-new Belgian assault rifles and hundreds of boxes of ammunition. Jones recognized the contents from the inventory list of the last shipment earmarked for the Citizens Action Committee.

Jones was on the verge of breaking up the drunken target practice when he spotted Fabrice at the far end of the swimming pool. The CAC commander sat on a lounge chair beneath an umbrella, accompanied by two women immodestly stuffed into tiny bikinis. Fabrice was wearing swim trunks, leather sandals, and a tailored dress shirt unbuttoned to his navel. As Jones stormed around the pools' perimeter, one of the bikini-clad women was rolling a joint on the table while the other was giving Fabrice a neck massage.

"Ladies, if you don't mind, I have some business to discuss with my friend," Jones said, arriving at the foot of the chaise lounge where Fabrice was napping.

The two women gave Jones a glassy-eyed stare, reluctant to move until he casually pulled aside his safari jacket, revealing the holstered SIG. The women quickly grabbed their clothes and retreated toward the manor house. In the commotion, Fabrice had been roused back to consciousness. He appeared annoyed by the abrupt end of the massage and startled to discover Jones standing at the foot of the lounger.

"Boss man! I didn't know you were coming out," Fabrice said, leaping to his feet and extending his hand.

"What the fuck is this, Fabrice?" Jones yelled, ignoring the greeting, waving angrily at the men out in the field, who were still busy shooting papayas with assault rifles.

"What do you mean, boss? This is the training camp, just like we talked about."

"The hell it is," Jones said, squinting suspiciously at the rolling paper, bags of weed, and empty bottle of Glenfiddich on the table. "Are those the weapons from the last shipment?" he asked, pointing at the open crates out in the field.

"Yeah, boss, we were just trying them out."

"Where are the rest of your men? You told me you had over a battalion signed up. All I see here is a goddamn pool party. Where is the Citizens Action Committee?"

"This is just part of it," Fabrice said, waving his hands manically. "We're on a training holiday. You know, a little break from the combat." He dropped into a crouch, pretending to shoot a rifle in a playful bit of pantomime.

"Cut the shit, Fabrice. We're running out of time. Do you have any idea what's going on right now at Green House?"

Fabrice shrugged sheepishly.

"For your information, your stepmother Charity is on the verge of taking over the country. A planeload of Chinese soldiers landed yesterday at the airport. We're knee-deep in a major fucking crisis. Meanwhile, you're out here hosting a poolside barbeque. Is this some kind of goddamn joke?"

"Come on, boss. We're just getting organized. I told you we'd be ready to go. We just need a little more time," Fabrice said, buttoning his shirt, trying to make himself presentable. "I'll have all the men out here tomorrow, I promise."

"Listen, Fabrice, I've staked my entire professional reputation on you and the CAC, but what I see right now looks like amateur hour," Jones growled.

"But boss, it's hard to find good help around here," Fabrice said, gesturing at the men out in the field, who had finished with target practice and moved on to a pickup game of soccer.

"Don't give me that crap, Fabrice. I booted the Russians out of Afghanistan with nothing but a ragtag bunch of illiterate goat fuckers."

Fabrice turned sullen, staring despondently at the soccer match, where the presumptive core of the Citizens Action Committee was arguing over a drunken own goal.

"Jesus! I can't waste any more time with this," Jones exploded. "I'm bringing in some muscle to jump-start this operation."

"Navy SEALS?" Fabrice asked, regaining his enthusiasm.

"Seriously?" Jones sneered. "Hell no! Some old friends of mine. Russians."

"The same ones you booted out of Afghanistan?" Fabrice asked, confused.

"That was a long time ago. Professionals don't hold grudges."

"Are these guys, like, mercenaries or something?"

"They don't like it when you use that term. People in the business consider it offensive," Jones admonished.

"So, what are they, then?"

"Technically, they're a biker gang, but they do management consulting on the side. I can have them on the ground in forty-eight hours. All you need to do is make sure your guys are here and ready to go. Can you handle that on your own, or do I need to be out here holding your hand?"

"No problem, boss," Fabrice said. "I promise we'll be ready."

"I hope so," Jones muttered, watching with disgust as the soccer match descended into chaos, one side carrying off the ball to the target range and placing it on a stump in place of a papaya.

CHAPTER NINE

The next day, Jones was back in the office, sitting at his desk after lunch, staring impatiently at his watch. At precisely two o'clock, he closed the door. By the time he was back in his chair, the red light was blinking on his classified telephone.

"Jones here," he said after picking up on the third ring.

"It's Congressman Burke. Is this a good time?"

"I'm always on the clock."

"Were you able to meet with Fabrice?"

"Hmmm, yeah," Jones murmured.

"How'd it go?"

"Not good. All the equipment was there, but not much else was going on. It was just Fabrice and his posse kickin' it by the pool."

"You're kidding me! You're telling me that our entire plan depends on this idiot? I thought coup plotting was one of your subspecialties."

"It's taken care of," Jones shot back. "I'm bringing in a mentoring team to help kick-start the operation."

"A mentoring team? For a coup?"

"Stop calling it a coup. This is a normal dynastic transition. That was the whole point of picking Fabrice in the first place."

"OK. Whatever. Who's this mentoring team?"

"Some old friends I used to work with in Ukraine. Actually, at the time, they were on the other side, but now they're doing freelance work."

"And you think they can get the CAC up and running in time? From the looks of things at Green House, we're already too late. What about finding someone else?"

"Like who?" Jones blurted out. "This isn't a fucking reality TV show. We're picking the next president of the country, for god's sake!"

"What about Mugaba, the defense minister? The guys over at the Pentagon love him," Burke said. "And he's not in bed with the Chinese, right?"

"Not as far as we know. But with Mugaba, it's anyone's bet whose side he's on," Jones said. "Besides, if we went with him, then it actually would be a military coup. We can't afford the bad press. Anyway, it's too late for that now. We're stuck with Fabrice and need to make the best of it."

"Even if you can get the CAC up to speed, what the hell are we going to do with it? Charity is already running the show over there," Burke insisted.

"Don't worry about that part. I can take care of Charity. I just found out some new information about her little project with the Chinese."

"Was she in on the drone attack?" Burke asked giddily.

"Not exactly, but it's still something we can use to our advantage. My surveillance team got some pictures of Charity meeting with her Chinese contacts."

"Was it about the secret prototype project they were discussing before the attack?" Burke asked.

"Yeah. But the prototype was a purse, not a bomb."

"A purse? You mean, like, a handbag?"

"Yeah. That's her game, high-end leather goods," Jones revealed. "Apparently, she's building a factory outside of town with some Chinese investors. She was carrying a sample from the new product line during the presidential address. I guess she was hoping for a little free publicity. Unfortunately for her, the paparazzi didn't get a chance to see the goods before the drone strike took out her husband."

"But if she didn't have anything to do with the attack, how is that going to help us?"

"On the contrary, she's the perfect foil for the Citizens Action Committee. Charity is pretty much the only person in the country who can make Fabrice seem reasonable by comparison. Don't worry. Just leave it to me," Jones reassured him.

"If you say so. What can I do on this end?"

"For now, just the same as before: Keep your mouth shut. You can crow all you want once we get Fabrice into Green House, but not until then. You got it?"

"Yeah, sure, I got it. But keep me in the loop. I want to know what's going on."

"No problem."

+++

Two days later, Claire and her staff huddled in the conference room with copies of all the local newspapers spread across the table—each with an identical set of headline photos. The first image was of Charity Namono standing between two Chinese men outside an industrial warehouse. One of them was handing her an envelope. A second picture showed Charity flipping through a thick stack of euro notes followed by a final image of her stuffing the wad of cash into an agate-blue ostrich leather clutch with an elegant hand-brushed silver clasp.

"What do we make of this?" Claire asked, holding up one of the tabloid-style broadsheets.

"That Charity thinks ATM stands for Asian Teller Machine," Jones said, chuckling.

Claire ignored the comment. "What do we know about the two men standing with her in the picture?" she asked Jake Baxter. "Do we have any idea who they are?"

"I called one of my contacts over at police intelligence, but they aren't saying much," Jake answered. "Same with the Chinese embassy. They're denying any involvement with Charity and trying to downplay the entire story."

"What's been the reaction on the street?" Claire asked.

"It was slow to pick up at first, probably due to the government's crackdown on social media. But now that the newspapers are circulating around town, it's starting to gather steam. We're expecting major protests later today once people start getting off work. Something about Charity seems to push people's buttons."

Claire turned to the political officer. "Stephen, what's the story coming out of Green House? How is the regime reacting to the news?"

"Somewhat as expected. President Namono invoked an old defamation statute and promptly suspended operations at all the offending papers. Beyond that, they're downplaying the pictures. The official line is that Charity has been involved in a private investment deal with some international businessmen. They insist that everything is above board and adamantly deny any connection between her business activities and the new base-leasing agreement with China."

"Until this morning, I would have said that the regime still had the upper hand," Claire said. "But I'm not so sure anymore. They're becoming reactive, and that's not a good sign. If Namono feels threatened, it's going to increase the chance of miscalculation."

"It certainly seems that Green House is raising the stakes," Stephen said. "Yesterday, the government made good on its promise to deploy the army into the streets. We've seen the military out conducting mounted patrols all around the city. So far, it's mostly been a show of force. We haven't heard of any confrontations with protesters. Nevertheless, deploying the army represents a major escalation."

"Thanks, Stephen," Claire said. "Jeff, what do you hear from your contacts over at the ministry of defense? I thought we were operating under the assumption that Mugaba wasn't going to send the army into the streets."

"Yes, ma'am. At least, that was the case as of a few days ago, when I last spoke with the minister. Either he was lying to me, or Green House overruled him."

"Which do you think it was?"

"I'm not sure," Sawyer said. "But there's one thing I know about Mugaba. The guy is always thinking three steps ahead of everyone else in the room. If he did agree to send the army into the streets, he didn't do it without having an endgame in mind. It's not his style to act on a whim."

"Given our history with the minister, I don't find that particularly reassuring," Claire said before turning to the station chief. "OK, Mike, your turn. All the papers report that these photos of Charity came from a group calling itself the Citizens Action Committee. I've been in DRoG for almost five years, and I've never heard of this group. What do we know about them and their agenda?"

For the first time during the meeting, Jones looked up from his notepad. "As much as I hate to admit this, we've been caught flatfooted on this one," he said with a shrug. "I went back through all our files. We don't have anything on this group. It's as if they just appeared out of the blue."

"You're telling me that the CIA doesn't have the slightest idea who these guys are or where they came from? How is that even possible?"

"DRoG is not a high-priority collection target for the agency. There are dozens of low-level activist groups operating below our radar. We don't have the resources to be tracking every single rinky-dink bunch of disgruntled revolutionaries."

"But this one seems to have a specific agenda. They released these pictures with the express intent of embarrassing Charity Namono and the regime, yet, as far as we know, they don't have any other grievances or political demands. Don't you think that's an odd basis for a revolution?"

"Not really. Plenty of people don't like Charity," Jones said. "Hating her is the one thing that almost everybody in the country agrees on."

"That's a surprisingly reasonable point," Claire conceded. "Nevertheless, I'm going to need more than that. By the end of the day, I want to know everything you can find out about this Citizens Action Committee: their history, their membership and agenda; anything that could be relevant."

Jones nodded, pretending to scratch a few lines in his notebook. "Is that it?"

"Well, since we're on the subject…based on everything we've seen over the few days, are we nearing the point of no return for the regime? It seems as if we might be entering a prerevolutionary moment."

"Hmmm, that's a tough call," Jones said, sucking his teeth.

"Is it really?" She cocked her head in mock disbelief. "We have a delegitimized regime ordering the army into the streets. An ailing president in the hospital recovering from an assassination attempt. Hyperinflation. Investors fleeing the country. A foreign power landing combat troops unannounced at the airport. Social media and newspapers shut down. Several hundred students leading a sit-in at the university. And now, a mysterious group trying to humiliate the first lady. I'm surprised to hear that the agency considers this a stable political environment."

"You know as well as I do that predicting regime collapse is a fool's game. If you want a definitive answer, let me get my dart-throwing chimp out of the closet. He'll be happy to tell you what's going to happen tomorrow."

"Do you have anything slightly better than that?" Claire asked, ignoring the display of gross insubordination.

"We've been beta testing an interesting new program called PUNTER."

"PUNTER? Dare I even ask?"

"Predictive Unstructured Networks for Trend Extraction and Reflection."

"That sounds perfectly obscure. What does it do?"

"Exploitation of low-level betting markets. It's the hottest thing going," Jones said. "We've been bankrolling bookies in the local markets, asking average citizens to wager on the prospects of their country's political future. It's still in the experimental phase, but we're getting some fascinating feedback across a wide range of social stability indicators."

"What are these indicators telling you?

"That President Namono should be warming up the hot tub at his villa in the south of France."

"And Charity?"

"As of this morning, she's a sixteen-to-one long shot."

"To occupy Green House?" Claire said with surprise.

"No, to still be alive by the end of the week."

"Thanks, Mike. Very helpful. Who's next?" the ambassador asked, looking around the room.

At the far end of the table, Emily Gates, the embassy's press officer, raised her hand. "Madam Ambassador, we just received a cable from Washington with some talking points and a draft press release. It was sent directly from Reid McCoy's office at the White House."

"Since when does the White House dictate the text for a local press release? Isn't that our job?" she asked rhetorically.

"Yes, ma'am. However, they're concerned that things are getting out of control."

Claire sighed and shook her head. "What does it say?"

The press officer cleared her throat and began reading from the prepared statement.

"The United States is deeply concerned about the rising level of violence in the Democratic Republic of Gisawi and strongly urges all sides to exercise restraint. We call on demonstrators to refrain from acts of instigation and for government security forces to avoid the excessive use of force. We encourage all parties to engage constructively in good-faith dialogue toward a peaceful resolution of the present unrest. Any such effort must include full transparency concerning the activities and intent of all foreign powers operating inside the country. The United States remains fully committed to supporting an open and constructive engagement whereby all sides may reach a mutually agreeable vision for the country's future."

Ambassador Roberts closed her eyes and took a deep breath. "You realize that statement is meaningless nonsense."

"Yes, ma'am. However, it's already been approved for release by the White House."

"Reid McCoy expects me to say those words with a straight face?"

"The mode of delivery was not specified," Emily said.

"Good. In that case, just fax a copy to the local papers."

"They've all been shut down."

"Right, I almost forgot."

"And social media too," Emily added.

"Of course. So why don't you nail a copy of the statement to the embassy's front door and we'll leave it at that. Anything else before we move on?"

"There's another issue," Emily said. "We just received an update on the student sit-in at the university. They're refusing to obey the government's order to end the protest and vacate the campus."

"Good for them," Claire said. "They must have gotten someone's attention over at Green House."

"Not only the government's attention. For the last several days, they've been getting significant coverage from the international media. The student leaders are doing interviews by phone from inside the campus. About an hour ago, they issued a new list of demands."

"What are they?"

"They've called on President Namono to step down. It's the first time they've come out directly against the regime."

"While I admire their courage, I'm afraid they may have pushed this to the point where the government won't be able to back down without losing face," Claire speculated. "They may end up getting more than they bargained for. Anything else?"

"One last thing," Emily said. "The students also demanded that we close our counter-terrorism operating base and end all US support for the Gisawian military. They're claiming that it represents tacit American endorsement of an illegitimate regime. Everyone is just waking up back in Washington, so I doubt they've seen the news yet. Should we give them a chance to digest the statement before responding?"

"You mean with some banal nonsense like what they just sent us?" Claire asked rhetorically. "No. I think the students deserve better than some patronizing diplomatic doublespeak."

"Should we ignore them?"

Claire thought about the options. "I think I'll pay a visit to the university and meet with them in person. There's an American woman on the faculty. I believe her name is DeVore. She knows the students who are leading the sit-in. Call her and see if they would be willing to meet with me."

"Madam Ambassador," Jake Baxter interjected, "I strongly advise against that course of action. The situation is too unstable right now. We can't guarantee your safety once you step foot on that campus."

"What on earth do you mean?" Claire said. "The university is surrounded by Gisawian police. There hasn't been a single incident of violence instigated by the students. The campus is probably the safest place in the country right now. Trust me, I'll be fine."

"I second the recommendation that you do not go anywhere near that campus," Mike Jones interrupted.

"Why? Does the CIA consider it a high-threat environment?" Claire shot back.

"No, I'm sure it's fine," he said, dismissing Jake's concerns for the ambassador's safety. "The real problem is the optics of your meeting with the students. It risks sending the wrong message."

"You mean the message that America supports the Gisawian people's aspirations to live in a free and democratic society that respects universal human rights?"

"Exactly!" Jones said. "This may not be the best time to be pushing those buttons. If you show up on that campus, it will be viewed as an affront to the regime. Green House can afford to dismiss a bunch of spoiled students, but they can't ignore an American ambassador joining their pajama party. With all due respect, it would be an utterly reckless move for you to go anywhere near that sit-in."

Claire took a deep, calming breath, somehow resisting the urge to throw her station chief out of the meeting. Instead, she calmly turned back to the press officer.

"Please call over to the university. Find a good time for me to meet with the students. That's all for now," she instructed, before getting up and leaving the room.

+++

Five minutes later, Jones was back in his office, slamming the door behind him. He punched an unmarked speed-dial button on his desk phone, snapping his fingers impatiently as he waited for someone to answer.

"This is Mike Jones calling from DRoG. Get me Congressman Burke right now!" he barked into the phone when a hapless staffer picked up.

"Sir, the congressman is out of the office," said the staffer. "He's in a breakfast meeting, and then he goes directly to the floor for a vote. I don't expect him back until after lunch."

"Send him a text. Tell him it's urgent. I'm staying on the damn line until he gets his ass to a phone."

There was silence on the line as the staffer weighed the options. "Sir, I'm going to put you on hold for a moment while I try to reach out to the congressman."

Jones switched the phone over to speaker and started working on his computer. Twenty-five minutes later, the staffer came back on the line. "Sir, I'm connecting you to Congressman Burke now. Thank you for waiting."

There was a click as the call was transferred, followed by the sound of the congressman's voice. "Burke here."

"It's Jones. We've got a problem."

"Fabrice?"

"No. Claire Roberts. She's gone rogue. It's time to take action."

"What the hell is she doing?" Burke asked.

"Trying to start a damn revolution. She's going over to the university to meet with the students."

"You mean the ones doing that sit-in thing?"

"Yeah."

"They're all over the news. The media is eating that shit up. Why the hell is she going over there?"

"Presumably to coddle their infantile sense of self-importance while at the same time selling out her country. Those little punks just released a new list of demands. They're calling for us to end our support for the regime and close down the counter-terrorism operating base."

"Who cares?" Burke said. "The last time I checked, the students weren't in charge of anything. As long as they're stuck there on campus, why the hell does it matter?"

"Because if the ambassador shows up there, it's going to keep them in the spotlight. That's the last thing we need right now. Trust me, these things work better when nobody's paying attention."

"OK, you're the expert on this," Burke said. "By the way, nice move on Charity. I saw the pictures in yesterday's paper. The one of her stuffing the euros into her purse was classic!"

"That was the easy part," Jones said. "The challenge now is making sure that Fabrice is ready to go when the time comes."

"Is he up to it?" Burke asked.

"I don't know. The mentoring team arrives tomorrow. Hopefully, that will kick-start the operation. They can get Fabrice to the steps of Green House, but once he's inside, there's not much more we can do. He'll need to man up and get things back in order," Jones said.

"What's the next move for the Citizens Action Committee?"

"For the time being, they need to lay low. The pictures of Charity got their name out on the street. That's enough for now, but we need to maintain the mystique. More importantly, we don't want to link Fabrice to the CAC until the last possible moment. We can't give the opposition time to react."

"Understood. Then you want me to go forward with the rest of the plan as discussed?" Burke asked.

"At this point, we don't have any choice. The ambassador is too much of a wild card. We can't take any chances. Do you know what to do?" Jones asked.

"Yeah, I can handle it. The paperwork is ready. I'll put the wheels in motion today. While I'm doing that, what happens on your end?"

"I'm still trying to figure that out," Jones said. "But you don't need to worry about it. The important thing is that when the time comes, she's neutralized."

"Wait. Who are we talking about again? Charity or the ambassador?"

Jones fell silent for a moment, then gave a deep sigh of exasperation before screaming, "Both of them!"

"Right. I knew that!" Burke blurted out. "I just wanted to be sure."

"Anything else?" Jones asked.

"Nope. I'm moving forward with the plan. I'll be in touch," Burke said.

"OK. And remember, no mistakes," Jones warned.

CHAPTER TEN

———

Two days later, Claire called Mike Jones to her office for an unscheduled meeting. When he walked through the door, she waved him over to her desk.

"Grab a seat," she instructed. "Reid McCoy wants to talk. He should be dialing in from the White House any minute."

"Anything I should be worried about?" Jones asked.

"I have no idea. His assistant didn't elaborate."

Jones shrugged and sat down. "I'm sure POTUS just wants somebody to wave a magic wand and make this all go away."

"No doubt," Claire agreed. "So, have you found out anything more on this Citizens Action Committee?"

"Nope. Whoever they are, they're keeping a low profile. I reached out to all my contacts around town. Nobody knows anything about them. No names. No history. Nothing."

"And we haven't heard anything from them since they released those pictures of Charity?" Claire asked.

"Nope. Not a word," Jones said, straight-faced.

"It's all very odd," Claire murmured, lost in thought, staring off into space.

"What is?"

"That this group doesn't seem to have any obvious political agenda beyond this vendetta against Charity. It doesn't make sense that they would go to all that trouble without some kind of follow-up. What exactly are they trying to achieve?"

"Maybe they're biding their time, waiting for the right moment to spring the next thing," Jones suggested.

"I suppose so," Clare said, sounding unconvinced. "Have you been able to get any more information about what was going on in those pictures of Charity?"

"Not much more than we already knew. However, we were able to identify the two Chinese guys who were with her."

"Anything interesting on them?"

"Not really. The official story we got from Green House checks out. They seem to be legitimate private businessmen with no official connections to the government back in Beijing. According to the Chinese embassy, they loaned Charity the money to open a purse factory outside of town, and they remain involved as silent partners. That's it."

"And the cash being exchanged in the photos?"

"Who the hell knows? Probably just a little something to grease the skids with the local permit office. That's business as usual down here."

Claire nodded but didn't press. "Let me know if you find out anything else."

As Claire finished speaking, the red light on the secure telephone began blinking. She put the call on speakerphone. "Hello, Reid. It's Claire. I've got Mike here with me in the office. What can we help you with?"

"Hey, Claire. I just wanted to give you advance warning on a story about to break here in the Beltway."

"Something involving DRoG?" she asked, surprised.

"Actually, it's about you. Congressman Burke is about to issue a press release calling for you to testify before his committee regarding the president's policy on DRoG."

"In person? Can he do that?"

"Maybe, if he can manage to get his committee chair to sign off on it. But that's not our biggest worry right now. He's also calling on the president to remove you from your post."

"That's ridiculous. On what grounds?" Claire said.

"Same crap as before, accusing the administration of giving DRoG over to the Chinese."

"Reid, everybody knows that's a load of shit. Even Burke."

"Well, Claire, you can say that all you want, but it didn't help our case when that fucking PLA plane landed at the airport last week, not to mention those pictures of Charity in the papers with her new Chinese buddies. Maybe you can tell POTUS how he's supposed to explain all that out on the campaign trail. Right now, Burke's got the upper hand, and he's playing it for all its worth."

Claire sighed. "Fine. So what am I supposed to do about it? Do you want me to get on a plane and rush back to Washington to testify?"

"No, we're not there yet. For now, the best thing we can do is nothing at all. You serve at the president's pleasure. Burke can't do much about that except make a lot of noise. But we've still got to tamp this thing down. As long as that ethics investigation is hanging over his head, Burke will do whatever he can to keep DRoG in the spotlight. He's already booked himself on all the Sunday talk shows. We can't afford to give him any more ammunition."

"Reid, in case you forgot, this isn't only about the midterms. We're in the middle of a crisis over here. I'm the senior US representative in this country. I can't just sit here in my office, twiddling my thumbs, while riots are happening in the streets. This is exactly when I need to be out there engaging with our partners. We can't let Burke dictate our diplomatic response for the sake of his re-election campaign."

"Nope, sorry, Claire. POTUS was absolutely clear on the plan," Reid insisted. "He doesn't want to hear the word 'DRoG' again until after midterms. As long as we don't hand Burke any more leverage, people will eventually get tired of hearing him shoot his mouth off."

"You want me to just go mute?"

"Do whatever is necessary to keep yourself and DRoG out of the news back here at home. I don't think that's asking too much," Reid instructed.

"You think I have control over that?" Claire asked.

"I'm only asking you to do your best. By the way, what's the latest on the drone attack investigation? Have the Gisawians stumbled over any leads?"

"I'll let Mike give you an update," Claire said with a nod to Jones.

"Hey, Reid. Mike here," he said, taking the cue. "We don't have anything more on the attack. Police intelligence is keeping this thing very close-hold. I can't get anything out of them."

"Nothing? Really? Not even a good rumor?"

"As far as we can tell, they're still treating it as an inside job. We know for sure that the drone came out of the army's inventory, most likely from a warehouse belonging to the Gisawian counter-terrorism force. We've heard through the grapevine that the entire unit has been confined to barracks since the attack. We're assuming that they must still be looking at suspects inside the camp."

"How about the Chinese troops? What they've been up to?"

"Mostly housekeeping and getting settled into their new home. They haven't been off the base since they landed at the airport. It seems like they're trying to keep a low profile after all the publicity over their arrival."

"Interesting. Have you been able to keep an eye on them?" Reid asked.

"Well, it's not too hard, since the Chinese base is right across the runway from our camp. The fucking Gisawians have basically turned the duty-free shop into a new Checkpoint Charlie."

"But what's their end game? Are we expecting to see them expand their military presence to other parts of the country? I'm guessing they didn't come all that way just to sit inside a walled compound out at the airport. Beijing must have something planned for those troops," Reid speculated.

"We still don't have a good read on that, but I've reprioritized our entire collection effort against the target. My top asset here in DRoG has already penetrated the Chinese camp. He's got people with good access working on the inside. I expect we'll have some reporting flowing from his network pretty soon."

"Excellent. Keep up the good work," Reid said. "Claire, you got anything else for me?"

"No. I think I understand your intent."

"Good. And just to reiterate, you have the president's full trust and confidence. Don't worry about the stuff in the papers. We'll take care of Burke on our end. You just focus on keeping things under control over there."

"Will do, Reid. And please give my regards to POTUS next time you see him."

"Right. Talk soon."

After Reid dropped off the line, Claire turned to Jones. "So, what do you think?"

"About what?"

"About everything. It seems obvious that the White House wants to wash their hands of this. Clearly, they'd prefer not to think about it between now and the midterms."

"In my experience, that's the best possible news you can get out of Washington."

"How's that?"

"The words 'Figure it out on your own' are music to my ears. It's more like the good old days," Jones said with a chuckle.

"You mean the days when you could casually overthrow the government of a small developing nation without even checking in with your boss?"

"It was a different time," Jones said, becoming misty-eyed with nostalgia.

"Was it? Because sometimes it doesn't feel like that much has changed."

Jones shrugged.

"All right, I think we're done here," Claire said. "I'll be out of the office tomorrow morning on personal business. My assistant can get ahold of me if anything comes up."

"Got it," Jones said, getting up from his chair. "We'll hold down the fort here while you're gone."

+++

Early the next morning, an embassy driver dropped Claire off at the front gate of National University. The campus was eerily quiet as she made her way to Anna's office. It had only been a few weeks since the shutdown, but the school grounds were already revealing hints of neglect, with dry palm fronds littering the sidewalk, weeds pushing up through the rock gardens, windblown piles of trash collecting along the edges of the buildings, and forgotten leaflets flapping on empty bulletin boards.

When Claire arrived at the building, she double-checked the number. The structure looked more like an underfunded rural health clinic than an ivy-covered institution of higher education. After confirming that the directions were correct, Claire went inside and began hunting for Anna's office. It didn't take long to find the only open office in the entire building. Claire knocked on the door and stuck her head inside.

"Madam Ambassador!" Anna said, rising from behind her desk. "Please come in."

Anna offered her a rickety wooden chair that appeared as if it predated the founding of the university.

"I'm sorry I don't have a better option," Anna said, glancing at the chair with an embarrassed shrug. "Unfortunately, the faculty lounge has been locked up for the last few weeks, along with everything else on campus."

"Don't worry. It's still better than spending the day feeling like a prisoner inside the embassy."

Anna smiled, already enjoying the company. "So, you've been in DRoG for quite a while now, haven't you?" she asked.

"Over four years, but sometimes it feels much longer," Claire sighed. "I think they're having trouble finding someone else willing to take the job."

Anna nodded, unsure if the ambassador was joking or being serious. "Well, I'm sure your experience is appreciated," Anna offered.

Claire laughed at the suggestion. "Unlikely. In fact, I suspect that I've long overstayed my welcome."

"How so?"

"I'll put it this way: No one in Green House will shed any tears when I leave. And I'm guessing the same is true back in Washington."

"Why is that?" Anna asked, curious about the inner workings of bureaucratic politics.

"It's complicated," Claire said, hesitating. "Let's just say that the White House prefers to keep our relations with DRoG out of the headlines. However, since I've been here, it's just been one thing after another: first the Operation Brushfire fiasco, now all this excitement with the protests. Generally, these are considered unwelcome distractions inside the Beltway. They would rather not spend too much time thinking about it."

"Unsurprising, I suppose," Anna remarked.

"You've been here in DRoG for a while as well," Claire said.

"Not as long as you, but a few years. I arrived just before the start of Operation Brushfire."

"I think we discussed that when we met a few weeks ago. That's why you came here, wasn't it? As an advisor for the operation?"

"It was meant to be a temporary gig," Anna said, laughing. "But then it turned into something else entirely."

"Life works that way sometimes," Claire said. Then she paused, considering her words before continuing. "If you don't mind me asking, how much do you know about what really happened during Operation Brushfire?"

Anna hesitated, unsure of how to answer. "Probably a lot more than I should," she finally said.

"I suspected as much. Then again, you weren't a casual observer. I mean, given your relationship with Lieutenant Colonel Bigombe," Claire prompted.

Anna nodded but didn't take the bait.

"Unfortunately, I'm not at liberty to discuss the version of the story that eventually made it into our classified reports," Claire continued. "However, I can tell you that it doesn't paint a pretty picture of what went down. On either side."

"Does it even matter at this point?" Anna asked. "You know, there's an old saying here in DRoG that my fiancé once told me."

"Louie?"

Anna nodded. "He said that a lie has many variations, but the truth none. That's the thing about Operation Brushfire. Everybody has their own version of what they think happened. It's like that old adage about the blind men and the elephant. The truth depends on what part of it you grab."

"I see your point. But there's one thing that shouldn't be in doubt."

"What's that?"

"That your fiancé shouldn't underestimate his uncle."

Anna was taken aback by the ambassador's bluntness. "I don't believe he does," she said.

"Yet after everything that happened, the two of you still decided to stay. Why?"

"Louie's an idealist," Anna said with a shrug. "Or at least he used to be. His brothers and sister all moved away years ago. They left at the first opportunity. Now they have their careers and families overseas. Louie was the only one who came back."

"To fix things?"

"Maybe that's part of it. I think he's trying to live up to some imaginary expectation."

"You mean because of his father?"

Anna nodded. "Did you know him?"

"Not personally. That was back before I joined the State Department. But I spent several years working as a journalist in Africa and remember hearing his name. From what I've heard, everyone always assumed that one day, he would be president. A heroic death on the battlefield only added to his mystique. That's quite a legacy for a son to live up to."

"In a way, I think it's even worse because Louie didn't know him very well. The army was his father's life, and he wasn't around much when the kids were young. Most of Louie's memories of him are based on this idealized legend. In fact, Louie was in the UK at boarding school when he heard the news about his father's death. Ever since then, his uncle has acted as a de facto father figure. Maybe that's why it's hard for Louie to be objective about Mugaba."

"Can I ask you a personal question about Louie?" Claire asked.

Anna nodded.

"Do you think that Mugaba may be scared of him?"

"Scared? Of Louie?" Anna asked skeptically.

"Maybe 'intimidated' is a better word."

"I don't understand what you mean. Mugaba is one of the most powerful men in the country—a lot of people think that he's the one running it. Why would he be intimidated by Louie?"

"Just a gut feeling. I always found it interesting that Mugaba decided to put his nephew at the center of the action during Operation Brushfire. Anyone could have pulled the trigger on the drone strike that supposedly killed Odoki. But Mugaba made sure that it was Louie at the controls. It kind of makes you wonder. If things had gone wrong, who would have taken the fall?"

Anna took a deep breath before venturing to answer. "Mugaba has always protected Louie. But of course, that protection comes at a price. For his uncle, loyalty is everything."

"But does that loyalty run both ways?" Claire asked. "I hope I'm not overstepping my bounds, but do you know why your fiancé hasn't left his camp in almost two weeks?"

"I won't ask how you know that," Anna said. "But since you do, you must also know that since the attack on the president, his unit has been on alert, awaiting orders."

"Are you sure that's the only reason?" Claire pressed.

Anna looked down at her desk and didn't answer.

"Louie isn't going to change anything by becoming a martyr for his uncle," Claire continued. "I'm sure it's not what his father would have wanted."

"I know that," Anna whispered.

"But does he know that?"

Anna shook her head, not sure if she knew the answer. The two sat in silence until a buzzing sound came from the ambassador's handbag. Claire glanced at the screen. It was a one-line text message from Mike Jones: "CALL ME ASAP!"

"Something you need to take?" Anna asked.

Claire shook her head. "No. Nothing that can't wait. Why don't we go over and meet with the students?" she suggested, looking to change the subject.

"I can't promise you a cheery reception," Anna warned.

"I didn't expect one. But that isn't a good reason not to show up. The students deserve better than some ridiculous statement like the one we put out yesterday. None of their demands are unreasonable. They might be the only ones in the county who are making any sense right now."

Anna was getting up from her chair when the office door burst open. Nesi was standing in the doorway, panting as if she had just sprinted across campus. Her eyes widened when she realized that she'd barged in on a meeting between her teacher and the American ambassador.

"I'm sorry!" Nesi blurted out between gasps of air. "Anna, you need to come quickly."

"What is it, Nesi? I was just bringing the ambassador over to meet everyone."

"There are soldiers outside the front gate. It's the regular army, not the police. They're surrounding the university!"

Anna, Claire, and Nesi rushed outside and headed toward the front gate. By the time they arrived, a small crowd of students was already gathered inside the entrance, watching nervously as the soldiers unspooled razor-sharp concertina wire across the street. Several armored personnel carriers were parked nearby. Up in the turrets, the machine gunners watched over their comrades as they constructed a line of makeshift barricades around the campus.

Near the gate, Didier was frantically taking pictures with his cell phone and texting them to his contacts in the local media, aid agencies, and human rights organizations—anyone who might be able to get the word out about what was happening. He was so focused on taking pictures of the soldiers that when Anna and Nesi showed up with the ambassador, he didn't notice.

"Didier, what the hell is going on?" Anna asked.

"What does it look like? We're being surrounded by the army," he answered without slowing the furious pace of his texting.

"I see that, but are they here to keep people out or keep us in?"

"They showed up about an hour ago and started putting up barriers. I went out to ask the officer in charge about what was going on. He told me that his orders were to allow one-way traffic only."

"What does that mean?"

"It means that we're free to leave whenever we want, but once we do, we don't get back in. The government is turning this into a standoff. They're trying to see how long we'll last."

"Has anyone left yet?"

"Just a few random people who happened to be wandering through campus when the soldiers started putting up the wire," Didier said. "No one from the sit-in has walked out. As soon as I send these photos, we're meeting to decide what to do next."

As they watched the soldiers establishing the perimeter, Anna noticed, off in the distance, a man on a motorbike approaching the checkpoint. His scooter was comically overburdened with grocery bags and plastic containers. Anna thought something about him looked vaguely familiar, but he was too far away for her to know for sure.

She saw him chatting with the officer in charge, then inexplicably, being waved through the security cordon. He maneuvered the motorbike through the obstacle course of razor wire and armored vehicles, crossing the no man's land between the soldiers and the students. When the scooter entered the gate, Anna recognized Sammy behind the wheel. He pulled to a stop next to where they were standing.

"Ms. Anna!" he exclaimed, cutting the engine and flipping up his tinted visor.

"Sammy, what on earth are you doing here?" she asked, marveling at the massive load of supplies balanced precariously on his moped.

"Lunch delivery," he said, nodding at the overstuffed bags filled with dozens of insulated food containers.

"SB Café has been catering the sit-in," Nesi explained. "Sammy is supplying the resistance!"

Anna turned back to her old friend. "The officer in charge told Didier that no one could come back on campus after leaving. How did you convince them to let you through?"

Sammy waved dismissively at the soldiers on the other side of the razor wire. "I know them from my café over on the army base. I gave them some gift cards, and they said no problem with me coming back and forth to deliver food."

"What about the rest of us?" Anna asked.

Sammy shook his head, looking sympathetic. "No. I'm sorry, Ms. Anna. The rest of you can only go out, not back in."

"Well, at least they aren't planning on starving us to death," Anna joked grimly. "Sammy, did you keep the café open during the protests?"

"Oh, yes, Ms. Anna!" Sammy exclaimed. "We're busier than ever with catering all the marches. And we just opened a new tea house on the Chinese army base at the airport. The Sujah Leaf Café. It's a new concept store," he said excitedly. "Small-batch, hand-picked premium tea from Sri Lanka."

"Never let a crisis go to waste, I suppose," Anna said in bemused disbelief at Sammy's entrepreneurial spirit.

The barista winked at Anna, flipped down his visor, and gunned the scooter's engine. He sped off in the direction of the building where the student government committee had established the headquarters for the sit-in. After Sammy had disappeared in a cloud of sooty exhaust, Anna turned to Claire.

"I guess you'll need to be getting back to the embassy," she said. "Presumably, the soldiers won't give you a hard time as long as you promise not to cross back through the lines."

"What makes you think I'm leaving?" Claire said.

Anna stared at the ambassador, uncertain whether she was serious. "Didn't you just tell me a few minutes ago that being a martyr wasn't worth it?" she asked.

Claire shrugged. "If I go back to the embassy, I'll be as trapped there as you are here. At least if I stay, I'll feel like I'm accomplishing something useful."

"I'm not so sure about that," Anna cautioned.

"If nothing else, maybe it will force President Namono to think twice before escalating the situation."

"You're volunteering as a human shield?"

"I guess that's one way of looking at it," Claire said, trying to decide if she was comfortable with the designation.

"Well, I'm sure the students will be happy to have you," Anna said, reaching out to shake the ambassador's hand. "Welcome to the sit-in. Give me a minute, and I'll take you over to meet the students. I need to call Louie first. Maybe he knows something about what's going on outside the gate with the soldiers."

"No problem. I should call the office and let them know that I'm going to be later than expected," Claire said, giving Anna a wink.

+++

Anna walked away from the crowd gathered around the gate and dialed Louie's number.

"Where are you?" Anna heard the worry in his voice.

"I'm at the university," she shouted, trying to drown out the background noise. "I was getting stir crazy at home, so I came over this morning to work in my office."

"It's not a good time to be out in the streets," Louie said, unable to hide his frustration.

"You can't expect me to sit alone all day in an empty house. I haven't had classes in weeks, and you've only been home a few nights since the attack. What am I supposed to be doing?"

"Did you know that the president ordered the army to start patrolling the streets?" Louie asked, ignoring her question. "It's not safe for you to be out driving around."

"You don't need to worry about that. I'm perfectly safe right where I am. In fact, I'm being protected by hundreds of your buddies."

"Anna, what on earth are you talking about? Are you feeling OK?"

"Haven't you heard? The army surrounded the university. They're not letting anyone in."

"What? When?" Louie exclaimed, clearly unaware of this turn of events.

"About an hour ago. Soldiers showed up and started putting razor wire across the main gate. They're letting people leave campus, but no one can get back inside once they go out. President Namono is trying to strangle the sit-in. He must be hoping that the students will give up and go home without a fight."

"I swear, Anna, I didn't know anything about it. If I did, I would have called you this morning and told you not to go there."

"Don't worry, I would have come anyway."

"Don't go anywhere!" Louie pleaded. "I'm calling my uncle right now. I'll have the officer in charge come inside and personally escort you off campus."

"Louie, that's not necessary," Anna protested.

"Yes, it is! You're an American citizen. What's going on there has nothing to do with you. You shouldn't be involved in any of this. It's not your place. What if the students try to provoke something, and the army is forced to respond? You could be killed!"

Anna could tell by his voice that Louie was beyond exhaustion; his words sounded almost frantic. She took a deep breath, hoping that if she remained calm, it would help ease his anxiety. "Louie, you don't need to worry about that. I promise you, the students aren't going to provoke anything. It's a peaceful demonstration. It's been that way since the beginning. I can assure you that if anything happens, it's going to start with the other side making the first move."

"You don't know that. There's no telling what could happen. I don't feel comfortable with you being the only American there."

"Is it about me being an American or me being a white woman?" she asked.

"Anna, you know that's not what this is about."

"But you told me once before that it put me in a special category. Isn't that what you're really talking about when you say that it's not safe for me to be here?"

"No, Anna. I'm saying that this is not your fight. It's not your country. You may think that you're helping to protect the students by being there, but it won't make any difference if the army comes through that gate. You're getting yourself involved in something that's not your business and could get you killed."

"Well, I happen to disagree. And I'm not walking away. The students asked me to stay. Besides, if it makes you feel any better, I'm not the only American here. Or even the only white woman."

"Who else is there?" Louie asked, having no idea what she was talking about.

"Ambassador Roberts is here with me. She came over this morning to speak with the students and got caught on campus when the army showed up."

"Anna, please tell me you're kidding," Louie said in exasperation. "Is the American ambassador trapped in there with you? Does anyone else know?"

"The students know, but I'm not sure who else."

"Wait a second." In the background, she could hear Louie fumbling around his office, followed by the sound of a television newscaster speaking in the background. "Well, everybody knows now," he continued. "One of the students must have texted a picture of her to the media. It's the breaking news story on every news channel. They're showing a picture of you and the ambassador standing together inside the wire, along with the students."

"Fuck," Louie muttered to himself, then said, "I'm calling my uncle. Both of you need to get out of there right now."

"I told you that it's not necessary. We can walk right out the front gate anytime we want. No one's keeping us here against our will."

"Good. Then let me send over one of my drivers in an armored vehicle to get you. I'll have them escort you home. They won't have any problems getting through the roadblocks."

"Louie, you're not listening to me. I told you that it's not necessary. We're both staying until this is over. Do you understand what I'm saying?"

There was silence on the line. In the background, Anna could hear the newscaster's voice describing what was unfolding right before her eyes.

Possible hostage situation in the Democratic Republic of Gisawi...unconfirmed reports of a senior American diplomat being held inside National University...army forces surrounding the campus...no statement yet from Green House... Chinese officials are urging a peaceful resolution to the crisis...

"Anna, please, don't fight me on this," Louie pleaded. "There is no guarantee this will turn out OK. I need to know that you're safe. Please, come outside the gate. I'll make sure that someone is there to take you home."

"I should be telling you the same thing. Except that there's one difference between our situations. I can walk out of here anytime I want. But that's not true for you, is it?"

Louie was quiet for a while, trying to decide how to answer. "It's a completely different situation," he finally said.

"Is it? You haven't left that camp in almost two weeks. You're a prisoner inside your own office. Do you even know why they're keeping you there? Has anyone told you anything about what's really going on?" Her voice quivering with emotion.

"Anna, you know why. They're still doing the investigation. We'll know something soon."

"Investigation? Are you serious? Louie, it's nothing but a farce! Do you honestly think that it matters what they find?

Someone is setting you up! You're nothing more than an insurance policy. And we both know who will be protected if it comes down to that."

This time, Louie was silent for so long that Anna wasn't even sure whether he was still on the line. "You were right," he finally said. "We should have left here a long time ago. I'm sorry that I've put you in this situation. It's my fault. I don't know why I thought I could fix things. It was a childish fantasy. I know that now."

"No, Louie, it wasn't. That's part of the reason I fell in love with you. Because you actually believe in something."

"Well, now we can see where that's gotten us," he said, sounding resigned to his fate. "So, how long do you plan on staying there at the sit-in?"

"I guess until it's over," she said.

"And how will you know when that is?"

"I suppose when I see you again."

Louie sighed, realizing that there was nothing he could say to change her mind. "Please be careful."

"You too. I love you."

"I love you too," Louie said.

+++

When Anna hung up the phone, Claire was still on hold with the embassy switchboard, waiting to be connected to Mike Jones. She had a finger to her ear, trying to block out the noise from the street.

"Jones here," he answered after a time.

"Mike. It's Ambassador Roberts. Can you hear me?"

"Not really. What the hell is that noise in the background?"

"Armored personnel carriers!" she yelled as one of the vehicles rumbled past.

"Ah, that makes sense," Jones said casually. "The BBC is reporting that you're a hostage. You know, I don't think this is what Reid had in mind when he asked you to keep a low profile. For your information, you're on the breaking news ticker of every network in the world."

"I'm not a hostage," Claire insisted.

"Sure. Whatever. Call it what you want, but the White House is fucking furious. I just got off the phone with Reid. He said POTUS is going through the roof. Congressmen Burke is in the middle of a live press conference, denouncing the administration's failed policy on DRoG. He's accusing you of coddling antigovernment radicals trying to overthrow the government."

"Jesus, Mike, that's completely ridiculous. Burke doesn't have the slightest clue what's going on here. I came over here to meet with some students. I had no idea that the army was planning on barricading the campus. Is that why you texted me earlier?"

"No. I didn't even know where you were until I turned on the TV a few minutes ago and saw the news. I was texting you about something else that came in overnight," Jones explained.

"Something more on the Citizens Action Committee?"

"No, some unrelated chatter that we picked up through intercepts," Jones explained. "It wasn't specific, but we have reason to believe that you may be under threat."

"What do you mean? What kind of threat?" she asked.

"That's not entirely clear. Possibly kidnapping. Maybe assassination. A network that we've been monitoring mentioned your name. It was similar to what we picked up right before the strike against Namono. We've had some nodes under surveillance since the attack. They've been quiet for the last few weeks, but recently one of the cells became active again and specifically mentioned your name. I can't go into the details over an open line, but we're taking this threat seriously."

"That makes absolutely no sense," she said flatly. "Why would the people who attacked President Namono want to kill me too? The logic is so convoluted that I don't even know where to begin."

"Listen, I'm not here to debate the rationality of their hit list. It doesn't make sense to me either. I'm just telling you the facts. And I'm sure you're aware that we can't disregard any substantiated threat against a senior American diplomat. POTUS has already been briefed on the situation."

"Actually, Mike, I'm feeling quite safe right now. I'm standing in an empty university campus, surrounded by the DRoG army. I don't think anyone is going to try to kill me here," she insisted.

"That's not the point. I've already spoken to Reid about this. POTUS has approved your immediate evacuation as a precautionary measure. The last thing we need right now is for you to get popped in addition to everything else going on."

"I can sense the concern in your voice," she said dryly. "Why are you the one calling me? Who's in charge there?"

"Don't worry about that, Claire," Jones said, pointedly using her first name. "The important thing is your safety. I have a direct line to the White House. I'll be running crisis management here until they find your replacement. What you need to do right now is walk out that front gate and go to the military checkpoint. I've already spoken with Minister Odongo. There's a DRoG army vehicle outside. They will escort you directly to the airport. We have a plane there waiting for you. We'll have you back home in time for dinner reservations in Georgetown. Don't worry, I've got everything under control here."

The conversation was interrupted by another convoy of military vehicles. "Are you still there?" Jones blurted out over the sound of revving engines. "We're running out of time. You need to walk out that gate and get onto that plane right now!"

"You can tell Reid that I'm staying," Claire shouted over the roar of the engines.

"I guess I should have been more specific," Jones replied. "I wasn't presenting this as an option. POTUS wants you out of the country immediately. Given everything that's going on, he's not going to take the risk of something happening to you."

"I think what you mean is that he's caving in to Burke, hoping to shut down the bad press. Well, forget it, Mike. I'm not leaving," Claire countered.

"Don't be unreasonable. We're already in hot water here. The entire world is watching this thing unfold on TV. Meanwhile, Burke is making hay back in DC. I don't think this is how you want to end your career."

"Maybe it is. What's the alternative? Giving in to the bluff and getting on the plane? Then going back to Washington to be shoved aside into a glorified desk job until I retire?"

"There are worse things than that," Jones offered.

"I'm not so sure. In any case, you can tell Reid that I'm not being held as a hostage, if he even cares. But I'm also not leaving. I'm going to see this thing through to the end."

"It should go without saying that if you stay at the university, we can't guarantee your protection. You're putting yourself in a dangerous situation, not to mention willfully undermining American policy toward a close regional ally. That's called insubordination. You'll have to answer for this back in Washington."

"Thanks, Mike, I'm aware of that."

Jones weighed his options. "You know, Claire, I have the authority to forcibly remove you from that campus and send you back to the States in handcuffs, if necessary," he bluffed.

"Go right ahead. As you said, the world is watching."

"Damnit!" he yelled into the phone. "You're making a big fucking mistake!"

Claire hung up on him without responding and calmly put away her phone. Then she walked over to where Anna was waiting. The two of them stood there for a moment watching as the soldiers continued unspooling strands of barbed wire across the road.

"Any change of plans?" Anna asked.

"Nope. I was just tying up a few loose ends back at the office," Claire said nonchalantly. "They won't miss me a bit."

"Great. Then shall we see what Sammy brought for lunch?"

Claire smiled and nodded, then followed Anna to the building where the students were staging the sit-in.

+++

An hour later, Louie was sitting in the reception area outside his uncle's office at the ministry of defense. He had arrived unannounced, and the secretary had informed him that Mugaba was unavailable. She relented only after Louie insisted that he was not leaving until he saw his uncle. After he'd been waiting for forty-five minutes, a blinking light on the secretary's phone signaled that Mugaba was ready for his next appointment. She nodded at Louie, letting him know that he was permitted to enter the office. He found his uncle hunched over his desk, working through a thick stack of papers overflowing from his inbox.

"Lutalo," he said, glancing up from his work. "I wasn't expecting to see you today, but my secretary said it was urgent. Couldn't you have called from the base?"

"I'm sorry, Uncle, but it wasn't something I felt comfortable discussing over the phone."

"Really!" Mugaba said, taking off his reading glasses and leaning back in his chair. "Our nation is in the midst of a crisis, and you demand a personal audience with the minister. In that case, it must be something important indeed."

"Uncle, why didn't you tell me that President Namono ordered the army to the university? I only found out when Anna texted me and said that soldiers were surrounding the campus. How could you have not told me about this?"

"Don't forget your place, Lutalo!" Mugaba snapped. "You are a lieutenant colonel in charge of one small unit in the army. Why do you think that you deserve to be informed of every national security decision? Just because you happen to be the nephew of the minister? Does that make you more important than all the others who must wait to receive their orders from the chain of command? For some reason, you must think that you are special."

"No, I don't think I'm special," Louie said. "But I am the commander of the counter-terrorism force. If the army is deploying into the streets, shouldn't I at least be informed about what's going on? No one has told me anything since the attack. I'm being treated like a prisoner, trapped inside my own camp. When I left the base to come here, I was followed by two men from police intelligence. They're waiting for me outside the gate right now. I can't even go to the bathroom without them tagging along behind me."

Mugaba shook his head, hissing through his teeth. "I am sorry for that, Lutalo. I know this has been a difficult time for you. But you must understand that I have no control over this matter. It is in the hands of police intelligence. Until they've finished their investigation, Green House has instructed me to keep the counter-terrorism force restricted to base."

"But Uncle, this is ridiculous! Do they suspect that someone in my unit was behind the attack on the president? Or are they just looking at me? The entire notion is preposterous!"

"I don't know what they think, Lutalo. I'm not privy to the details of the investigation. But certainly, you can appreciate why they are taking such precautions. The drone used in the attack came from your warehouse. It was assigned to your unit. It's only logical that the investigation would focus on those who had access to the device."

"But it doesn't seem that they're interested in anyone else but me," Louie protested. "The investigators have gone through my office half a dozen times. They confiscated my computer and searched through my cell phone. Last week, they even showed up at our house and went through all my things while Anna had to sit in the living room. She was terrified. She thinks I'm going to jail. What am I supposed to tell her?"

"The fact that they're looking closely at you should not be surprising."

"How can you say this, Uncle? I have a spotless record. I have served honorably for many years. But what they're accusing me of is treason. I could be put to death!"

"Don't you understand? The reasons you have stated are exactly why you have drawn their attention. You have been an exemplary officer in every way."

"That doesn't make any sense," Louie muttered, shaking his head.

"Think about it, Lutalo. After Operation Brushfire, you were the hero of the country for killing Daniel Odoki. Your name was on the front page of every newspaper, and people at the highest levels took notice of this, even inside Green House. It was inevitable that this kind of attention would arouse jealousies, perhaps even concern over your ambitions."

"But Uncle, you know that I never asked for any of that. I wanted to be in the field with the soldiers, not at the controls of a drone, like some coward. I have no desire to be a general. That's not why I came back here after school."

Mugaba threw back his head and chuckled as if he'd heard a good joke. "Lutalo, you know the old saying from the village: Any soldier who doesn't see a future general when he looks in the mirror is not a good soldier. And one thing

I know for sure is that you are a good soldier. Just like your father was."

"Are you suggesting that I would try to kill the president to position myself for Green House? That idea is beyond reason! You said yourself that I am nothing but a lieutenant colonel, one of many in the army. Who would be foolish enough to believe that I had such ambitions?"

"Lutalo, it's not about your rank. It's about your name. People still remember your father. They also remember that he was destined for great things. When he was killed, many felt that our county had lost the best of that generation."

"I know that, Uncle," Louie said, staring down into his lap. "But I still don't see what that has to do with me."

"It has everything to do with you. I know that you are tired of hearing my old village sayings, but let me tell you just one more. It is possible to kill a man but impossible to kill his name. Do you understand what that means?"

Louie shook his head.

"It means that your father may be gone, but his name is still remembered. And as long as you carry that with you, people will see him when they look at you. That is why some men will always be suspicious of your motives."

"They suspect me of something that I didn't do. What is my defense if I am only guilty because of my name?"

"Lutalo, you know that I will always protect you. On the day your father died, I promised my sister that I would never let any harm come to you. I intend to keep that promise if it's the last thing I do. But for that to happen, you need to trust me. You must always remember that family comes first, no matter what."

"You said yourself that you don't have any control over the investigation. How can you possibly protect me if police intelligence decides that I am guilty?"

"We are in dangerous times right now, not just for you, but for everyone, the entire country. Green House is in chaos, and there is no telling what tomorrow will bring. Soon, there may come a time when someone will need to step forward and take hold of the reins. Do you understand what I am saying?"

Louie nodded.

"When that time comes, it will demand that we all make difficult decisions," Mugaba continued. "The future of our nation may depend on it. But the most important thing is knowing who you can trust. Knowing which side to be on when the knives come out. Do you understand me, Lutalo?"

Louie closed his eyes and nodded again, feeling sick to his stomach. "Thank you for seeing me," he murmured. "I must return to the base."

"Of course," his uncle said. "And please, have courage. I know that in the end, justice will prevail. Things will turn out right."

"Yes, Uncle," Louie said. He stood up and headed for the door, leaving Mugaba to his paperwork.

CHAPTER ELEVEN

Mike Jones stormed into his office, slamming the door behind him. At his desk, he punched the speed dial button for the White House Situation Room.

"Get me Reid McCoy. Now!" he barked the instant someone answered.

"I'm sorry, sir, but Mr. McCoy is meeting with the president right now. Can I have him call you back when—"

"I don't give a fuck if he's getting a pedicure from the pope!" Jones screamed. "You send somebody in there right now to pull him out. Tell him Mike Jones is on the line, and it's urgent!"

Sixty seconds later, the deputy national security advisor was on the phone. "Mike, this had better be good news."

"Sorry to burst your bubble, but it's worse than we thought."

"What's worse than an American ambassador being held hostage and the president of the United States looking like a dickless idiot?"

"She's not a hostage," Jones said.

"What the hell do you mean, she's not a hostage? I'm watching a live shot of the university on TV right now, and I don't see her walking out that gate."

"What I mean is that no one is keeping her there against her will. She's gone full Kurtz on us. We need to send someone up the river to bring her back."

"Jesus fucking Christ," Reid muttered. "POTUS is going to have my ass when he hears about this. Listen, I can't walk back into that room without giving him some options. What have you got for me?"

"We can get a detachment of SEALS down here from Europe by tomorrow morning," Jones said. "We could send them in for hostage rescue."

"I thought you just said that she's not a hostage. Wouldn't that be kidnapping?"

"We'll tell the press that she's suffering from Stockholm syndrome."

"No fucking way," Reid said. "I'm not sending a bunch of juiced-up gunslingers in to break up a student pajama party. We can't risk a military fiasco right before the midterms. We need to push this thing off on the Gisawians. What's the chance of convincing them to go in there and get her out?"

"The army's got the campus surrounded," Jones said. "I guess we could ask Defense Minister Odongo to send them in there and get her."

"Minister Odongo? Remind me again whose side he's on? I can't keep these fuckers straight."

"Technically, ours. But he's more of a free agent."

"If his soldiers have the place surrounded, it should be a piece of cake. Have them go in, grab her, and put her on the first flight back to DC."

"I'm not sure that's such a great idea," Jones cautioned. "Things could get dicey in there. The Gisawian regular army isn't trained for that kind of operation. They'd be hard-pressed to extract kittens out of a cardboard box without botching something. If the students put up any kind of resistance, the entire thing could turn into a bloodbath. The only Gisawian unit capable of pulling it off would be the counter-terrorism force."

"Great. Who do they work for?" Reid asked.

"Also for Mugaba. His nephew is the unit commander."

"Then let's talk to Mugaba and see if we can get them on board to pull Claire out of there with minimal drama," Reid proposed.

"One slight problem. The counter-terrorism unit has been confined to barracks for the last two weeks, under surveillance by police intelligence," Jones explained.

"What the hell for?"

"Reid, we've been over this several times," Jones said impatiently. "It was one of their drones that almost killed President Namono."

"Jesus, I can't keep any of this straight. OK, then who's left?"

"I think the only other force in DRoG trained for that kind of technical operation would be the presidential guard."

"And who do they work for?"

"Funny that you should ask. I just got a report from one of my sources inside the Chinese compound. Apparently, the presidential guard received training from the PLA at their camp out by the airport. Looks like the Chinese are getting a little anxious about protecting their assets inside Green House," Jones speculated.

"Damn. I need some kind of diagram to keep track of all this. So, it sounds like you're telling me that our options are: A, sending in the untrained Gisawian army to instigate a massacre; B, using a counter-terrorism force that's under suspicion of trying to kill the president; or C, deploying the presidential guard, which is working for Beijing."

"Yup. That sounds about right," Jones confirmed.

"I can't go to POTUS with those shit options! I'll get fired on the spot. Are you telling me that's all we've got?"

Jones stayed silent, letting the tension build before delivering his pitch. "There may be one other option."

"Something that will get Claire off that campus and onto a plane back home?" Reid asked hopefully.

"Eventually, but that won't be the first order of business."

"What other business is there? The press is going crazy over this. We've got to shut this down ASAP. Congressman Burke is having a field day with this shit show," Reid said, a hint of panic in his voice.

"Don't worry about Claire," Jones reassured him. "She's not going anywhere. I'm talking about the whole enchilada. Bringing in an entirely new dance card over at Green House."

"A coup? Are you fucking crazy? I thought our whole plan was to keep a low profile and maintain the status quo."

"Well, that plan kind of went out the window, didn't it? My sources inside Green House are saying that Namono is in bad shape. He's got no fucking idea what's going on. It's only a matter of time until someone spots an opportunity and decides to take it. My preference would be that we get a say in who that's going to be rather than giving it to Beijing wrapped up in a bow."

"Jesus, Mike. I can't even believe we're having this conversation. Who the hell do you have in mind?" Reid asked.

"For right now, I don't think we need to be focusing on any one person in particular," Jones said. "But there's a group that could potentially be helpful. The Citizens Action Committee."

"Wait a second, aren't they the guys who leaked those photos of Charity to the newspapers?"

"Yup."

"But we don't know a damn thing about them. They could be a doomsday cult for all we know."

"I have reason to believe otherwise," Jones hinted.

"Are you suggesting that I walk back into the Situation Room and tell POTUS that we're backing a coup plot by an organization that we know nothing about?"

"Well, it's either that or toss the keys over to Beijing and put them in the driver's seat." Jones countered.

"Correct me if I'm wrong, but you're proposing that we sell out President Namono after thirty years of loyal subservience to American geopolitical interests. Is that something you're comfortable with?"

"Come on, Reid. This is child's play. My first job in the agency was managing Manuel Noriega's Christmas shopping list. Do you think he held that against me when I had to put him on that plane to Miami? Fuck no! We're all consenting adults here. That's how the game is played. Namono is way past his expiration date. We need to bring in a new generation, somebody who's got the cojones to stick it to the Chinese."

"But Mike, if we turn on Namono, how do we know what we're getting in his place? We could easily go from bad to worse."

"Don't worry about that. I've got it under control. You tell POTUS that we're negotiating with the Gisawians to ensure Claire's safe passage out of the country. We'll get her on a plane back to DC as soon as possible. In the meantime, I'll reach out to the Citizens Action Committee and explore their viability."

"I'm telling you, POTUS isn't going to like this," Reid warned.

"Give me forty-eight hours. And tell POTUS that if we pull this off, we'll have the Chinese packing their bags and beat Burke at his own game," Jones promised.

"Fine. Forty-eight hours. That's it."

"You won't be sorry," Jones said before hanging up. He grabbed his jacket and sprinted for the door.

+++

Two hours later, Jones was pulling into the presidential retreat where Fabrice and the Citizens Action Committee were training. As he parked the car in the driveway, he could hear the sounds of automatic gunfire and flash-bang grenades echoing across the plateau. Jones moved quickly toward the sound of the guns, sprinting around the manor house with his weapon drawn. Rounding the corner, he stopped dead in his tracks, staring in awe at the scene before him.

Since his last visit, the manicured lawn and swimming pool had been bulldozed and turned into a military-style obstacle course. The topiaries had been burned to the ground, and the rose garden replaced with a knee-high horizontal trellis made of concertina wire. He could see CAC fighters crawling on their bellies through the mud underneath the razor wire, AK-47s cradled in their forearms.

The next obstacle was a foul-smelling cesspool excavated from an old bocce ball court. Jones watched as a group of men struggled through the waist-deep muck carrying logs on their shoulders, emerging from the other side looking like feral pigs that had been rooting in the mud. Next, the would-be revolutionaries were paired up in teams of two, hauling sandbags through a maze of burning car tires. Then, after fixing bayonets to their rifles, they fought their way through a static formation of department store mannequins buried in the ground up to their knees.

The penultimate task involved swinging on a rope across the swimming pool, now a septic stew of sludge and debris. Once over the water, the men sprinted to their final station, a shooting range of pop-up targets set at a distance of two hundred meters.

Around the obstacle course, a dozen ruddy-faced white men were supervising each station. Looking like soccer hooligans, the men were dressed in camouflage cargo pants, black T-shirts, and leather biker vests. Puffy, bloated physiques hinted at a steady diet of steroids and vodka. The lead consultant wandered around the course, firing a pistol into the air and throwing flash grenades at anyone who seemed to be lagging behind. Meanwhile, the other trainers were yelling at the CAC recruits in a mixture of Russian and heavily accented English, offering technical critiques peppered with genitalia-themed insults.

Jones was reluctant to interrupt the highly productive training session but eventually caught the lead consultant's eye and signaled for a break in the action. The boss let off several loud blasts from an air horn, causing everyone on the course to freeze in place. He announced a ten-minute smoke break and called Fabrice out from the ranks.

Jones could barely suppress a smile when he saw the CAC commander emerging from the thick ooze of the old bocce court. Fabrice was covered from head to toe in mud, dragging himself across the yard to where Jones was waiting.

"It's a good look for you," he said as Fabrice collapsed onto one knee.

"Boss, these fucking Russians are crazy!" he whimpered. "They're trying to kill us."

"They're just doing what they get paid for. This should have been happening all along. Unfortunately, we were getting way behind schedule. There was no way your guys were going to be ready without some extra help."

"You expect me to thank you for this?" Fabrice said, spitting on the ground. "Fuck you!"

"Hey, take it easy," Jones said, grinning from ear to ear. "I bet you'll be thanking me when you're sitting in Green House."

"So, this is the great CIA plan!" Fabrice exploded. "You think that swinging on some damn rope over a pool and getting yelled at by drunk Russians will get me to Green House?"

"No, of course not. Don't be ridiculous," Jones chuckled. "This is just for esprit de corps. But don't worry, I'm working out the rest of the details as we speak."

"Oh, is that so? Because so far, all I see are a bunch of white folks talking bullshit and telling the black man to run around in the mud. That's what your damn plan looks like to me!"

"Come on, Fabrice, there's no need to turn this into a race thing. You need to trust me."

"Why the fuck would I trust you? There isn't anybody you wouldn't lie to. That's your thing, man. I bet you don't even know what the truth is anymore."

"That's a bit harsh," Jones said, for an instant appearing almost aggrieved. "Especially for someone who spotted you on a five-thousand-dollar bar tab a few weeks ago. And you don't even know the half of it. This morning, I gave you the biggest gift you're ever going to get."

"And what was that?"

"I pitched the Citizens Action Committee to the president of the United States."

Fabrice caught a second wind as the words sunk in. He rose to his feet and looked Jones straight in the eye. "What the hell does that even mean?"

"It means that when this thing goes down, nobody is going to be taken by surprise back in Washington. We don't want them to hear about the CAC for the first time on the day you walk into Green House. You've got to socialize the concept first, give people some time to get used to the new brand."

"You're saying that the president knows about me?" Fabrice asked, momentarily forgetting that he was covered in mud and smelling like a compost pile.

"Well, not you specifically. We've got to take this one step at a time. The first stage is introducing the movement. It's all about reassuring people that you guys are legit. Once we get them comfortable with the concept, then we'll start getting down to specific personalities. This kind of thing works best when you roll it out incrementally. But that's not your problem. You just leave that part to me."

"What am I supposed to be doing in the meantime?"

"Exactly what you're doing right now: getting your men ready for the operation," Jones said, nodding across the yard at the hardened core of the Citizens Action Committee. The men, covered in mud, were taking a break on a pile of old car tires. Several of them were smoking cigarettes while chatting on cell phones. Jones was distracted by the scene and stared at the men before turning back to Fabrice.

"Please tell me those aren't the same cell phones that I sent out here last week," Jones said.

Fabrice looked at his men and saw them talking on several cheap Nokia phones delivered to the compound by courier the week before. "Yeah, so what?" he said. "They still had minutes left on them after we did what you asked."

"Fuck! I told you those were burner phones. You were supposed to throw them away after your guys dialed the numbers and read through the scripts."

Fabrice shrugged, still not seeing the point.

"The NSA!" Jones exploded. "Maybe you've heard of them?"

Fabrice nodded.

"They're monitoring all those SIM cards, you idiot! Why do you think I sent them way out here to make those calls?

It's a goddamn miracle that a Tomahawk hasn't leveled the place. Tell them to pull the SIM cards out of the phones and throw everything into the swimming pool. We can't risk having the Citizens Action Committee associated with threats against the ambassador. You got it?"

"OK, OK. I got it. But what happens next? Does your president give us some kind of secret signal when it's time to move on Green House?"

"Yeah, that's exactly how it goes down," Jones said sarcastically. "Listen, Fabrice. The White House doesn't give a shit about the CAC, or, frankly, anyone else who might decide to overrun Green House. As long as they're not in bed with Beijing, that's all that matters. If you can manage that, we can look forward to a few decades of doing business together, just like your old man before he let things go to shit."

"Yeah, boss, I'm on board. But what about the plan?"

"Relax. I'm working on a few final details before we get rolling on Operation Hermes."

"Hermes?"

"Yeah, that's the code name," Jones confirmed.

"What does it mean?"

"I don't know. Nothing. But when you hear it, you need to be ready to go."

"Go where?"

"I'll let you know when the time comes."

"To do what?"

"I'll let you know that too. Until then, keep an eye out for a text with the code name. Then get your boys ready to move."

"What about the Russians?"

"They'll be going with you, providing adult supervision."

"Fuck them!" Fabrice said. "They've been riding our asses since the day they showed up. Why do we need them?"

"We can't afford to screw this up. They may not look it, but these guys are pros. Did you happen to check out their CVs?"

Fabrice shook his head.

"The Crimea? Libya? Syria? Ever heard of those places? These guys consulted on every single project. They work chaos like a scalpel. You just need to put up with them for a little longer. Trust me, once you're in Green House, they'll be on the first plane out. So, are we good?"

"Yeah, we're good."

"OK, then wait for my text," Jones said. "Operation Hermes. Don't forget it."

The big Russian boss blew the air horn, calling the Citizens Action Committee back to the obstacle course. Fabrice sighed, picked up his rifle, and turned back to the muddy bocce court, visions of life in Green House fading from his mind.

+++

An hour later, Colonel Sawyer walked through the front gate of the defense ministry to meet with Mugaba Odongo. As soon as he arrived, the receptionist led him into the minister's office. Mugaba was waiting behind his desk. His three cell phones were nowhere to be seen, and his inbox was empty.

"Good afternoon Minister Odongo," Sawyer said, shaking Mugaba's hand. "Thank you for meeting on such short notice. I'm sorry to be making a habit of this."

Mugaba smiled, dismissing the apology with a wave of his hand. "It's no problem at all, Colonel. I always make time for my American friends," he said, motioning Sawyer to one of the chairs in front of his desk. "I presume you're here to discuss the situation at the university?" he said, moving directly to the matter at hand.

"Yes, sir. As you can imagine, my government would like to see the situation resolved as soon as possible."

"Indeed. As would we. However, there seems to be some confusion concerning the status of your ambassador and the other woman. The international press keeps referring to them as hostages. However, that's not our understanding of the situation. May I ask how your government views it?" Mugaba asked.

"Officially, we're not using that term. And frankly, we think the press is blowing this way out of proportion. Nevertheless, the sooner it's over, the better for everyone involved. But given the political sensitivities, we think the optics would be better if this were a Gisawian-led operation."

"I fully concur," Mugaba agreed. "It would send the wrong message if American forces were to go in unilaterally. However, that still leaves the question, how should we go about getting your ambassador off campus?"

"I've received guidance from Washington asking if your military could lead the operation."

Mugaba rubbed his chin. "Even under ideal conditions, that would be a risky operation. There's no telling how the students might react once we go in."

"My government shares your concerns. Clearly, this is something that needs to be handled delicately. Of course, that would require a specially trained unit," Sawyer hinted.

"I assume you're referring to our counter-terrorism force?"

"Yes, sir. The United States has invested considerable resources in training and equipping that force. We know their capabilities. It's the best unit in your army, and probably the only one able to pull off a mission like this."

"I don't disagree with your assessment, Colonel Sawyer. However, there are other issues that must be considered. Given the unstable political situation, I am limited in my ability to deploy military forces. Approval for such an operation could only come from the president himself."

"And what are the chances of that happening?"

Mugaba leaned back in his chair, smiling and shaking his head. "Please do not take this the wrong way, Colonel Sawyer, but the fate of your ambassador is not foremost on the list of concerns at Green House."

"I don't expect that it would be," Sawyer replied. "However, it was the lead story for every major news outlet in the world this morning. Like it or not, people are paying close attention to what is going on inside the university."

"That may be the case, but we are in the midst of a serious crisis. People are waking up each morning not knowing what the day will bring. They are tired of the uncertainty and chaos. They need a strong leader who can take control of the situation and do what is best for the county."

"It sounds as if you don't believe President Namono is up to the task," Sawyer speculated.

"Don't put words into my mouth," Mugaba warned, waving his finger at the colonel. "All I am saying is that we are standing on the edge of a cliff. Do we jump, or do we pull back from the edge and return to business as usual? I fear that we are running out of time to make that decision."

"Minister Odongo, I think I understand what you're getting at. I know my government shares your concern about the path that DRoG is on. And quite frankly, we're confused about what is happening inside Green House, especially since the arrival of the Chinese soldiers at the airport."

"I've already told you, that decision was made at a higher level than me," Mugaba said defensively. "I was not even consulted on the matter. I was as surprised as you were when it happened."

"I take you at your word. But now we're hearing rumors that Chinese advisors are training the presidential guard. Did you know about this beforehand?"

"Colonel Sawyer, I know you're aware that the presidential guard is an entirely separate entity from the army. They don't answer to my ministry. I have no control over what they do or who they do it with."

"But the issue isn't just about who trains the presidential guard. We're concerned about the big picture—whether the Chinese are using this crisis as an excuse to increase their influence inside Green House."

"I cannot speak to the deliberations happening inside Green House," Mugaba insisted. "Unfortunately, I'm no longer privy to these discussions. However, I do know that the Chinese are playing the long game. They have much more patience than Washington. I expect they'll wait for the right opportunity, then move when they feel that the odds are in their favor."

"Do you share our concerns about what's happening? The United States has been a close ally of DRoG for many, many years. Our ties go back to the Cold War. But at the moment, we don't have any idea where the relationship stands. It seems like Green House wants to have it both ways."

"Colonel, as I said, these decisions are made above my level. Therefore, it would be inappropriate for me to comment. However, it does bring to mind an old proverb that I used to hear people say in the village: One should always hold a true friend with both hands."

"Do they know this saying in Green House?"

Mugaba shrugged. "At some point, a choice must be made between old friends or new."

"In that case, may I ask your preference? Old friends or new?" Sawyer asked.

Mugaba gave a sly smile and chuckled. "As the risk of causing offense, my preference is always for the devil you know over the one you don't."

"And what about the situation at the university? Do you think that this is something that can be resolved discreetly on your side?"

"Perhaps," Mugaba said. "But there are two separate issues involved."

"I'm not sure I understand."

"The two Americans, and then the students. The first issue is a matter of mutual concern. However, the latter is strictly an internal matter, something that we will resolve our way," Mugaba explained. "Nevertheless, I can assure you that we will make every effort to extract the ambassador and her companion safely. It's in no one's interest for this situation to drag on any longer."

"We're in full agreement on that point," Sawyer confirmed.

"But Colonel Sawyer, I feel compelled to mention that what you are asking me to do is not without risk. And not only for those inside the university."

"How so?"

"I don't think it's a secret that the counter-terrorism unit has been confined to camp since the attack on our president."

Sawyer nodded. "Yes, we understand that some restrictions have been placed on the unit's movement and its commander."

"I assumed you were aware of that. But what you may not know is that I have been restricted in my authority to deploy them. Since the attack, all orders must be reviewed by Green House. Even low-level decisions are now under scrutiny. I have little power to direct such an operation."

"What exactly are you getting at, Minister Odongo?" Sawyer pressed.

"If I were to order the counter-terrorism unit to enter the university and retrieve your ambassador, there are some inside Green House who would view it as an act of mutiny, a direct challenge to the president's authority. If you wish me to go forward with such an operation, I must have some assurance from your side that my loyalty will be acknowledged. Otherwise, the risks are simply too great for me, as well as the soldiers who follow my orders."

"Minister, surely you know that I'm not empowered to make any promises on behalf of my government."

"No, of course not. I didn't expect that you would be. But given the present instability, almost any action on my part could set off an unpredictable chain of events. If I order this operation, I can't promise that there won't be unintended consequences."

"I understand that, and I appreciate the risks. But I also know that my government wouldn't have sent me here unless they were confident that you could resolve the problem. I feel certain that anything you can do to bring about a quick resolution will be greatly appreciated in Washington."

"Of course. I will do my best, Colonel Sawyer," Mugaba said, standing up and extending his hand. "I always support my American friends."

+++

Later that evening, Sawyer was back at his house, an American-style duplex situated inside a gated enclave reserved for diplomatic families. He was in his underwear, sitting at the computer, eating a dinner of cold Spam, saltine crackers, and imported beer. Since his family's evacuation, he had quickly regressed to a bachelor's existence. Sawyer was just about to start a video chat with his wife back in the States when his cell phone buzzed with an incoming text from Louie Bigombe.

Meet me at the camp front gate ASAP. Please bring a pizza. Hold the anchovies.

Sawyer stared at the message, trying to make sense of what he was reading. When he couldn't come up with any plausible explanation, he assumed that Louie was intentionally being cryptic. Rather than pressing for details, he simply texted back "OK." He ordered a pizza from a takeout place down the street, then got dressed to go out.

About an hour later, Sawyer arrived outside the camp. He waited in his car, checking out the scene for anything that seemed out of the ordinary. The base appeared deserted, dark except for the dim glow of a single lightbulb dangling from a wire in the guard shack. A sleepy soldier sat at a table, listening to the radio and drinking a bottle of soda.

Sawyer texted Louie to let him know that he was waiting outside the fence, then got out of the car, pizza in hand, and walked over to the gate. This roused the soldier in the guardhouse. He rushed outside with his rifle, alarmed to find a visitor sneaking around the fence at night. He pointed his weapon into the darkness and ordered Sawyer to move forward into the light.

"I'm here to see Lieutenant Colonel Bigombe," Sawyer yelled out, holding the pizza box high up in the air over his head, hoping not to get shot.

The soldier nodded suspiciously and slowly lowered his weapon, apparently assessing a white man carrying a pizza box as a low probability risk. He ordered Sawyer to wait at the gate, then went back into the guard shack to make a phone call. A few minutes later, Louie appeared on the other side of the fence, waving for Sawyer to join him beyond the guard's earshot.

"Thanks for coming, Jeff," Louie said, speaking softly through the wire fence. "Sorry about all the secrecy."

"No problem. I figured you had a good reason for acting so weird. Are you coming outside, or are we talking through the fence?"

"We're not alone," Louie whispered, glancing over his shoulder.

Sawyer noticed two men standing nearby, smoking cigarettes, watching from the shadows. "Who the hell are they?"

"My escort from police intelligence," Louie grumbled. "They go with me everywhere."

"Really? So you're still on double-secret probation?"

"Yes. More or less."

"And you just happened to have a craving for pizza tonight?"

"Thanks for bringing it," Louie said, taking the pizza box from Sawyer through a gap in the fence meant for deliveries. "Here, let me give you some money." He passed a few bills through the fence.

"Sure," Sawyer said, stuffing the money into his pocket. "Anything else I can get you while I'm here? Maybe some nachos or something?"

"Actually, I'm not hungry. The memory card from the drone wreckage is taped between the bills I just gave you. Sorry, it took so long to get it. It was a little tricky for my friend over at police intelligence to get access to the evidence locker."

Realizing what had just transpired, Sawyer glanced nervously at the two men watching from the shadows.

"Don't worry," Louie reassured him. "I've had someone deliver a pizza every night for the last week. That way, they wouldn't be alarmed when you showed up here."

"Good thinking. So what now?"

"How long do you think it will take to get the information off the data card?"

"Not long," Sawyer assured him. "I'll download it on my computer as soon as I get back home. I know a guy in DC who can decrypt the file. He should be able to get it back to me in a day or two at the most. What do you want me to do with it when I have it?"

"On one of the bills, I wrote a web address for an encrypted data transfer portal. Drop the files in there. I'll get an automatic notification once you make the transfer."

"Wow, you've really thought this through," Sawyer said, impressed with Louie's planning.

"I've had some time on my hands over the last few weeks."

"That may be about to change," Sawyer said.

"What do you mean?" Louie asked.

"I met with your uncle today. My government is asking for his help concerning the situation at the university." Sawyer explained.

"You mean the student sit-in? The army is already surrounding the campus. What more can we do?"

"Listen, Louie, I know you have a personal connection to all this, with Anna being inside the campus. But this is spinning out of control. We have an ambassador who's refusing to come out. It's the lead story on every news outlet. We've asked your uncle for help in getting this resolved."

"What do you mean, 'resolved'?" Louie asked, uncomfortable with the choice of words.

"I mean getting Ambassador Roberts and Anna the hell out of there. We can't afford to have anything happen to them. This is coming all the way from the top. The White House wants this over as soon as possible."

"What did my uncle say?"

"He said that he'd try to help."

"How? By sending the regular army in to confront the students? That's crazy," Louie protested.

"Yeah, that's what he thought too," Sawyer agreed. "I think that's why he's planning on sending your unit in to bring them out."

Louie said nothing, his eyes drifting down to the box of cold pizza in his hand.

"We don't have any other choice," Sawyer continued. "Look at it this way: You're the best one to do this. Maybe you can even convince Anna to come out and bring the ambassador along with her. We need to get this thing over with as soon as possible."

"What happens to the students once they're out?" Louie asked.

Sawyer shrugged. "I hate to be harsh about this, Louie, but that's not our problem. My orders are to get the two American citizens off that campus. Once that happens, it becomes a Gisawian internal matter."

"So, you don't care at that point?"

"Of course, I care. But it's not my job to tell your government how to run its business. We all want a peaceful resolution. Right now, my priority is getting the ambassador and Anna out of there with minimal drama."

"My uncle can't order my unit anywhere as long we're still under investigation," Louie insisted. "There's no way that Green House will approve the operation."

"That's what he said too, but at this point, maybe he thinks there's nothing left to lose. It's not like you'll be in any more trouble than you already are. Might as well pile it on," Sawyer said, trying to sound lighthearted.

"Thanks for the vote of confidence," Louie said with a sigh.

"No problem. I figured you needed a little pep talk. Hopefully, I won't be delivering the next pizza to you through steel bars."

"Yeah, I hope not," Louie said, finally cracking a smile. "Thanks for helping me out with the memory card."

"Sure, no problem. By the way, do you have any idea what you expect to find out from the flight data?"

"I have a few suspicions, but nothing that I'm willing to put money on."

"Well, I hope there's something there that will help you out. I'll get the data uploaded to the file transfer portal as soon as possible. Until then, enjoy the pizza, and good luck with the mission."

"Thanks," Louie said, then turned and walked back toward his office.

Sawyer lingered at the fence, watching the men from police intelligence stub out their cigarettes and follow Louie into the darkness. Once they disappeared into the shadows, he reached into the pocket where he had stuffed the money. Sawyer fingered the bills until he felt the bump of the memory card between them. His heart was racing as he jogged back to the car. Sawyer slipped into the driver's seat, double checked that the chip was still in his pocket, and then raced home to his computer.

CHAPTER TWELVE

———

The morning after he visited the training camp, Mike Jones sat in the office, drinking coffee and reading through the overnight intelligence reports. On the wall above his desk, an array of flat-panel televisions were tuned to international news channels. Every few minutes, Jones glanced up to check the headlines scrolling across the bottom of the screens. The standoff at the university was still the lead story on every channel, the world waiting to see who would blink first.

Jones checked his watch and did some quick time-zone math. Then he picked up the phone and dialed Reid McCoy's home number. The deputy national security advisor answered on the tenth ring, sounding groggy.

"Reid. Mike Jones here. Got a minute?"

"Its three-thirty in the fucking morning. Couldn't this wait a few more hours?"

"Things are moving fast over here. I need some feedback before moving ahead with the plan. How did POTUS react to the pitch on the Citizens Action Committee?" Jones asked.

"You want the truth?"

"Hmmm, I guess that depends," Jones said, still watching the TV, looking for updates on the situation at National University.

"I would say that POTUS was less than enthused about the plan. To be honest, the entire thing seems kind of half-baked. We hardly know anything about these guys except that they hate Charity Namono, and frankly, that's not much of a resume to go on."

"I'm working on a full dossier right now. I was able to make contact with one of their representatives. It's looking better than we thought. I think these guys could fit the bill."

"What the hell does that mean?" Reid asked, unconvinced.

"They're technocrats. Good-governance types. That's why they were trolling Charity. They were trying to make an example of her."

"That's all well and good, but it doesn't mean that we're backing them to take over the damn country. Do we even know who's in charge of the organization?"

"They have a leader, but they want to keep his identity under wraps until the situation ripens," Jones explained. "That's the way things work over here. Once you throw out a name, the next thing you know, they're lying dead in a ditch."

"OK, so what's this guy like?"

"A strong leader. He's got a vision for the country but isn't going to be kowtowing to Beijing."

"You realize why that's funny, don't you?" Reid said, chuckling on the other end of the line.

"Dammit, Reid! You know what I mean. This guy's not going to sell us out like Namono did. He's sort of like a black Chiang Kai-shek. Someone we can do business with."

"Mike, I don't know if POTUS will buy this thing without kicking the tires first. Don't we have any other options?"

"We're running out of time," Jones pressed. "Namono could knock off any minute. If we don't have something lined up and ready to go, we're screwed."

"All right. I'm not making any promises, but here's what I need: Put together what you have on this group and send me a decision memo ASAP. I'll try to get something in front of the principals today. But I don't want you moving forward on anything until I give you the word. Understand?"

"Yeah, I got it. The dossier will be sitting in your inbox by the time you get to the office," Jones promised.

"OK. What about Claire? Any progress on that front?" Reid asked.

"No. She's still refusing to come out. The media is going crazy. The story is pushing into the next news cycle."

"Dammit!" Reid spat. "What about the Gisawians? Aren't they going to make a move?"

"Maybe. Yesterday, I sent the military attaché over to talk with Mugaba. From the sound of it, they want this over as much as we do. I'd say there's a fifty-fifty chance that he sends in the army to bring her out."

"We can't afford to have them botch it," Reid warned. "The entire world will be watching. But no matter what happens, I want Claire on the first flight back to DC. Got it?"

"Right. No problem. How do you plan on spinning it when she comes out? Her face is going to be all over the media."

"That depends on how things go down. Somewhere between Joan of Arc and Patty Hearst? Anyway, whatever you do, don't let her talk to the press when she gets out. You put her ass on that plane before she has a chance to open her mouth," Reid warned.

"Don't worry. I've got it under control."

"You better. Anything else, or can I try to get another hour of sleep before heading into work?"

Jones fell silent, distracted by something happening on the televisions. "Wait a second," he mumbled. "Something is going on over at the university. The news channels are broadcasting a live feed from somewhere inside the campus."

"What the hell is it?" Reid asked.

"It's one of the students. I think it's the leader of the sit-in. Hold on a second. Let me turn the sound on."

Reid waited on the line while Jones flipped one of the TVs off mute. Didier Kengo appeared on the screen, speaking from inside a classroom. The shaky video looked as if it was being shot from a smartphone. Standing behind a podium, Didier began reading from a prepared statement.

"What's happening?" Reid shouted into the phone.

"They're calling Namono's bluff. The students are threatening to walk out through the security cordon in twenty-four hours unless the president agrees to step down and hold free elections. They're calling for a mass march on Green House."

"Jesus, this can't be good," Reid muttered.

"Don't be so sure. This may be the opportunity we're looking for," Jones said. "Let me try to get in touch with Claire and find out if the students are serious about this."

"Then what?"

"If they're trying to get rid of Namono, then somebody's got to take his place."

"The Citizens Action Committee?" Reid asked.

"It's now or never. We'll see if they're ready for the big leagues."

"Don't make any promises you can't keep."

"I promise."

"Very funny. Keep me updated," Reid said and hung up.

+++

After getting off the line with Washington, Jones dialed the ambassador's cell phone. He expected to get her voicemail and was surprised when she picked up on the first ring.

"Claire. Mike Jones here. We need to talk."

"I'm listening," she said without enthusiasm.

Jones could hear a roomful of voices engaged in animated conversation in the background. "Are you somewhere private? It sounds like there's a party going on over there."

"Mike, have you been paying any attention to what's going on? We're all stuck in classrooms without air conditioning. The students have been sleeping on the floor for the last two weeks. Just say what you need to say," Claire demanded.

"That was a nice little bit of theater on TV a few minutes ago. Did you coach them on their list of demands?" Jones asked.

"No. They don't need any help from me. They've got a pretty clear idea about the kind of country they want to live in."

"Well, they might be getting more than they bargained for. The news is reporting that people are starting to gather outside Green House. The kiddos may have just kicked off a revolution." Jones said, still watching the break news tickers scrolling across the TV screens.

"I guess that means they're not alone in wanting things to change," Claire insisted.

"Listen to me. They may not realize it yet, but they're playing with fire. You and I both know that there's a good chance this doesn't end well for anyone. You're the grown-up in the room. You need to take responsibility and talk some sense into them."

"And tell them what, Mike? To give up their hopes for a better life?"

"Don't be so fucking naïve. You're surrounded by several hundred poorly trained Gisawian soldiers whose paychecks are signed by President Namono. Do you think they're going to let those students stroll through the perimeter tomorrow and march on over to Green House? This could end in a bloodbath. And if it does, you'll bear a good deal of the blame for encouraging it," Jones threatened.

"How do you figure that?"

"You're an enabler, a senior American diplomat who's sided with a bunch of delusional student radicals."

"You're seriously accusing me of being an enabler? Mike, we've been on the wrong side of things over here for almost thirty years now. I don't particularly want my name added to a long list of people who looked the other way and let the charade continue."

"Oh, that's great," Jones said sarcastically. "I guess you'll be able to leave here with your virtue intact. And when this country descends into bloody chaos, you'll have the satisfaction of knowing that you did the right thing."

"And what will you remember when you look back on it, Mike?" she shot back.

"I'll remember that I did what was necessary to protect the interests of my country. Because, in case you've forgotten, that's what we get paid to do."

There was silence on the line. Jones could hear the students talking excitedly in the background. Then his cell phone buzzed with an incoming text.

"Are you still there?" Jones asked.

"Yes, I'm here. But I don't think there's anything left for us to discuss."

"I just got off the phone with Reid. He wants you on the first flight back to Washington. This is coming straight from the top. We're not playing games anymore."

There was a long pause before she finally answered. "Tell Reid that I'll get on the plane once the students get safely past the army perimeter and not before."

"Dammit, Claire! You're making a big fucking mistake. This is gross insubordination. You are defying a direct order from the White House."

"Just tell him that I'll gladly get on the plane tomorrow once the students are out, but not until then. Goodbye, Mike," she said.

When Jones realized that she'd hung up on him again, he slammed down the phone. He fumed, then remembered the text message. Glancing at the screen, he recognized the number as a burner phone he'd given to his deep source in case of emergency.

Presidential guard force mobilizing. Reinforcements moving toward Green House. ETA 45 minutes.

"Shit," Jones mumbled. He reread the message, going through a mental list of his rapidly diminishing options. He picked up the desk phone and dialed Colonel Sawyer.

"It's Jones," he said when the colonel picked up. "Listen up. I need you to get everybody into the conference room ASAP. I'm calling an emergency action committee."

"Is the ambassador back?" Sawyer asked, confused as to who was giving the order.

"No. And she's not coming back. I'm in control here. This is under my authority. Any questions?"

Sawyer pondered the numerous breaches of protocol that had occurred during the first twelve seconds of the conversation. However, the sheer audacity of the gambit seemed designed to steamroll any possible resistance.

"Yes, sir," Sawyer said, unsure what else to do. "I'll round everyone up."

"Good. I've got a few things to finish up, then I'll meet you all in the conference room," Jones said before hanging up.

+++

Thirty minutes later, the entire staff was assembled, minus the ambassador. Everyone was riveted to the television, watching live footage of events unfolding around the city. With each passing minute, the crowd outside Green House was growing. Protesters already outnumbered the thin line of presidential guard troops manning the perimeter around the mansion. With everyone glued to the TV, no one noticed Mike Jones slipping into the room and casually claiming the chair usually occupied by the ambassador.

"OK, team, what's the latest?" he blurted out, startling everyone in the room.

Jones ignored the expressions of surprise and stared pointedly at Colonel Sawyer, leaving him no choice but to respond.

"Things are getting tense outside of Green House," Sawyer reported. "The presidential guard has reinforced the exterior perimeter, but they're already outnumbered by the protesters. More people are arriving by the minute. The students from the sit-in have fired up the street."

"Any statement from inside Green House?" Jones asked.

"Nothing yet," Sawyer reported. "We haven't heard a word from President Namono for several days. But a few minutes ago, state media reported that the ministry of defense was about to make some kind of special announcement."

"Any idea what it's about?" Jones asked.

"No. I called my contacts over at the ministry, but no one is saying anything. Either they don't know what's going on or they're too scared to talk."

"Anything new from the kiddos at the university?"

"Same as before. The army still has the place surrounded, and there's been no word from the ambassador. As far as we know, the students are still planning to walk out through the front gate tomorrow morning."

As Sawyer spoke, the news broadcast cut away from the chaos outside Green House to a live shot of an empty podium in a drab conference room. On the wall behind the lectern was the circular crest of the Gisawian ministry of defense. Seconds later, Minister Mugaba Odongo entered the picture and made his way to the podium. He calmly flattened out a page of notes and donned a pair of reading glasses, pausing dramatically before looking into the camera.

"My fellow citizens," he intoned, "it is my solemn duty to inform the nation that our beloved leader, President Jean Mutara Namono, is in grave condition and must seek immediate medical attention outside the country. I have ordered the army to escort President Namono from Green House directly to the international airport, where he will be evacuated by military aircraft. Per article seven of the draft constitution, an interim military committee will oversee governmental affairs until a formal order of succession can be approved and signed by the council of consultation. Until such time, I call on all Gisawians to join together in unity and prayer for the speedy recovery of President Namono and his return to Green House. In this time of crisis, we must not allow petty grievances and superficial divisions to cripple our great nation. God bless President Namono and the Democratic Republic of Gisawi. Thank you."

Mugaba took off his glasses and calmly folded the notes. He left the podium without another word as the broadcast ended.

Jones shook his head in disbelief and turned to the political advisor sitting a few seats away. "Stephen, please tell me what the fuck just happened."

"Your guess is as good as mine," Stephen said with a shrug.

"What the hell is article seven of the draft constitution? I didn't even know DRoG had a constitution."

"It's a well-kept secret. The draft has been under review by the council of consultation for the last eight years. There was a rumor going around that they had copied the entire thing from Tajikistan. I think we can safely assume that it's some kind of vaguely worded fig leaf for dynastic succession. But since no one has seen the document, there's no way of knowing what's inside."

"Give me your best guess on how this plays out," Jones urged.

"If the draft constitution provides some framework for hereditary succession, then presumably Charity or Fabrice would be next in line for Green House. However, there's always a chance that Namono will leave the country without formally appointing an interim ruler."

"Why would he do that?"

"He doesn't want to give away something that he may not get back. If it looks like a formal transition of power, it will give instant legitimacy to whoever is named interim leader. I'd say there's a fair chance that whoever gets it won't want to relinquish the job if Namono ever comes back."

"What happens if he leaves the country without putting anyone in charge?"

"In that case, I guess it's a jump ball for Green House once he's gone," Stephen said.

"OK. Keep monitoring the situation," Jones said, getting up and moving toward the door. "I've got to step outside for a quick phone call. I'll be back in a few minutes."

+++

In the embassy courtyard, Jones began scrolling through a list of cryptically named contacts on his phone. He dialed one of the numbers and began to pace back and forth, waiting for someone to pick up. After a dozen rings, Fabrice answered.

"Where the hell were you?" Jones yelled. "I told you to stay close to the phone."

"I was in the bathroom."

"Are you ready to move?" Jones asked.

"Yeah, we're ready," Fabrice confirmed.

"You understand the plan?"

"Yeah, I got it boss."

"OK, good. Give me a few minutes to confirm the target location," Jones said, glancing at his watch. "I'll text you the coordinates as soon as I have them. Any last-minute questions before we start this?"

"What about the Russians?"

"What about them?" Jones said impatiently.

"Are they going on the operation?"

"What the hell do you think? We've already been through this, Fabrice. Their contract runs through the end of Operation Hermes. I brought them on board to make sure that everything goes according to plan. That was the deal from the start. Why? What's the matter now?"

"Their women have been living here at the house for the last two weeks. They've emptied my father's entire wine cellar."

"I can't do anything about that," Jones said. "There's a rider in the contract for on-site therapeutic massage services and an open bar."

"Yesterday, they went on a hunting expedition in our private nature preserve and killed an entire herd of endangered antelope."

"All right, Fabrice, I get it! I won't let them count that as billable hours. But right now, we've got bigger things to worry about. We're running out of time. Your father is about to be medically evacuated from the country. Green House is going to be empty."

"Where did you hear this?" Fabrice asked, sounding panicked.

"Defense Minister Odongo just came on TV and made the announcement."

"Is Mugaba making a play?"

"Sure, why the hell not? Everyone else seems to be. He might as well join the party," Jones said sarcastically. "As long as Mugaba still controls the army, he must think he has a chance. But we've still got one advantage."

"What's that again?" Fabrice asked, sounding uncertain.

"The Citizens Action Committee!" Jones exploded with impatience. "We've already planted the seed at the White House. Trust me, if we can seize the initiative, they'll go along with it before ever admitting they had no idea what was happening. POTUS will pretend like it was his idea all along."

"When is my father leaving?"

"Soon. We've got a narrow window of opportunity if we're going to make this happen."

"But what if Operation Hermes doesn't work?"

"Then we're shit out of luck. But there's an old saying back home: Possession is nine-tenths of the law. I'm telling you, Fabrice, whoever gets to Green House first is going to be the one who keeps it. We've got to move now, while there's still time."

"OK, but as soon as it's done, the fucking Russians are out of here."

"Yeah, no problem. It'll be your country by then. You can run them out of town on a rail for all I care. Listen, we're burning daylight. Give me a few minutes to confirm the target location. I'll send you a text. As soon as you get the coordinates, you need to be rolling out the door. Got it?"

"Yeah, boss, I got it."

"OK. Good luck. Let me know when the package is secure."

As soon as Jones hung up, another text message from his deep source popped up on his cell phone.

Gisawian counter-terrorism forces are deploying from the base.

Jones quickly tapped back a message to his asset.

Where to?

A moment later, the reply popped into the message queue.

National University

"Dammit! Mugaba is making his move," Jones muttered, shoving the phone into his pocket and heading back inside the embassy.

+++

In the conference room, everyone was exactly where Jones had left them fifteen minutes before: sitting around the table, fixated on the television. The live news broadcast showed a split-screen view, with one camera stationed on a rooftop across the plaza from Green House. Its panoramic shot showed protesters flooding into the square, the crowd growing by the minute. The thin line of presidential guard troops was still holding the perimeter outside the mansion but inching backward as the protesters pushed forward. On the other half of the TV screen was a live shot from a camera overlooking the international airport's runway. In the distance, a Gisawian military transport plane was parked on the taxiway, and technicians scurried around the aircraft, doing preflight checks.

"What'd I miss?" Jones asked, reoccupying the seat at the head of the table.

"Looks like they're waiting for Namono to come out of Green House," Colonel Sawyer said.

"Have they said where they're taking him?"

"Not yet. There haven't been any more statements since Mugaba broke the news."

"I've got to hand it to him; that was a brilliant move. He caught everyone off guard," Jones said. "Now he's trying to seal the deal before anyone has time to react."

Sawyer gave him a skeptical look. "That's what you think this is about? Mugaba making a play for Green House?"

"Are you kidding me?" Jones said incredulously. "Of course it is. I don't believe for a second that he hasn't been planning this all along. By the way, I just got a message that the counter-terrorism unit is on the move. Apparently, Mugaba has sent them over to the university. He's seizing the initiative and sending everyone a clear message."

"Sorry, you've lost me," Sawyer said, shaking his head. "What exactly is the message?"

"First, he's letting Green House know that they're not calling the shots anymore when it comes to controlling the army. Second, he's letting the folks in Washington know that he can be counted on to take care of business."

"You mean getting Ambassador Roberts off campus?"

"Yup. He's about to score some big brownie points back inside the Beltway, and he knows it. But still, that may not be enough to win the prize."

As Jones was speaking, he was distracted by the political officer, who was reading updates from his phone and raising his hand to speak. "What is it?" Jones asked.

"The AP is reporting that the Chinese have called for an emergency session of the UN Security Council to discuss the deterioration of the security situation in DRoG."

"Yeah, I bet they have," Jones said, shaking his head. "Beijing is stalling for time while they try to figure out what the hell is going on. It's nothing but a delaying tactic."

Stephen began reading out loud from his phone. "The Chinese foreign minister urges the international community to respect DRoG's sovereignty and to warn against any attempt at foreign-imposed regime change. They're calling for the establishment of a transitional government per article seven of the draft constitution under review by the council of consultation."

"They're bluffing," Jones scoffed.

"Do you want me to request a full translation of the foreign minister's comments?"

"Don't bother. I don't need to speak Mandarin to know what's going on here. This is all about them getting Charity into Green House. They're trying to buy time so they can get their Peking ducks in a row."

On the television screen, there was a flurry of activity outside the presidential mansion. An ambulance backed up to the front door, and a medical team rushed inside. A short time later, the medics reappeared with a wheeled stretcher and quickly loaded it into the ambulance. Once the doors were closed, the convoy began inching toward the front gate of Green House, which was blocked on the other side by the mob of angry protesters. From the camera's vantage point, the road leading out from Green House appeared impassable.

A gunner sitting atop the lead vehicle ripped off a burst of fifty-caliber machine gun fire into the air. Panicking, the crowd dropped to the ground and scrambled for cover. The front gate of Green House opened wide, and the military convoy raced through the gap, with the ambulance following close behind.

At the same time, the television camera out at the airport showed the crew finishing final preparations for departure. A refueling truck pulled away from the plane as ground technicians yanked the chock blocks from under its landing gear.

The embassy staff watched in silence as the convoy carrying President Namono sped through the city in the direction of the airport. Fifteen minutes later, the ambulance arrived on the tarmac, and the medical team quickly transferred the stretcher into the belly of the aircraft. The cargo door closed, and the plane began taxiing to the end of the runway. The camera captured the puffs of sooty exhaust as the engines revved. The final shot showed the aircraft speed down the runway and gradually lift into the sky for an unknown destination.

"What now?" Colonel Sawyer asked. "Do we have any guidance from Washington?"

Jones looked at him with a raised eyebrow. "Do you think anyone back there has the slightest clue how to play this?"

Sawyer shrugged, uncertain of the answer. Jones leaned back in his chair, watching President Namono's plane disappearing into the horizon. The other half of the television screen showed the angry crowd closing in around Green House.

"Mark my words," Jones said, "the first person who gets in there is going to keep it. All we can do now is sit back and watch the show."

CHAPTER THIRTEEN

The next morning, Louie was standing outside the university, watching the sunrise. The air over the city was hazy from fires burning through the night, and they cast an ominous red glow across the campus. Louie looked through his binoculars, scanning the buildings for any sign of activity. Nothing appeared to be happening on the far side of the barricades. He checked his watch for the third time in as many minutes. Only a few hours remained until the deadline when the students had threatened to march through the perimeter and on to Green House.

The Gisawian counter-terrorism force had deployed under cover of darkness. Shortly after midnight, they had relieved the regular army soldiers, who had been manning their positions since the start of the sit-in. Louie had personally positioned his teams of sharpshooters on the adjacent rooftops under the light of a full moon, giving them an unobstructed view of the campus. After that, he had walked the entire perimeter around the school, reinforcing the gaps and ensuring that his defensive positions had interlocking fields of fire.

An olive-drab tent had been set up behind the lines to

serve as their makeshift command center and was filled with maps, bulletin boards, and communications equipment. On a table in the center of the tent was a crude three-dimensional model of the campus grounds. The leaders of Louie's assault teams huddled around the mock-up, discussing a strategy for accessing the building where the students were staying.

Louie looked through the binoculars at the rooms where the students had been sleeping. The windows were covered with bedsheets to deter unwanted observation. A few times during the night, he had seen flashes of light from behind the makeshift curtains, perhaps someone using a flashlight to find their way to the bathroom.

Shortly after Didier's televised speech, the government had cut off electricity to the campus. Then, just before dinner, they had stopped Sammy's food deliveries through the perimeter. There had been some discussion about turning off the water supply; however, cooler heads prevailed.

As the sun peeked above the horizon, Louie walked up to the edge of the perimeter, getting as close as he could without entangling himself in the strands of razor wire. He dialed Anna's number, hoping that her phone had enough power left to receive his call. To his relief, she picked up.

"Louie, where have you been? I tried calling you yesterday until the power went out," Anna said. She sounded as if she had been awake all night.

"I'm sorry. We received orders to deploy. I've been going nonstop since yesterday afternoon," he explained.

"Deploy? I thought you were still confined to base. What happened?" Anna asked, anxious about what he was going to tell her.

"I'm not exactly sure. The call came right after the president left Green House. There was no explanation, they just told me to get the unit ready to move. We left camp a few hours later."

"What did your uncle say?"

"Nothing. I wasn't able to get ahold of him. The orders came down through the chain of command."

"What about your minders from police intelligence? Are they still with you?"

"I think they're around here somewhere, but they didn't try to stop us from leaving the base. I guess someone told them to back off."

"Are you allowed to tell me where you are?" Anna asked, her voice cracked, betraying her worry.

"I can do better than that. Pull back the bedsheet and look out the window."

Louie waited until he saw a hand pushing aside one of the curtains. When he saw Anna silhouetted in the morning light, he raised his hand and waved.

"Louie, what are you doing here?" she asked, sounding panicked.

"We were ordered to relieve the regular army last night."

"Why on earth would they send an elite counter-terrorism unit to babysit a bunch of college kids?"

"We're not babysitting. My orders are to get you and the ambassador out before the deadline."

"You're kidding, right?"

"Anna, this isn't a joke. Those are my orders. One way or another, you and the ambassador need to be out of there before ten-thirty this morning."

"What happens if we don't come out?"

"That's not an option. I'm to take the ambassador directly to the airport where there's a plane waiting. That's all I know."

"What about the students?"

Louie was silent.

"Are you still there?" Anna asked.

"Yes, I'm here. I don't know what's going to happen to them. They haven't told me anything except that the ambassador needs to be on that plane. But if I had to guess, I don't think the government will allow them to march on Green House. They'll be detained before it goes that far."

"Louie, this isn't right. We need to do something!"

"Listen to me, Anna. It's not my place to judge whether it's right or wrong. I'm just telling you what's going to happen. I'm begging you, please come out now. And if you care about your students, you'll convince them to come out too. This has gone on long enough. They've made their point. Besides, Namono is already gone. What more are they going to prove by marching on Green House? They're just going to get someone hurt, or worse."

"I can't believe what you're saying. Is this why we stayed here after Operation Brushfire? So your uncle could continue using you for his dirty work? You told me that you wanted to make things better. That you wanted to make a difference."

"Anna, please stop," Louie said, sighing with exhaustion. "We've been through this so many times. We never had any evidence to prove that it was my uncle behind Operation Brushfire. It was all just speculation. That's not what this is about."

"Yes, it is! Don't you see what's going on? You're the perfect pawn. You always have been. That's why your uncle uses you. For him, it's only about power. That's all that matters. But you actually believe in something, and he uses that against you."

"You mean the same way that the students are using you? Don't be naïve, Anna. Do you seriously believe that the world would be paying attention to them right now if it wasn't for you and the ambassador being in there with them? No one would give a damn. The army would have already gone in there days ago and ended the entire thing. They're using you for protection and publicity."

"OK, fine, then I guess we're both suckers. But that doesn't make it any better."

"What do you want me to do, Anna? I'm in the army. I can't just decide which orders to obey and which ones to ignore. That's not how this works. I was ordered to get the ambassador out and take her to the airport. That's what I'm going to do."

"What happens after we're gone?"

"I told you, I don't know," Louie whispered.

"Guess."

Louie hesitated, reluctant to say the words out loud. "The regular army soldiers will come back once we're gone," he said. "One way or another, they're going to take back the campus."

"That's what I think too," Anna said. "And yet you still want me to come out?"

"This isn't your fight, Anna. You should never have gotten involved."

"Well, it's a little late for that now."

"No, it's not too late. Just walk out the door. As soon as I get the ambassador to the airport, I promise you I'll go straight to see my uncle. I'll try my best to make sure that the students are treated fairly. I know he's not perfect, but he's not a killer. He'll listen to me."

"You have a lot more faith in him than I do."

"So, are you coming out?"

"My phone's about to run out of power," Anna said, avoiding the question.

"It's less than three hours until the deadline. Just tell them that you're leaving. They'll understand. And for their sake, please convince them to come out with you."

Anna was silent for so long that Louie thought her cell phone's battery had gone dead. "Louie, I'm staying here," she finally said. "I'm not leaving unless we all come out together."

"What about the ambassador?" he asked.

"I'll tell her what you said, but I'm guessing that her answer will be the same."

"Please, Anna."

"I'm sorry, Louie. I love you. I know you'll do the right thing. I'm trying to do the same," she said, and then her phone went dead.

+++

Meanwhile, Mike Jones was sitting in his office back at the embassy, working on his computer. He glanced up at the television, checking the latest news from the standoff at the university. He had tried calling the ambassador earlier in the morning, but she hadn't picked up the phone. On TV,

Louie's soldiers were preparing for the operation. The camera panned to a shot of the building where the ambassador, Anna, and the students were sequestered. The windows were dark and the curtains drawn, giving no sign that anyone was coming out.

The news broadcast cut away from the university and went live to the situation outside Green House. Thousands of protesters had maintained their vigil through the night, undeterred by President Namono's departure the day before. The demonstrators had turned Independence Square into an impromptu encampment, gathering around campfires, cooking food, drinking, and singing. The presidential guard troops had held their nerve through it all, risking their lives to protect an empty house whose occupant was at an undisclosed location overseas.

Jones stared at the TV, lost in a trance, when his cell phone began buzzing on the desk. He glanced down at the number and saw that it was the call he had been waiting for all morning.

"What the hell is going on?" Jones yelled into the phone. "You were supposed to check in last night. Where have you been?"

"We're back at the compound," Fabrice said.

"You've got the package?"

"Yeah, we got her."

"Any trouble?"

"Hmmm, you could say that," Fabrice hinted.

Jones closed his eyes and clenched his jaw, trying to imagine what could have gone wrong. "Dammit, Fabrice! Did you listen to the Russians? They were supposed to make sure everything went OK."

"Yeah, boss, everything was fine until we woke up this morning."

'Why? What happened?"

"We're surrounded."

"What do you mean, you're surrounded? You just told me that you were back at the compound, right?"

"Yes. Everything was going according to plan. We found Charity exactly where you told us she would be. Then we brought her back here and locked her in a room. But when we woke up this morning, there was a bunch of presidential guard soldiers outside, along with some Chinese-looking dudes."

"Dammit, Fabrice!" Jones repeated. "Why didn't you strip her down and check her out first?"

"What? She's my stepmother!"

"I mean for trackers, you idiot. I bet the Chinese had her all wired up and followed your stupid asses right back to the compound."

"Sorry, boss. I didn't think about it."

"Jesus. OK, let's try to figure this out. Did they give you any demands?"

"Yeah, they want Charity back. They said they're taking her to Green House. They've given us twenty minutes to send her out, or they're coming inside to get her."

"Goddamn Chinese!" Jones fumed. "I knew they weren't going to sit this one out."

"What do you want me to do, boss?"

"Are the prostitutes still there? Maybe you can send them out to stall for time."

"We tried that. The Chinese don't want them, just Charity."

"Fuck! Give me a minute to think. Do you still have those burner phones I gave you? Maybe we can use them to draw in an airstrike."

"They're at the bottom of the swimming pool," Fabrice said before becoming distracted by something going on in the background. "Boss, the Chinese are saying we only have fifteen minutes left."

"Dammit! OK, let me see what I can do. I'll call you right back," Jones said, slamming down the phone.

Jones had just started sketching out a plan when the phone rang again. He checked the caller ID and saw that it was Fabrice. "Jesus, what now?" he shouted by way of greeting. "I'm trying to work something out."

"It's over, boss."

"What do you mean, it's over? I thought they were giving you fifteen minutes."

"The Russians made a deal with the Chinese."

"They can't do that! It's not in the contract. They're only consultants. They have no negotiating authority."

"Boss, we didn't have a choice. They had us surrounded. They said they weren't leaving without Charity."

"I can't fucking believe this! What kind of deal did they make?"

Jones could hear Fabrice unfolding a piece of paper. "Do you want me to read the entire thing?"

"No. Just give me the highlights."

"In return for Charity, the Russians get safe passage to the airport, a direct charter flight to Cyprus, and six million euros cash."

"Goddamn Russians! They don't even have the professionalism to call me for a counteroffer? You tell them that they're on the blacklist. As long as I'm around, they'll never work for the CIA ever again. You got that?"

"Yeah, boss, I'll tell them. But they're already packing up and getting ready to leave."

"What about the Citizens Action Committee?" Jones asked.

"The Chinese said that all my men are free to go once we turn over Charity."

"You tell the Chinese that they've got another thing coming if they think they can just drive Charity over to Green House and drop her off. You're the rightful heir to the throne. She's nothing but a two-bit gold digger. This isn't going to change our plan. POTUS is on board with the CAC. The deal is as good as done."

"Boss, I'm not going to Green House," Fabrice whispered.

"What?"

"I'm going to Cyprus with the Russians. The Chinese offered me a deal too."

"Don't fucking do this to me, Fabrice! I've staked my entire professional reputation on you and the CAC. I did all the legwork and sold this thing back in the Beltway, and now you want to throw it all away? Think about what you're doing."

"I've made my decision."

"How much are they offering you?"

"Five million euros, plus an EU passport."

Jones chuckled. "You'll burn through that inside three months. Then what's the plan, huh? Don't you realize that

I'm offering you a chance at long-term security with almost unlimited upside potential? Green House is a guaranteed money maker."

"More like a guaranteed bullet in my head. Look at the TV, boss. You see those crowds outside the front gate?" Fabrice said. "If Charity wants it so bad, she can have it."

Jones sighed. "Fabrice, I'm disappointed in you. But I know it's not entirely your fault. It's a generational thing. You kids today aren't cut out for the business. You've all gone soft. There's no fire in your belly. You just don't have what it takes to succeed in geopolitics these days."

"I'm sure you'll find someone else," Fabrice said, sounding almost sorry.

"Fine! Have it your way. But don't come crying to me in six months when you're out of cash, and life back at Green House isn't looking so bad anymore. I'm telling you, you're making a big fucking mistake."

Fabrice didn't respond, and Jones heard a commotion in the background. The Russians were arguing over a missing piece of luggage and what to do with the prostitutes. Finally, Fabrice came back on the line. "I'm sorry, boss. The Russians are ready. It's time to go. We're bringing Charity out to them now," he explained.

"Goddamn it, Fabrice! I'm giving you one last chance. Don't fucking sell me out!"

Before Jones could say anything else, the line went dead. He took a deep breath and exhaled slowly, trying to gather his thoughts. Then he reached out for the secure telephone on his desk and pressed the speed-dial button for Reid McCoy's home number. On the eighth ring, the deputy national security advisor picked up.

"Mike, why can't you ever call me during the daytime?" Reid said.

"Time zones. Are you familiar with the concept?"

"Whatever. This really couldn't wait until morning?"

"Nope. The fat lady's singing. We've got less than an hour to get this thing back on track," Jones said.

"Wait a second. Yesterday, you said that we were all set with the Citizens Action Committee. I told POTUS that it was all under control. Now you're telling me that it's not?"

Reid was now wide awake and pacing in his bedroom.

"We had a minor hiccup this morning with the CAC," Jones explained.

"What the hell does that mean?"

"It turns out they didn't pass vetting," Jones clarified. "They weren't the right guys for the job."

"When I went to bed a few hours ago, President Namono had left the country, and there was an angry mob gathering outside Green House. Are you sure this is when we want to be switching teams?" Reid asked, sounding panicked.

"We don't have any choice," Jones insisted. "The CAC is no longer in play. Listen, I don't have time to go into all the details. We've got to make a quick adjustment. I need your approval for a switch to plan B."

"Plan B? Mike, we never discussed a plan B. I went to the mat for you on this Citizens Action Committee thing. Now you're coming to me with something completely different?"

"Shit happens. The CAC turned out to be unreliable. Now we've got to shift focus."

"And who are we going to shift it to?" Reid asked.

"Mugaba Odongo. The defense minister. He's the only good option left," Jones explained.

"I thought you told me that he couldn't be trusted."

"He can't, but otherwise, we might as well give Green House over to the Chinese. They're getting ready to put in Charity unless we act now," Jones warned.

"You honestly expect me to walk into the Situation Room tomorrow morning and tell POTUS that we're now backing Mugaba?" Reid shouted into the phone. "Just two days after I convinced him that we were going with the CAC?"

"I know this doesn't look good, but we don't have a choice. This is a very dynamic situation I'm dealing with over here. You can tell POTUS that Mugaba is willing to play ball. In fact, right now, he's about to do us a pretty big favor."

"What's that?" Reid asked, skeptically.

"He's deployed the counter-terrorism unit to pull Claire out of the university. I should have her wheels-up to DC in a few hours."

"Mike, you're killing me," Reid groaned. "This entire thing is turning into a three-ring circus. I'm going to look like a dumbass when I walk into the White House tomorrow and try to explain this to the President."

"Believe me, this wasn't my first choice either, but things on the ground are moving fast. If we don't seize the opportunity, we're going to lose the entire ball game."

"OK. So, what needs to happen to unfuck this situation?" Reid asked, impatiently.

"I need the authorization to send some of the American troops from the base out to intercept a military convoy," Jones said, matter-of-factly.

"What the hell are you talking about?"

"The Gisawian presidential guard and some Chinese advisors are transporting Charity to Green House. I need to run some interference to buy us a little time so that Mugaba can get his shit together."

"Hell no! I'm not risking a superpower confrontation just to keep Charity Namono from getting into Green House. Mike, you've completely lost all perspective on this. Do you even realize how crazy that sounds?"

"Reid, we don't have a choice. They're on the way there now. If Charity gets to Green House before Mugaba, it's all over."

"I don't give a shit! POTUS is never going to authorize sending US forces to intercept a Gisawian convoy and their Chinese advisors. He's not going to start World War Three over who gets to sit in Green House. It's not going to happen. End of conversation."

Jones mentally sorted through options before coming back with a counteroffer. "All right, you win. No American troops. But I need something I can work with. That convoy is less than two hours away from Green House. I've got to slow them down."

"Don't even think about asking for an airstrike," Reid threatened.

"Don't worry. I already thought about that. There isn't enough time. I need you to call over to the NSA and get all the social media turned back on."

"You're kidding, right?" Reid asked.

"Nope. Namono cut it off a few weeks ago when the protests started. There's only one data pipe coming into the country, and I know the NSA can override the kill switch. Just have them turn it back on for a few hours. That's all I need. I can take care of the rest from here," Jones pleaded.

"You know there's about zero chance of that happening, right?" Reid said, trying to keep his cool.

"Well, if you can't make it happen, then Congressman Burke will wake up tomorrow morning a happy man. All his bullshit about giving Green House over to Beijing will have turned out to be true. He's going to have a field day sticking it to POTUS until the midterms," Jones said, trying to find leverage.

"You're blackmailing me, Mike. I thought we were on the same side."

"We are! I'm just trying to do what's best for everyone involved. Don't worry, there won't be any fingerprints. Just turn it back on for a few hours. That's all I need."

"You remember a few weeks ago when I told you that our goal was keeping DRoG out of the headlines? This isn't exactly what I had in mind," Reid sighed.

"So, you're saying that you'll call over to the NSA?" Jones asked, hopefully.

"You better have Claire on that plane by the end of the day," Reid said, not answering the question. "But if anything goes wrong, I'll deny that we ever had this conversation. It's your ass on the line, not mine."

"I wouldn't expect anything less. Thanks, partner," Jones said.

+++

An hour later, Louie was inside the command tent with his senior noncommissioned officers, going over final details of the mission. They were busy conducting preoperational checks and reviewing contingencies for anything that might go wrong. Outside, the assault teams prepared their equipment, cleaned weapons, and put fresh batteries in their radios. The soldiers were loading rubber bullets into magazines and stuffing stun grenades and tear gas canisters into various pouches on their body armor. Meanwhile, on the rooftops, the sharpshooters were making adjustments to their scopes and checking windage, preparing for the worst-case scenario if something went wrong down on the ground.

With his men focused on final preparations, Louie stepped outside the tent, found a quiet spot away from the others, and tried calling his uncle for the third time that morning. He was surprised when Mugaba finally answered. "Uncle, it's Lutalo," he said. "I'm sorry to bother you. I'm outside the university. We're getting ready to start the operation."

"Yes, Lutalo, I know where you are. I'm busy right now. Is there something I can do for you?" his uncle asked.

"I need to ask a question before this begins."

Louie heard his uncle sigh before asking, "What's your question?"

"I haven't been given any rules of engagement. We don't have guidance about what do if we encounter resistance from the students."

"Your orders are clear. I signed them myself. You've been tasked to secure the American ambassador and take her to the airport. Then you will neutralize the student protest. This nonsense has gone on long enough. The students will not be permitted to march on Green House. What part of this task do you find unclear?"

"Uncle, I understand the mission. But no one has said anything about what tactics have been authorized. It's less than an hour until the students walk out through our lines. I need to tell my soldiers what to expect, how they should react if threatened."

"Lutalo, it's not my place to dictate your tactics. My job is to define your overall objective, which I have given you in no uncertain terms. How you achieve this must be left to your judgment. This is why you were entrusted to lead this unit. When you took command, certainly you must have understood that one day something like this would be expected."

"This isn't a military operation. There's no enemy inside the university. They aren't terrorists. It's just a bunch of kids. And Anna's in there with them," Louie said, his voice cracking with emotion.

"You are a soldier, Lutalo. You are paid to make difficult decisions. Life and death decisions. Isn't this what you wanted when you decided to follow in your father's footsteps? He was not a man who was afraid to follow his orders, and he followed them to his death."

"I am not afraid for myself. That's not what this is about."

"What else could it be about?" his uncle asked, frustration in his voice. "This is what you've been waiting for: a chance to prove yourself. I know that you've grown tired of hearing my village sayings, but let me give you one last proverb to consider: One who wishes to follow in the path of his father must learn to walk like him. Now is that moment, Lutalo.

Now is the time for you to live up to his example. You have your orders. It is up to you to accomplish the mission. Can you do this, or must I call in another officer who is up to the task?"

Louie said nothing, taken aback by the harshness of his uncle's words.

"Lutalo, I don't have time to play games!" Mugaba yelled into the phone. "I need your answer now!"

"Yes, Uncle," Louie finally whispered. "I can do it."

"Good. Your father would have expected nothing less. Call me when the ambassador has arrived at the airport. Do you understand?"

"Yes. And what about the students? What happens to them?"

"It will be handled as a criminal matter. Once you have detained the students, you will turn them over to police intelligence. They will handle it from there. Once this task is complete, you will report back to me."

"At the ministry?"

"No. I've just received an important call from the American embassy. I must go to Green House right away. Once you're done at the university, take your men directly there. I will meet you and explain everything once you arrive. Is that clear?"

"Yes, Uncle."

"Very good. And do not forget, Lutalo, the nation is depending on you. And I depend on you too," Mugaba said.

CHAPTER FOURTEEN

———

Minutes before the deadline, Louie was still going through the final checklists with his soldiers. Throughout the morning, they had continued reinforcing the perimeter and double-checking all their equipment, leaving absolutely nothing to chance. The nearby streets had been blocked off with concrete barriers. Chest-high strands of razor wire encircled the entire campus. Overgrown shrubbery had been cut back to clear the field of view for the sharpshooters stationed on the rooftops.

A line of sandbag bunkers was positioned near the entrance to the university. Helmeted soldiers could be seen poking their heads above the makeshift fortifications like baby birds sitting in a nest, waiting to be fed. Just outside the front gate, the Kevlar-clad assault teams were crouched behind the armored vehicles, awaiting orders to advance.

Louie was looking through his binoculars again, hoping that he might see Anna and the ambassador emerging from the building. He had not heard anything from her since their conversation earlier in the morning. He surprised himself by silently asking God for some kind of divine intervention, anything to avoid what he feared would be a disastrous ending.

At the precise moment of the deadline, the auditorium door opened, and several students stepped outside into the light. About fifty of them gathered in a tight group. Their clothes looked slept-in and their faces haggard, but otherwise, they might have been heading off to a morning class instead of getting ready to walk toward a heavily armed perimeter.

Louie spotted Anna and the ambassador standing together in the center of the group. Even from a distance, he could tell that Anna was exhausted. Louie wished that he could snap his fingers and make it all go away, that he and Anna could disappear forever and leave this all behind.

In unison, the students began walking forward into the center of the plaza. One of them moved to the front of the group and appeared to be giving orders. Through his binoculars, Louie recognized Didier Kengo from his televised speech the day before. He looked almost like a drill sergeant leading a formation of new recruits. Didier gave a loud whistle, and the group marched in a straight line toward where Louie and his men were positioned outside the front gate.

When the students reached the halfway point between the building and the barbed-wire perimeter, Louie nodded at one of his soldiers, who was manning a microphone. The soldier turned on the mike, sending an ear-splitting squawk of feedback echoing across the campus. He cleared his throat and began reading from a prepared statement. His voice reverberated from the loudspeakers mounted atop an army jeep.

"By order of the Gisawian Army, you are directed to cease your activity and assume a prone position. You will lie face down on the ground with your arms extended, and remain in this position until you receive further instructions. When approached, do not make any sudden moves. If you comply with these instructions, you will not be harmed."

When the solider finished speaking, Didier Kengo raised a hand and brought the group to a halt. Louie looked over at his assault teams. Several men armed with tear gas grenades raised the launchers to their shoulders. Louie made eye contact with the team leader and shook his head, signaling them to lower their weapons.

When he turned back, he saw that Didier had stepped away from the group and was advancing alone into the center of the plaza. His hands were at his sides, palms forward, making clear to everyone that he was unarmed. When he closed half the distance to the wire, Didier stopped in his tracks, lowered his arms, and waited.

As he watched the situation unfold, Louie played through a dozen scenarios in his mind, trying to guess what Didier was trying to achieve. Meanwhile, his soldiers kept one eye fixed on Didier and the other on Louie, waiting for his command. Then, without warning, Louie stepped through a gap in the razor wire and began walking toward Didier.

The soldiers exchanged nervous glances, presented with a contingency that had not been discussed during their rehearsals. The sharpshooters on the rooftops followed Louie's advance, watching every step through their telescopic sights. Louie continued until he was standing directly in front of Didier, blocking any chance for a clean shot. Then something else unexpected happened: Didier smiled and reached out to shake Louie's hand.

"You must be Lutalo," he said.

At first, Louie didn't know how to respond. Then he shook Didier's hand. "I've heard a lot about you from Anna," he said.

"It's good to finally meet. I'm only sorry it's under these circumstances."

"Maybe not knowing each other makes this easier," Louie suggested.

"That might be true if you really believe that we're on different sides. But from what Anna has told me about you, I don't think that's the case."

"Don't confuse empathy with acquiescence. I have my orders, and I don't enjoy the luxury of deciding which ones to follow and which to ignore."

"Never?"

"Listen, Didier, I didn't come out here to have a student debate with you. We're not discussing hypotheticals. What's happening here is deadly serious. You're putting all their lives at risk," Louie said, nodding at the other students, "including Anna's. You've got what you asked for. Now it's time for this to come to an end."

"What makes you think it's over? Didier asked. "Just because Namono is gone? That's all the more reason to continue."

"Why? You've made your point. The entire country saw you on TV yesterday. Now Green House is empty. Isn't that what you wanted? What more are you going to accomplish by leading your friends into danger?"

"I'm surprised to hear you, of all people, say this." Didier shook his head, looking disappointed. "Anna told me you were different. That you would understand what we're trying to do."

"I do understand, Didier. But I'm worried that you don't. You don't know the kind of people you're dealing with. The men protecting Green House aren't going to put down their guns and come out for a little chat. If you insist on marching, people are going to get hurt—maybe worse. Will it still be worth it to you if that happens?"

"That depends on whether or not it makes a difference."

"And they all agree with you on that?" Louie asked, nodding at the students again.

"We didn't come this far to give up now. We still plan on marching to Green House. I've come out here to ask that you let us pass."

"I don't have that option. I'm taking the ambassador to the airport. There's a plane there waiting for her," Louie said.

"Then what?"

"Then, you and the others will be detained and turned over to police intelligence."

Didier shook his head in disbelief. "Do you think that's safer for us than marching to Green House?" he asked. "You know the stories about what goes on during questioning by police intelligence."

Louie didn't reply. He glanced at his watch, then back at the soldiers, who were baffled by what was happening. He realized that the longer he stood there with Didier, the more likely the chance of a deadly miscalculation.

"What are the charges against us?" Didier pressed. "At least tell me why we're to be detained."

"I don't have that information."

"But you're still going to turn us over? Without even knowing why? Although I'm assuming this doesn't apply to Anna."

"Those are my orders," Louie replied, ignoring the personal jab.

"In that case, our conversation is over."

"I need to speak with Anna," Louie said before Didier had a chance to turn around. "Can you please ask her to come over?"

Didier nodded, then walked back to the others. Louie watched as Didier and Anna had a brief conversation. Then she left the group and walked out into the plaza, where Louie was waiting. For a moment, the two of them stood there without speaking. Anna broke the silence. "Didier said that you aren't letting us through."

"It's for their own safety. He doesn't understand the risks."

"That's bullshit, Louie, and you know it. They won't be safe with police intelligence either. You'll be lucky if you aren't stuck in there with them sooner or later."

"This isn't my decision," Louie said flatly.

"If that's the case, there's nothing more for us to discuss."

"Wait!" Louie said as Anna turned and starting walking away.

He reached into his pocket and pulled out his phone. He turned the screen toward her, but at an angle, so the sharpshooters couldn't see it through their long-distance scopes. Anna reluctantly turned back and looked at what Louie was trying to show her. Her eyes widened as he scrolled through the pictures.

"Where did these come from?"

"A memory card from the drone wreckage. Police intelligence didn't have any idea what they were sitting on. My old friend was able to retrieve the card from the evidence locker."

"Who else knows about it?"

"Almost no one. Someone from the American embassy helped me get the data off the card. He sent me the pictures a few minutes ago."

"And that's still not enough to convince you?"

Louie let out a deep sigh. "I'm not sure I needed convincing, but now it's more than just suspicion. But I'm afraid it's too late to make any difference. He's already on his way to Green House. I'm supposed to meet him there after taking the ambassador to the airport."

"Did he tell you why?"

"No, but I'm sure you can guess the answer."

Anna glanced over her shoulder at the students before turning back to Louie. "Are you actually going to hand them over?"

"It could be worse if I let them march to Green House. The army's never going to let them get there."

"What if they had an escort?" Anna asked, staring at Louie's soldiers waiting beyond the wire. "If you give the order, I know they'll follow you."

Louie closed his eyes and grimaced as if pained by what she was suggesting. "That's mutiny," he murmured. "Disobeying a direct order."

"Mutiny against who?"

Louie ignored the question. "I need to get the ambassador to the airport. She's not part of this anymore."

"Can I tell her about the pictures?"

Louie shook his head. "No. I still haven't decided what to do."

"If the students are safe and allowed to walk out of here, I know she'll agree to leave with you and go to the airport, no questions asked."

Louie stared at his phone, at the last image taken by the drone's camera in the instant before it crashed. He slid it into his pocket and looked back at Anna. "Tell Didier that my men will escort them to Green House. But he needs to understand, I can't guarantee what will happen once they get there. He has to tell that to all the others before they walk out through that wire. I won't do it unless they're all in agreement."

"I'll make sure they know," Anna said. "And the ambassador?"

Louie pointed at an armored jeep parked just outside the perimeter. "The plane is waiting for her at the airport. She needs to go now."

Anna nodded and was about to turn around, then stopped and leaned into Louie's arms. He held her tightly, not wanting to let go. For a moment, they forgot they stood in an open plaza in the crosshairs of sniper rifles.

"I'm going with you to Green House," she whispered to him.

"Can I convince you to reconsider?"

"Nope. We're in this together," Anna said, smiling at him.

"OK. Let Didier know it's time to go. Otherwise, it will all be over before we get there."

+++

In the embassy conference room, the staff watched a live broadcast of the chaos outside Green House. The crowds were growing by the minute. During the morning, the mood had transformed from a boisterous celebration into something more menacing. Sensing the shifting tide, the presidential guard troops had retreated inside the walled compound, opting for a more defensible position within the perimeter. The executive mansion now resembled a besieged fortress, with its guardians nervously watching from towers high above the square.

Emboldened by the retreat, gangs of young men began probing the outer defenses of the compound. Some of them gathered up old car tires and piled them at the base of the wall, doused them with gasoline, and set them aflame. The smoldering rubber sent thick clouds of black smoke swirling into the air, obscuring the television camera's view of Green House. Meanwhile, other protesters were launching volleys of makeshift projectiles over the walls, including rocks, beer bottles, and an assortment of ladies' handbags.

The protest appeared to be teetering on the edge of mayhem when Jones sauntered into the conference room and claimed his seat at the head of the table.

"What's the latest?" he asked Colonel Sawyer.

"Same as before. Green House is under siege, the country is in full revolt, and no one knows who's in charge. Other than that, everything's going great."

"From chaos comes order," Jones said, seeming strangely unconcerned with what was taking place outside Green House. "We just need to give things a little time to sort themselves out. Any update on Charity's whereabouts?"

"We've been monitoring social media posts claiming that she was last seen in a convoy traveling toward Green House," Sawyer said. "Some reports said that she was stopped at an intersection and surrounded by an angry mob, but we haven't been able to confirm that."

As he spoke, the news broadcast cut away from Green House and began showing a shaky video clip taken from a cell phone camera.

"Speak of the devil," Jones said, nodding at the television.

Over the crowd's heads, they could see several military vehicles stopped at an unmarked street somewhere on the edge of the city. A platoon of soldiers from the presidential guard formed a tight perimeter around several black SUVs and held back an angry crowd at gunpoint.

"Strange how all the social media suddenly turned back on this morning," Sawyer said, glancing over at Jones, who watched the standoff with a look of satisfaction.

"Yes, very coincidental," Jones mumbled, appearing surprisingly unsurprised.

"People started blocking all the roads leading into the city once the word got out about Charity's location," Sawyer explained.

"Let Beijing suck on that," Jones said, gleefully watching as the mob began closing in on Charity's SUV. "This ain't Tiananmen Square. They aren't going to shoot their way out of this one."

"Any word from the ambassador?" Sawyer asked.

"Everything is going as planned. The Gisawians extracted her from the university about twenty minutes ago. She should be on her way to the airport right now. We're just waiting on one other passenger; then it's wheels-up for DC."

"Another passenger?" Sawyer asked, confused.

"A minor hiccup. One of my assets blew his cover. In all the excitement, he got a little sloppy with tradecraft. I had to pull him out before the Chinese, or somebody else rolled him. No biggie. Just the cost of doing business."

"So, what happens to him now?"

"Standard exfiltration protocol for a high-level asset. We'll debrief him back at Langley, then set him up with a green card and new identity. After that, he goes off on his merry way, knowing that he did a great service to God and country."

While Jones spoke, the news broadcast cut away from Charity's imperiled convoy and back to a split-screen view. One half was a live shot outside Green House. The situation was deteriorating rapidly as the presidential guard soldiers started firing tear gas into the crowd, hoping to drive the protesters away from the outer wall. The other half of the screen showed a group of marchers moving in the direction of Green House. They waved Gisawian flags, chanting through bullhorns, and called for people to join them in the street. As the camera view widened, they could see that a convoy of military vehicles escorted the procession.

Colonel Sawyer squinted at the screen, trying to make out the insignia painted on the bumpers of the military jeeps driving alongside the marchers.

"That sort of looks like the Gisawian counter-terrorism force," Sawyer said. "It's almost like they're protecting the marchers."

"Turn up the volume," Jones ordered, his giddiness over Charity's situation evaporating.

"It's that guy from the student sit-in," Sawyer said as the camera panned across the marchers' front line. "The one who was on TV yesterday. And I think that's Louie Bigombe walking next to him."

"Fuck," Jones muttered under his breath. "Have you heard anything from Mugaba?"

"No. Should I have?" Sawyer asked. "If you want, I can call over to the ministry and see if I can reach him."

"He's not there," Jones clarified. "He should be on his way to Green House."

"If that's the case, I doubt he'll be getting there anytime soon," Sawyer said, nodding at the television screen. "All the streets are blocked. He's probably stuck in traffic somewhere."

Jones sprang out of his seat and moved toward the door. "I'm going to Green House," he said over his shoulder.

"Are you crazy? That mob is about to go over the wall. It's gonna be a bloodbath," Sawyer called after him. "There's nothing you can do."

"Send a text to Mugaba!" Jones yelled as he left. "Tell him I'll meet him there!"

+++

The convoy of armored SUVs was inching its way through the crowd at a snail's pace. Driving along the road was like moving through a deep canyon during a thunderstorm, except that it was people rather than water flooding in from every tributary. The alleyways and side streets were sending a surging deluge of humanity in the direction of Green House. Although the presidential palace was less than a mile away, there was no clear path to maneuver the SUV through the sea of demonstrators.

Mugaba sat in the front seat, fuming over the creeping pace of their advance. Throngs of chanting protesters surrounded the vehicle. The driver had no choice but to drift along at the same pace as the marchers. Through the bulletproof windshield, Mugaba could see billowing plumes of black smoke rising from fires burning outside the mansion. Worried that he might have already missed his opportunity, he pounded ineffectually on the dashboard, urging the driver forward.

Outside in the street, the mood was ebullient. It was like a Carnivàle parade without the costumes. People were waving Gisawian flags and banging makeshift drums made of trash bins and paint buckets. Teenagers blew noisemakers and tossed firecrackers into the air while younger children zigzagged through the crowd, playing games of tag. Along the sidewalks, small-time entrepreneurs seized on the unexpected business opportunity, mingling with the marchers and selling snacks and bottles of water. Mugaba ignored the jubilation and stared straight ahead through the tinted windshield, avoiding eye contact with the curious revelers pressing their faces against the bulletproof glass.

As the crowd drew closer to Green House, the mood gradually began to change. The number of women and children in the procession dwindled as the celebration took on a darker edge. At one point, a gang of young men armed with cricket bats and bike chains raced past the SUV in the direction of the plaza. Occasionally, a rock or piece of rotten fruit bounced off the vehicle's hood, causing the driver to wince and slam his foot on the brakes.

As they neared the entrance to the plaza, they saw a handful of bloodied protesters retreating from the battlefield while urging others forward to take their place on the front line. By then, the road had turned into a virtual obstacle course of rubble, broken glass, and burning car tires. Finally, the driver stopped the SUV and turned to Mugaba.

"I'm sorry, sir," he said. "We can't go on. It's not safe. There's no way through."

Mugaba pounded on the dashboard again, infuriated, but realized that the driver was correct. "Call my security detail in the other vehicle. Tell them I'm walking," he announced. He bolted out of the passenger seat and disappeared into the mass of protesters.

Seconds later, several burly bodyguards with automatic weapons appeared beside the SUV. Their facade of quiet professionalism quickly turned to panic when they realized that Mugaba was already gone. The driver shrugged and pointed in the general direction where he had disappeared into the crowd. The leader radioed for backup, then the team bullied their way into the crowd in fast pursuit of their asset.

Somewhere up ahead, moving in the direction of Green House, Mugaba pushed through the swarm of revelers. After a few minutes of fighting through the crowd, he was panting and drenched in sweat, his large body unaccustomed to such bouts of exertion. He stopped on the side of the road to catch his breath. Hunched over his knees, he pulled out his cell phone and dialed Louie's number. When his nephew didn't answer, Mugaba jammed the phone back into his pocket and continued through the chaos.

When he was within a few hundred meters of Green House, his eyes began watering from the noxious fumes of burning car tires and tear gas. The presidential guard troops were nowhere to be seen, having already retreated inside the compound. Over the crowd's heads, Mugaba could see them cowering up in the guard towers, hiding behind bulletproof plexiglass shields and concrete blast walls. With his security detail nowhere in sight, Mugaba was powerless to move any closer. He was anonymous in the crowd but unable to advance toward his goal without running the risk of being swept up into the melee.

Mugaba began frantically searching the plaza for signs of his soldiers or anyone who would recognize his authority. He tried once more to reach Louie, but again, he got no answer. For a moment, he just stood there, trying to decide whether to make his way back to the convoy. Then he noticed a commotion across the plaza. Unable to see through the crowd, Mugaba scrambled up on a low concrete wall to get a better view.

From atop the wall, he recognized the students from the university. They were marching into the plaza as the crowd wildly cheered their arrival. At the front of the column, Mugaba spotted the young man who had read the list of demands on TV. The students were surrounded by a protective phalanx of soldiers marching along beside them. Mugaba squinted, trying to make out the patches on their uniforms. It only took a second for him to confirm his suspicion. The soldiers escorting the students were from Louie's unit. He spotted his nephew walking at the front of the column.

Mugaba climbed down from the wall and pushed his way through the crowd in the direction of the students. When he reached Louie, he grabbed his nephew by the collar and shook him hard. "You haven't answered my calls!" Mugaba screamed over the din of chanting protesters.

At first, Louie was speechless, shocked to see his uncle in such a state of torment and disarray. Mugaba was breathless and sweating profusely, his eyes full of rage, seemingly on the edge of mania. Louie glanced at his cell phone and saw that there were several missed calls from his uncle. "Why are you here?" he asked.

"I've been summoned to Green House. I must get inside now!" his uncle yelled, pointing his finger over the heads of the protesters. Even through the clouds of smoke and tear gas, it was apparent that there was no way through the siege.

"Why are you here alone?" Louie asked. "Where is your security detail?"

"We couldn't get through by car. The crowds were too thick. I must get inside before it's too late."

"I don't think that's possible. The presidential guard won't open those gates for anyone, not even you."

"Lutalo, gather up your men!" Mugaba ordered. "You will take me to the front gate. The guards will let me in once they realize who I am."

Louie glanced over his shoulder and saw that Didier and the other students were now mingling with the other protesters, waving flags and chanting in victorious celebration. Louie's troops were standing among them, hopelessly outnumbered but mostly ignored by the demonstrators, neither threatening the revelers nor encouraging their enthusiasm.

When Mugaba realized that Lutalo was making no move to rally his troops, he grew furious and began shaking his nephew by the lapels. "Lutalo, I am ordering you to gather your men and take me to the gate! Do you understand?" he screamed.

Louie didn't even acknowledge his uncle's demand. He was staring at the crowd, watching the students joining an impromptu dance party that had broken out in the street.

"You are disobeying a direct order!" Mugaba bellowed. "How dare you disobey me? I am the only reason you are not at police intelligence headquarters right now. I am the only one protecting you!"

Louie calmly turned and met his uncle's eyes. "It's not true. You are only looking out for yourself," he said. "Just as you always have."

"How dare you!" Mugaba exploded. "After all the years that I protected you! I was the one who looked after you when your father died. I was the one who brought you into the army and gave you success. You would be nothing without me! And now this is how you repay me? With disloyalty? You are done, Lutalo! Finished! Do you understand me?"

"No, Uncle. It is you who is done," Louie said, taking his phone from his pocket and turning the screen so Mugaba could see it. He began scrolling through the photos from the drone's camera. The first few images had been taken in a field somewhere outside the city, just before the drone took flight. Several of the frames had captured the image of the tired old colonel who usually sat at the desk outside Mugaba's office: his chief of staff, supervising the launch of the aircraft.

Mugaba's eyes grew wide with surprise; then he turned his head and spit defiantly on the ground. "What is this, Lutalo? Some kind of joke?" he scoffed.

Louie scrolled through a few more pictures, slowing down when he came to the final frames. The last shot was of the ceremonial stage the second before the drone struck its target. At the center of the picture was President Namono, standing behind the podium. The drone was close enough to capture the moment of recognition when the old man realized what was happening. Seated just behind him was Charity, oblivious to the danger, reading something on her smartphone. To the immediate right of the podium was the president's entire cabinet, all of the country's most senior officials sitting together in a line—all except one. There was one empty seat.

"You knew it was coming," Louie said. "If the explosives on that drone had fully detonated, it could have killed everyone on that stage, including the president and Charity."

Mugaba smiled and shook his head, defiant in the face of the accusation. "You're a fool, Lutalo. No one will ever believe it. For all you know, I stepped out to take a piss. An empty chair means nothing."

"Your chief of staff supervised the launch of the drone. He was one of the few people who could have gotten access to the warehouse where our drones were stored."

"Then maybe you should be talking to him!" his uncle shot back.

"No. I'm not going to let you do this. You demand loyalty from everyone around you, but only to protect yourself."

"You're taking a great risk, Lutalo. You don't understand the danger of what you are saying."

Louie shook his head. "Uncle, you've always told me the old village sayings. Now I have one for you: A hunter with one arrow should not shoot with careless aim."

As he spoke the words, Louie saw his uncle's confidence turn into fury. Mugaba ripped the cell phone from Louie's hand and smashed it to the ground, stomping it to pieces under the heel of his boot.

"No one will ever believe you!" Mugaba screamed.

"That's not for me to decide. I've already sent the pictures to the media. These people," Louie said, motioning to the crowd around them, "they can decide who to believe."

Mugaba glared at his nephew, clenching his fists. For a second, Louie thought that his uncle might kill him with his bare hands, in front of thousands of witnesses. He would become just another casualty of the day's overheated passions. But Mugaba pulled back from the edge, regaining his composure.

"Lutalo, look at what is going on here!" his uncle pleaded, gesturing at the mob attempting to scale the walls of Green House. "Someone must take charge. These people need a strong leader. If we wait any longer, everything will be lost. Please, help me now. For the sake of the country."

As Mugaba was speaking, Louie noticed several young men hoisting one of their compatriots atop the wall, breaching the last line of defense between the protesters and Green House. Lying on his belly, the man reached down, grabbed the hand of another protestor, and pulled his comrade up alongside him, then did the same with another.

The soldiers up in the guard towers panicked as they realized what was happening. It was unclear who fired the first shot, or if it had been intentional, but it was followed by several more. Within seconds, the entire plaza erupted into chaos as people scrambled for cover. Bullets flew, and the air filled with choking gas, but it was too late to stop the onslaught. Dozens of young men seized the opportunity to pour over the wall and drop down into the compound.

Louie's eyes began burning as the wind shifted, enveloping them in a cloud of tear gas. He turned back to his uncle, who finally seemed to grasp that his moment was slipping away.

"I'm sorry, Uncle. I won't do it," Louie said.

As he spoke the words, Louie saw a change come over Mugaba's face. It was an expression that he had never seen before, a look of vulnerability.

Louie heard several quick bursts of gunfire from somewhere inside Green House. The young men, who had gone over the wall, managed to overpower the guards and opened the front gate. Louie and Mugaba watched in stunned disbelief as a wave of protesters swarmed into the compound.

"This is not over, Lutalo," his uncle said. "You may think you have done the right thing, but you're wrong. You have no idea what you've unleashed."

Mugaba turned and began walking back in the direction of his convoy. Louie said nothing and made no effort to stop him. He simply stood there watching as his uncle fought his way upstream against the tide of humanity flooding toward the open gate of Green House.

+++

Claire stared out the window of the army jeep as it pulled up to an unmarked gate outside the international airport. The security guards must have been expecting their arrival. They glanced briefly inside the vehicle, then waved the driver through. Once past the gate, the jeep sped along a taxiway, bypassing the main terminal and customs police. Several commercial jets were sitting on the runway, with lines of passengers queueing up behind the mobile staircases, waiting to board their flights.

It dawned on Claire that after nearly five years in the country, she was leaving without a single piece of luggage. She opened her handbag and did a quick inventory of her possessions. There was some loose change and a few Gisawian bills, now virtually worthless except as souvenirs. A dead cell phone, its charging cord back in her office. Keys to a house that she would never see again, along with her blue embassy identification badge, presumably already deactivated. Staring into the bottom of the bag, Claire realized that she didn't even have her passport. However, she knew that would be the least of her concerns on landing back in Washington.

The jeep continued past some maintenance hangers, toward the far end of the airport, into a restricted area reserved for military aircraft. A few Gisawian fighter jets of questionable airworthiness were parked on the tarmac. Claire could see the Stars and Stripes waving in the wind over the American base. Directly across the runway was a similar-looking compound where a red flag with five yellow stars was flying above the new Chinese military camp.

When they reached the end of the taxiway, the jeep stopped outside an unmarked hangar. The driver looked at Claire and nodded at an open door leading into the building.

"We are here, Madam Ambassador," he said.

Claire grabbed her handbag and got out of the jeep. After she closed the door, the driver sped away, leaving her standing there alone. With nowhere else to go, Claire walked through the door into the hangar.

The cavernous bay was empty except for a single, unmarked Gulfstream jet. The N alphanumeric identifier stenciled on the tailfin was the only visible hint of its provenance. Standing next to the aircraft was a pilot straight out of central casting, wearing aviator sunglasses and a blue jumpsuit without any identifying nametag or insignia.

"Good afternoon, Madam Ambassador. We've been expecting you," the man said, waving her to the stairs leading up into the jet. "We have one other passenger joining us on the flight today. He's already on board, so we'll be taking off as soon as you're buckled in."

"Another passenger?" Claire asked, surprised.

"A colleague of Mr. Jones," the pilot said, his tone making it clear that no other information would be provided.

Claire climbed the stairs into the executive cabin. The window shades were drawn, and the interior lights dimmed. When her eyes adjusted to the darkness, she saw the other passenger sitting in a leather lounge chair facing the rear of the aircraft.

The pilot came up the stairs behind Claire and disappeared into the cockpit, locking the door behind him. A moment later, the jet's electrical system powered on, and a tow vehicle began pulling the aircraft from the hangar bay. Claire made her way to the back of the cabin and slid into the seat opposite her traveling companion.

"So you're the other one," she said, nodding at the man across the table.

"Good afternoon, Madam Ambassador," he replied.

"Please, call me Claire."

"As you wish," he said, smiling warmly. "Can I offer you something to drink? A coffee, perhaps?"

"Maybe after we take off," Claire said, sinking into the plush leather seat.

Sitting in the posh surroundings, Claire realized that she hadn't bathed or brushed her teeth for several days. In the seat pocket, she found a complimentary travel kit with a few moist towelettes and a package of Chiclets gum.

"I gather you worked closely with Mr. Jones?" Claire inquired, chewing on one of the stale Chiclets. "That must have been an interesting experience."

"I was happy to be of service," the man replied evasively.

"Indeed," Claire said, nodding. "I must apologize," she continued. "I know we've met before, but for some reason, I don't recall your name."

"Sammy," the barista answered. "At least until we land. After that, I don't know what."

"OK, then, Sammy. Nice to see you again. It's a long trip to Washington. I look forward to hearing about your plans for America."

"It will be my pleasure," he said, taking a sip from an espresso sitting on the table between them.

As the jet taxied away from the hangar, Claire raised the window shade and looked toward the horizon. She could see plumes of thick, black smoke rising into the air from the direction of downtown. A few minutes later, the plane was accelerating down the runway, pressing Claire into her seat as the nose gently lifted skyward. Once airborne, the jet banked sharply. The pilot circled once over the city, giving them a final look at what they were leaving behind.

From a few thousand feet, Claire could easily make out the landmarks down below. She followed a mental map as they passed over the American embassy, Independence Square, and finally, Green House. When the executive mansion came into view, Claire pressed her face to the glass. The view was partially obscured by smoke rising from the fires burning around the compound. She searched in vain for a sign that the students had made it. However, there were too many people packed into the square to make out any individuals. The crowd was so large that she couldn't even venture a guess at its size.

The pilot briefly turned into a steeper bank, enabling Claire to look directly down at the presidential mansion. Only a glance was needed to understand what had happened. The front gate leading into Green House was wide open, with hundreds of people streaming through the breach. At least one of the watchtowers appeared to be on fire, and there was no sign of resistance from the guard force.

Claire strained for one last glimpse as the jet leveled off and began climbing into a layer of clouds. As Green House faded into the mist, she glanced at her traveling companion, wondering what was going through his mind as his country descended into chaos down below. But the barista was already sound asleep, reclined in the leather chair, his espresso half-finished on the table.

+++

After his uncle fled the square, Louie stood watching as the protesters stormed through the gates of Green House. He felt strangely numb, like a detached observer, removed from the chaos around him. In the pandemonium, he had lost sight of Anna and the students. He reached into his pocket, thinking he would call her, then remembered that his cell phone had been smashed to pieces on the ground. Louie looked up, suddenly aware that he was not alone. A gaunt white man wearing a blue windbreaker and a floppy hat was standing beside him.

"Quite a day, isn't it?" the man said, smiling at Louie with an odd familiarity.

"Indeed," Louie replied unenthusiastically.

"I think we've met somewhere before," the man pressed, reaching out to shake Louie's hand.

Louie ignored the gesture and shook his head. "I don't think so."

"Maybe it wasn't here in DRoG. You were at Georgetown for grad school, right? We must have crossed paths somewhere in DC."

"You seem to know a lot about me, considering that we've never met," Louie said, unable to hide his annoyance.

"Sorry. I didn't mean to be presumptuous," the man backpedaled. "I guess I just read something about you on Wikipedia and was certain that we'd met somewhere before."

"I'm not on Wikipedia," Louie muttered.

"You are now," the man said, holding up a smartphone so Louie could see the detailed biographic entry of his entire life, including a recent photo. "They're calling you the Soldier of Democracy. You're the top-trending topic on Gisawian so-cial media right now. You've just become famous, my friend."

Louie said nothing. He was about to walk away when the man offered him a business card. Despite his annoyance, Louie instinctively took the card.

"The name's Mike. Mike Jones. I work over at the embas-sy," he said, neglecting to name which country, as if stating the obvious would have been an insult to them both.

"Should I assume that means you're with the CIA?"

"The letters aren't important," Jones said with a shrug. "We're all on the same team, after all."

"What exactly do you want, Mr. Jones? If you haven't noticed, things are a bit busy right now," Louie said, nodding at the mobs rushing through the gates of Green House. On an upper floor of the palace, wisps of smoke could be seen escaping from a shattered window, yellow flames dancing behind the shards of broken glass.

"Wow," Jones marveled, shaking his head. "It brings back memories of the Maidan. Kiev—now that was a fuck-ing party," the old spy said wistfully. "Of course, hopefully, things will turn out better here. In fact, I may be able to help you with that."

"Is that right?" Louie said, still on the verge of walking away. "And how might you do that?"

"We should have a little talk about elections," Jones hint-ed. "I think it's pretty obvious that Namono's never coming back. Somebody's going to need to step up to the plate. I'd say that you're as good a candidate as anyone out there."

"If you hadn't noticed, I'm a soldier, not a politician," Louie said, nodding at his uniform. "Things work best when those two job titles don't mix."

Jones chuckled. "There's something kind of refreshing about that kind of naiveté. But surely you realize that refreshing nonsense isn't going to get us anywhere useful—at least, not if you want to keep this from turning into a complete debacle."

"Mr. Jones, are you implying that my country is incapable of finding its way without your help? Believe it or not, we can get along just fine without the CIA."

Jones shrugged. "To each his own, I suppose. Although your father had a somewhat different view on the topic."

Louie shot him an icy glare. "Who the hell do you think you are? You don't know a damn thing about my father!"

"Oh, I suppose in one sense, that's true. Of course, I didn't know him personally. DRoG wasn't in my portfolio back then. But you must have known that your old man was on the payroll, right? Back during the border wars? Come on! Don't be so naïve. Guns don't grow on trees, after all."

Louie said nothing, staring straight ahead, watching as the fire spread to the other Green House floors.

"Your uncle never mentioned anything about it?" Jones asked in disbelief. "Didn't you ever wonder about your tuition fees at that fancy boarding school? Your father sure as hell wasn't paying for that on his army salary. But I can assure you, he was looking out for the best interests of your country. In fact, we considered him a rising star. I don't think it's an exaggeration to say that your country's entire history would have been different if he hadn't been killed. It might have been him sitting in Green House all those years instead of Namono."

Louie's mind was reeling as he listened to the man's words. His heart was pounding in his chest, and tears welled in his eyes. "Why should I believe anything you're telling me?" he said through gritted teeth.

"Because I've got all the files. It's all there in black and white if you want to see them. Of course, some of the other names have been redacted, but I can assure you, everything's right there: your dad's psych profile. His polygraph. Even the bank receipts for your tuition fees at school."

"Why are you telling me this?" Louie said, unable to look Jones in the eye.

"Because we've got another chance to get it right. From what I gather, your father was a good man, one of the best this country ever produced. He should have been the one leading DRoG to a bright future. Instead, you got thirty shitty years of Namono."

"But you backed him too. America supported him the entire time."

"Hey, sometimes you make do with the least bad option. After your father got killed, there wasn't a good plan B. By then, Namono had dug himself into Green House like a tick. It was easier playing the cards we were dealt."

The two of them stood there in silence, watching as clouds of smoke began billowing from the top floor of the palace. Looters streamed out the front door of the mansion, carrying an assortment of high-end electronics, priceless antiquities, and presidential paraphernalia. Meanwhile, under orders not to interfere, Louie's soldiers stood by and watched as flames slowly consumed the building.

"Listen," Jones finally said, gazing at Green House. "Humpty Dumpty has fallen off the wall, and it ain't gonna be easy putting him back together. We've got a narrow window of opportunity here. Are you with me on this? Can we work together and try to turn this into something positive?"

"What's in it for you?" Louie asked. "Presumably, you recruited my father back then to keep the Russians out. Now you want me to do the same with the Chinese? Is that the angle?"

"Oh, I wish it were that simple," Jones said with a sigh. "But things aren't so black and white anymore. Let's just say that DRoG is at a critical juncture. We want to do what we can to ensure a smooth political transition. I think we can all agree that's in everyone's best interest."

Louie realized that he was still holding the man's business card. He stuffed it into his pocket and turned away. "If you'll excuse me, Mr. Jones, I need to get back to my soldiers," he said. "This area is now under military jurisdiction. For your own safety, I advise that you return immediately to your embassy."

Jones nodded as Louie gave the palace a final glance, then began walking off toward his soldiers. "I'll be in touch," he called before Louie moved beyond earshot.

Without turning around, Louie raised his middle finger high into the air and continued walking away.

"Ha! Just like his father!" Jones laughed out loud. "You've got my card!" he yelled as Louie disappeared through the crowd. "Give me a ring when you're ready to talk business!"

Jones waited a moment, giving Louie one last chance to change his mind. Then he turned and began the long walk back to the embassy.

ABOUT THE AUTHOR

Glenn Voelz served in the Army as an intelligence officer. He now lives in Oregon with his family. *Operation Hermes* is Book 2 in the Gisawi Chronicles series.

THE GISAWI CHRONICLES

War Under the Mango Tree
Operation Hermes

GlennVoelz.com